PRAISE FOR JOY ROBERTS-PIERRE'S NOVEL

"Artfully written with vividly descriptive scenes and colorful characters that captivates the readers mind, and create a visual landscape for the imagination. A real page-turner."
– *John Pease, Arthur of* A Few Things About Hippos

"A captivating story with unexpected twist and turns!"
– *Valada R. Morris*

"So real and artfully descriptive, I felt as though I was watching a movie."
– *Delores Chapman*

JOY ROBERTS-PIERRE

JOURNEY TO
THE EDGE OF LOVE

JOURNEY TO
THE EDGE OF LOVE

JOY ROBERTS-PIERRE

Safari Multimedia, LLC

To my loving husband, Patrick Pierre, whose belief in my ability gave me the determination to remain focused; thank you, my darling, for your encouragement.

To my mother Grace B. Fergus and my sons John A. Pease, Jeffrey D. Pease, to my daughters-in-law, Nina Yip Pease, Sandra Pease, to my brother Joseph S. Roberts, to Stevenson Pierre, Natasha Pierre. To all my grandchildren: Andrew, Miles, Jaiden, Soraya, Jaidyn, Naya, Mariah and Shar all my love.

To The Union Baptist Church in Society Hill, S.C., my church family, thank you all for your prayers and support.

MONDAY MORNING

J ustine lay snuggled in her bed as the sunlight invaded the darkness gently nudging her further away from sleeps embrace when the alarm sounded abruptly snatching her from the cocoon of peaceful slumber. Her hand fumbled to find the switch to quiet the noise that wrenched her from the elusive world of dreams. She threw back the cover and sat up on the side of the bed. Lowering her head into her hands, she resigned herself to the fact that an end had come to the night's dormant bliss and exhaled.

A rich terra-cotta hue drenched the walls of the bedroom, and a plush armless chair sat cater-cornered facing a slated bed. A stain glass floor lamp exquisitely cut into various sized triangular shapes stood alongside the chair. Slowly she rose and stretched her arms in the air gradually edging away from the bed that was dressed with a creamed-colored chiffon bedspread, which draped onto a Persian rug. Stretching her arms outward, she went onto her toes taking baby steps toward the bathroom door.

She emerged from the bathroom bare skin beaming from the sun light that was shining through the shear-laced curtains in her bedroom. She removed a bra and sweatsuit from an antique bureau drawer and began to dress hastily. With forty-five minutes to complete her daily ritual of a two-mile jog before preparing for work, she grabbed her keys off the hook by the door and went outside into the hall. While waiting for the elevator to come she gave herself another good stretch. The bell chimed, the doors opened and Justine stepped inside.

Downstairs in the lobby she greeted Joe, the doorman, before heading out into the street. As she reached the corner, she noticed a chill in the air. She zipped up her jacket, pulled the hood over her head, and began to jog across the street toward the park. The sky was clear and the smell of dogwood trees filled the air. She inhaled taking in a healthy dose of the sweet fragrance looking forward to the journey that lay ahead of her. She ran down the hill to the corner where she began jogging in place waiting for the light to change. When it turned green she started across the street spotting a fellow jogger running in the opposite direction. She smiled and gave him the thumbs-up. He returned the favor and gradually she picked up momentum as she entered into the park.

Invigorated and armed with renewed strength Justine returned from her Monday morning workout, with minutes to spare to get ready for work. Quickly she undressed leaving her clothing on the bedroom floor and revisited the bathroom.

Justine stepped from the shower onto the bathmat. Water streamed down her body as she grabbed a towel, wrapped it around herself and scurried out of the room. When in the bedroom, she allowed the towel to slide off onto the floor. Tracking wet footprints on the parquet floor she approached the full-length mirror station in the far corner of the room. She took a bottle of body oil from her mahogany dressing table and poured some into the palm of her hand. As she rubbed the oil onto her skin, she noticed her once rounded breast had begun to sag ever so slightly. She was prideful of the body reflecting back from her mirror, but now that body was giving her cause for concern. At forty-eight Justine was undergoing changes; though she looked much younger than her age, there were subtle differences she found to be unsettling. Justine calculated every morsel that she consumed and had managed not to put on weight. Although she had to admit that while maintaining weight had never posed a problem in the past, it was now proving to be a bit of a challenge. Quickly she dressed and went into the bathroom to apply her makeup and fix her hair.

Ready to leave Justine picked up her towel and workout clothes and dropped them into the laundry bag that was hanging on the doorknob in the bathroom. Scurrying down the hall, she took her keys off the hook, grabbed her jacket and hand bag, and dashed out the door.

Justine reached the station just in time to catch her 8 a.m. train into Manhattan. She worked as operations manager of Sales at "Right Look" advertising company in Manhattan. The company was undergoing a financial crisis. Lately all staff meetings were about cutbacks. People who had worked there for years were scheduled for termination and various departments had been eliminated.

At 8:35 a.m., Justine arrived at the office. She had 20 minutes to go over one of the reports that lay on her desk. She walked across the room to where the coffee machine was located. Salina Diaz had brewed a fresh pot as was her custom for years. She poured herself a cup and took it over to her desk and sat down.

Halfway through the report, Salina popped her head in the door. "Good morning Ms. Parker," she said smiling. Salina was only eighteen when she started working for the company. She was a Puerto Rican woman in her late twenties who always seemed to be in a pleasant mood.

She was all of four feet eleven and three forth inches in height and she always wore very high stilettos heels, which made her appear taller. Her skirts were usually short and tight, making her legs which were very shapely, look much longer. Salina took great care in making a proper presentation of her legs because she believed them to be one of her best assets.

Justine looked up from her report and said, "Good Morning. Is it 9 o'clock already?"

"Yap, it is. Are we still going to have a staff meeting this morning?"

"Yes Salina, we are. Would you do me a favor and set-up the conference room and send out a memo to everyone that the meeting will start at 10 a.m.?"

"Already done," she said as she walked over to the coffee machine and poured
herself a cup. "You think we'll get a chance to get away for lunch today?"

"I don't know, Salina. Let's just play it by ear. We might have to send out for sandwiches and eat while we work. We have so much to get done," Justine said, sounding a little frustrated.

Salina was a close friend of Viola Banks who also happened to be Justine's lifelong friend. A little over nine years ago, Salina was in need of a job and Viola sent her to Justine. Salina interviewed for Justine's old position; the rest is history. Salina became Justine's right hand and Justine couldn't imagine running the department without her.

After the meeting, Justine and Salina warily went over all the changes that were implemented entailing cutbacks which would render a few more of the employees jobless. Justine had done everything in her power to save those positions. Some of the people scheduled for termination were loyal employees who had been with the company long before many of the managers. Poor Salina would have to meet with the unfortunate souls before the end of the day and execute the terminations. As bad as Justine was feeling, she was glad that the unpleasant task was Salina's.

Finding herself at the end of a long day, she sat back in her chair sipping on the remnants of her coffee. In front of her lay a stack of paperwork that had to be finished by the end of the week. She stood up and peered out of one of the windows that overlooked the ally way, which was sorely lined with discarded paper-cups, soda-cans and various articles of debris. She sighed and thought, I should be leaving now, but if I leave, I'll never be able to complete the work by the deadline. Because of the cutbacks, everyone's workload was tripled and that meant late nights for all who remained.

She picked up her cup and walked over to the small corner table where the coffee pot sat warming and poured another cup. Salina stuck her head in the door to say good night. Justine smiled at her and gave her the thumbs-up.

"Are you sure you don't want me to stay and help?" she asked.

"No, not tonight. I need to concentrate. However, I will need you tomorrow night."

"OK, then I'm out of here. Don't work too hard, Ms Parker."

"Oh stop with the Ms Parker thing, Salina, everyone is gone home."

Salina laughed and whispered, "We're never safe until we're off the property." She gave her a quick wink and they both chuckled. Justine then turned her attention toward the mountainous stack of paperwork on her desk. She had worked for the company for fifteen years. She started as a temp, after working for a large motion picture studio company for five years prior as an assistant to the Marketing Director. The company she worked for went out of business and she needed a way to pay her bills fast so she took a temporary job at "Right Look." If she didn't have the responsibility, of the children, she would have taken the time to look for a more suitable job as she was over qualified for that position. But she had two daughters in junior high school and a son in grade school. Although she was eligible for unemployment, she knew that it would hardly cover the expenses that the kids generated on a daily basis even with the child support money. She told herself that she would find a better job later. However, after three months of working for the company, they offered her a permanent position in Sales. The salary was considerably more than what she made as a temp so she settled; two years later the Sales Manager resigned due to pregnancy and Justine was promoted to that position. Three years after that when the General Manager was fired she was offered his position and the rest is history. Looking back, she had no regrets. The children were all grown and on their own. She was alone with yet another promotion under her belt as Operations Manager of Sales and Marketing. She was exceedingly over worked, however, well paid. After taking a sip of her coffee, she picked up one of the documents and began to deal with the task. She decided not to answer the phones so she could leave the office by nine o'clock.

Exhausted Justine reached her apartment building at 10 p.m. She lived on the 19th floor of a high-rise building in the Bronx. She picked up her mail and boarded the elevator. Approaching her apartment, she saw her neighbor Keith Huston's door swing open, "Hi Justine, how are you?"

"Hi Keith, I'm fine thank you, how are you?"

"Oh, I'm fine, fine," he said smiling.

Justine was tired and was in no mood for chitchat. Wanting to get straight to the reason he was in the hall, she asked unsmilingly, "So, what can I do for you?"

"Actually, I have a package for you from UPS," he said smiling broadly, happy to have an excuse to talk to her. She sighs, and thanked him for accepting the parcel and extended her hand to collect it. Keith cleared his throat as he handed her the parcel and said, "Yeah, well it's no problem. Look, Justine, I was just wondering..."

Before he had a chance to finish his sentence she cut him off saying, "Listen Keith, I am grateful that you signed for the parcel, but I really had a long and rough day and I just want to go inside and unwind. You understand, don't you?"

"Oh, oh, yeah, yeah, I understand. It's late, you're tired."

Justine cut in, "Yes, I'm beat, so thanks again, for your help." Hugging the package, she looked at him smilingly, this time, and turned the key in the lock, entered the apartment and shut the door.

Keith had just moved into the building six months ago, and as hard as he tried, he could not get close to Justine. He inquired about her to a neighbor across the hall, Mr. Fox, who told him that if he had any romantic notions concerning Justine, he would do well putting them to rest. She was a cold fish and he knew that firsthand, because he had also tried. Furthermore he had never seen her with any man. But Keith had not believed him. He thought she was a great looking woman and he believed that with persistence, he would be able to break down the wall she so clearly built around herself. However, after six months of trying, he was beginning to believe

Mr. Fox had a point. Keith, who was normally quite charming to the ladies, stood in the hall before retreating into his studio apartment and wondered how Justine always managed to make him feel so ridiculous. His studio apartment was small. It consisted of a kitchen, which was off to one side, a living space and a bathroom. There was a small corridor upon entering the apartment where the kitchen was the first room you saw on the right. The bathroom was on the left a few feet down the hall opposite the kitchen. One had to bypass it to enter the main room. A bed with four posts stood in the corner of the room against the wall; it faced a large picture window. There was a small terrace and its door stood alongside the window so you could walk right out onto it. In the middle of the ceiling, rods divided the room in half. Hanging from the rods were four red paneled curtains tied back on both sides of the bed, causing it to appear throne like. When entertaining, the curtains could be closed hiding the bed, creating a dramatic backdrop behind the black loveseat, whose back was parallel the bed facing a flat-screen TV on the opposite side of the room. The TV itself was housed within a built-in mahogany entertainment center on the wall which was also equipped with a CD player, computer and play station.

Keith sat on the loveseat and tried to interest himself in the program on TV. However, he could not concentrate. He found his mind wondering about Justine and what she was doing. Maybe she had taken off all her clothes and was preparing to take a bath. He imagined her naked, clothes strung on the floor around her feet. She was really built man, he thought. I would give anything to be the one to wash her back. He could imagine her full breast in his hands, in his mouth, on his face. If he could only run his tongue up and down her back, he would make slow circular movements until he reached the curve of her spine. Wow what an ass, he thought. Boy it was big. He wondered how it would feel in his hands. Now he was fully erect. He couldn't keep this up. Maybe he could call Sylvia? Nah she wouldn't come, he thought. I messed up the last time she was here. Why do I always fall asleep right afterward? Hell, what did she expect from me anyway? he thought. We don't have anything in common, we can't talk about anything. He believed her to be a birdbrain, however, a good lay. I'm going to call her, he thought and leaned across his bed and picked up his cell phone and dialed her number. The phone rang and Sylvia answered, "Hello."

"Hi baby, how you doin?"

"Who is this?" a squeaky high-pitched voice commanded.

"Ah, come on girl, stop play'n."

"Keith, is that you?"

"Girl you know it's me."

"Huh, I can't believe you're calling after the way you treated me the last time."

"Come on girl, you know I'm crazy about yah, now stop play'n."

"I'm not talk'n to yah no more, Keith," she said pouting.

"Ah, baby, please? Come on," Keith begged.

"I should hang up the phone on you, right now," she said sulkily.

"Baby you know you don't mean it. It's not my fault you're so good you take away all my strength," he said whining.

"I don't care," Sylvia yelped unyieldingly.

"Come on baby, I'll do better this time, I promise."

After a few minutes of this routine, Sylvia agreed to

come to his house providing he paid for her cab.

Just what he wanted to hear so he hung up the phone, hopped off the bed, and sprang into the kitchen. He grabbed a bottle of wine from the cabinet and placed it in the cooler on the counter; at his entertainment center; he popped in a CD and "Ooh, Baaaby, ♪ ♫, I'm hot just like an oven, ♪ ♫, I need some Love'n" ♪ ♫, filled the airways. In the bathroom, he stepped into the shower, turned on the water, and joined Marvin Gay in song.

Twenty minutes later as he stepped from the shower, the doorbell rang. Wow, he thought, that was quick. He grabbed a towel and tied it around his waist. He went to the door, swung it wide open, and said, "Hey Babb…" Stopping short he stood frozen in the doorway; streams of water flowed down the center of dune like craters of perfectly sharpened muscles forming streams of moisture all over his sculpted body. Justine stood outside his door clothed only in a house-robe. Her hair parted naturally and flowed down the side of her face with the ends barely feathering the tip of her shoulders. Her hair was full and black, with a single silver patch of hair framing one side of her face, creating a striking contrast to her chestnut brown skin. She could hear the soulful lyrics of "Sexual Healing" spilling out from inside his apartment and was instantly embarrassed for her intrusion. She stood in the doorway for what seemed to her an eternity before she was able to utter the words, "Oh, oh, ah, Keith, I'm so sorry, to disturbed you," unable to stop her eyes from scoping his manly physic.

Keith jumped in, "No, no it's OK, what can I do for you? Really, it's OK; tell me, how can I help you?"

"Oh no, it's late, I feel so silly. You're not even dressed, I mean you're getting ready for bed, I mean, I didn't mean to…."

Before she could finish, Sylvia stepped off the elevator and approached the door. Justine recognizing her as one of Keith's lady friends, retreated within the walls of her apartment.

"That's OK, I'll handle it. I'll call maintenance," she said, instantly closing the door behind her feeling incredibly awkward.

"Hi Baby," Sylvia sang in her squeaky high-pitched voice. Keith stared at Justine's shut door for the second time that night. Shit, shit, shit, was the only thought his mind could conjure. Sylvia glanced at Justine's door, and asked "What did she want?" as she stepped past him into his apartment. Her eyes began to scan the room. She simultaneously fussed with her hair while tugging at the fabric on her skirt, which clung to either side of her hips. "Ooh," she exclaimed. "The place looks nice, he, he. And Marvin Gay is playing. Is all this for little ole me?" Sliding out of her jacket she laid it on the loveseat along with her Gucci hand bag, she turned toward Keith, and her long curly hair bounced with the movement as it cascaded down her back like a waterfall to her waist. Keith was still standing in the doorway. "What are you waiting for?" she squeaked. "Come over here, he, he," she said with outstretched arms. Ah man, he thought to himself. This is going to set me back another six months with Justine. Why did this bimbo have to arrive at the exact same time? Unmindful that Justine was the intruder and not Sylvia. After all Sylvia was his invited guest. He wondered what Justine could have wanted all dressed up in her house robe, and she didn't appear to have anything else on underneath. "What's wrong with you?" Sylvia shouted.

It was clear that he was distracted. "No-nothing, baby," he said, shutting the door and walking over to her and planting a kiss on her lips.

But, Sylvia pulled away frowning, "What did she want?" she inquired.

"Oh, I don't know. Who cares?" he said, kissing her again hard on the lips.

But Sylvia would not be put off and pulled back in order to continue her query, but Keith never stopped. He continued his assault of kisses to her neck, gently pulling on its soft tender skin with his lips as he fondled it with his tongue. Finally he worked his way upward until he reached her mouth. Unable to maintain her focus she surrendered returning his kiss darting her tongue in and out of his mouth while she slid her hands down his moistened back until she reached his bum and squeezed it.

His penis stiffened and she swayed her hip grinding them firmly against his hardened member. He moaned, and she pulled the towel from his waist letting it drop to the floor. Lips locked, he walked her backwards toward the bed while tugging at her cashmere sweater. He skillfully pulled it over her head, shoved her onto the bed, and mounted her. Running his hands up her skirt, he noticed she wasn't wearing underwear. She groaned and pulled him down on top of her, parting her legs and rapping them around his back. He leaned forward and kissed her breast, taking her nipple into his mouth and pulling on it gently with his teeth, while vigorously flogging the tip of it with his tongue. She caressed his head tenderly as her arousal increased then slowly allowed her hands to slide down his back. He released her nipple and lifted her bottom upward. Taking hold of her skirt he pulled the elastic waist down over her hips. She assisted him by pulling her legs out of the garment and pulled him down on top of her. Thrusting her hips forward, she cried out with pleasure as she felt the hardness of his member enter her with a fury. Quickly she pushed forward in sequence with the rhythm of his dance that evoked pleasure with every thrust.

"Oh, oh," she cried. "Don't stop, don't stop!"

Justine walked into her kitchen, which was located fairly close to the door, and opening a drawer, pulled out a flashlight. Her apartment was in complete darkness. I feel like an idiot, she thought. Knocking on Keith's door in the middle of the night, and him coming to the door half naked; he probably thought that I was his girlfriend, she chuckled, but she was not amused. Some date, she thought, candle light whoopee in his boudoir. He is such a player. What must he have thought of me standing in the hall in my house robe?

He probably thought I had nothing on underneath; she was wearing panties but no bra. And what was I thinking? It was all so embarrassing. I hope he didn't think I was coming on to him. I had better learn where these fuses go so I can fix it myself. The trouble was that it happens so seldom that she always forgot where to place the fuse when it happened again. She shined the flashlight into the drawer while she foraged around looking for the box of fuses. Finally, she found the little square box with four fuses inside. She took it over to the fuse box and shined the flashlight inside so that she could see. She puzzled over which fuse was responsible for the darkened rooms. She had been preparing to take a bath when everything went dark. She had to figure this out because she didn't want to call maintenance just to screw in a fuse. After several tries, she finally placed the fuse in the correct slot and the lights came on in the apartment.

"Hah," she said, relieved that she had figured it out and walked down the hall past the main room and into the bathroom. Untying her robe, she removed her panties, and stepped into a tub of hot soapy water and sat down.

THE LUNCHEON

Taking her cell phone from her white Chanel hand-bag, Viola Banks ascended the bowels of the subway and stepped onto the busy sidewalk of Lexington and 59th Street. While the sun kissed sky warmed the concrete city of bricks and mortar, streams of people scurried by in opposite directions somehow managing not to bump into one another as they journeyed to their various destinations. Cars and buses sailed up the Avenue like big fish and whales in a sea of blowing horns. Like schools of sharks in search of a meal, cabs bob and weave in and out of traffic in search of a fare.

At the corner of 60th Street along the side of Blooming-dales, under April skies, a group of African American boys break danced to the sound of music generated from a boom-box seated on the side walk. Crowds of people slowly encircled them creating an arena for the street show. Across the street a steady flow of pedestrians descended the stairwell of the subway while their counters ascended out of its mouth like worker ants with intent of purpose. Jay-walkers dashed across the street while car-horns blasted their deafening song of protests. And the street show commenced, while a group of people lined up in single file a few feet away, to board one of the cities many buses. All of this creating a mosaic cluster of activities that come together weaving a symphony of chaos that is in keeping with the rhythm of the heartbeat of the city of New York.

Viola was dressed in black and white except for her red Michael Kors stiletto heels that allowed one toe to peer through a peek-a-boo opening in the front of the shoe. Viola wasn't someone you would off handedly call beautiful, but she was pretty in her own way, and she had style. Her hair was bobbed. It formed a geometric V at the nape of her neck. One side of her hair swept down hugging her cheek. The other side was much shorter and was cropped midway her ear, revealing the lobe, which was embellished with a black diamond encrusted earring. The platinum white hair that covered her head spoke drama against her ebony skin.

Approaching Bloomingdales she immediately dialed a number and waited patiently. After several rings, a voice answered, "Hello"

"Hi Justine, where are you?"

"I'm on 55th and Lexington, where are you?" answered Justine.

"I'm on 59th."

"OK, I'll be there in about five minutes," Justine said.

"Is Salina with you?"

"No I'm going to call her now," Viola said.

"OK then, bye." Justine hung up the phone picking up pace with the other pedestrians who breezed alongside her. As she neared the corner she hastened in order to catch the light. Her hair, which was pulled back in a ponytail, swayed and bounced to the rhythm of her stride as she journeyed forward. Anticipating a joyful reunion, she trailed Lexington as she passed the Fitzpatrick hotel, Kenneth Cole's, and Barami's, marching along happily toward 58th Street. Viola spotted her as she crossed 58th Street and started walking toward her. Justine crossed the street picking up her pace with both women smiling broadly, as they approached one another in the middle of the block. They offered kisses to the air on either side of each other's cheek. Then they hugged one another fondly. It had been a long time since they had seen each other.

Their last meeting was in December at a Christmas party. Now they stood under the warmth of April's sky drinking in each other's essence with their eyes.

"Hey gurl-l-l you look great, how are you?" inquired Viola.

"Thank you. I'm good, same O, same O, you're looking fab. How are you doin'?" replied Justine.

"I'm doin' great and thanks for the compliment darling … G u r l, I've been up to quite a bit since last we met," Viola said smiling devilishly.

"Which way are we going?" Justine asked as she studied Viola's body language. "Well I phoned Salina after talking to you and she's at Brasserie on 60th and third," Viola said.

"Then I guess Brasserie's it is."

"OK, let's go," Viola said. They began walking toward 60th Street.

"Don't think I didn't notice that look on your face."

Viola, trying to look innocent replied, "What look?"

"The cat that swallowed the canary, look when I asked you how you were doin'," Justine said, wearing a knowing grin.

Viola laughed and said, "I'll tell you all about it when we get to the restaurant."

Brasserie stood on the corner of third and 60th Street. When they arrived it was crowded, but Salina had managed to get them a table by the window. She waved them over grinning widely. She hadn't seen Viola in months and could barely contain her excitement. The restaurant was reminiscent of the early 40's with wood paneling surrounded subway tiles along the walls, and in the middle of the room, spherical lightings hung from the ceiling gently illuminating the wood paneling that framed the windows that looked out on to the sidewalks of 60th street. As they approached the table, Salina stood up with out-stretched arms that were eager to cradle Viola. "Hey," she cried as she and Viola embraced. "I really missed you," she said as they rocked each other from side to side. "How the heck are you?" Salina asked smiling from ear to ear.

Viola attempted to give her one of her chic kisses to the air, but Salina wasn't having it. She planted a big red kiss directly onto Viola's cheek. Viola squealed, "Ah girl, you messed up my make up." Then she laughed and they all sat down at a table, which had a window View of the Street. A sign at the curb read NO STANDING ANY TIME and across the street, a stream of people ascended and descended the subway. The busboy placed fresh bread on the table, added two glasses, and filled them with water. "The server will be with you in a minute," he said as he laid two more menus on the table.

Viola took a tissue from her purse and immediately began removing Salina's red lip prints from the side of her face. Placing the tissue into her purse, she murmured as she picked up a menu and fixed her gaze. The cling clang of dishes rang in the background while she studied the menu with great intent. Salina only glanced at her menu and promptly closed it laying it on the table. She sat back in her chair looking around the room. Viola looked up at her and said, "You know what you're ordering?"

"Ah hah", she said smiling. "All I had to do was study the menu while waiting for you two."

Justine studied her menu intently and then smiled and said, "I think I see what I want."

"Oh, really?" said Viola, stretching her eyes wide to inject humor.

"Yep, I'm getting the shrimp linguini and broccoli with garlic sauce."

"Me too," exclaimed Salina.

"Sounds like you two had this all planned," Viola said, looking at them smiling broadly. Viola had quite an over bite with her full lips resting upon her teeth when smiling and whenever she closed her mouth, it appeared to be somewhat strained. She was wearing those invisible braces on her teeth which she hoped would eventually correct the problem. It was amazing how, even with that flaw, she was still quite attractive.

Justine laughed and said, "No nothing's planned. I just like linguini. You're not getting off that easy, Viola. What have you been up to?"

Viola laughed throwing her head back allowing her tongue to cross her lips as she leaned forward eyeing the other two women and whispered, "I went to Brazil in February." Her eyes shifting from side to side, as if she had a secret she didn't want anyone to hear.

Justine smiled as she slowly leaned forward. "Thanks for inviting a sister," she stated jokingly.

"No it wasn't a joy trip, I went on business," Viola said seriously.

"Yeah right, Viola. I wasn't born yesterday."

"Yeah," Salina said. "Everyone knows that February is Carnival in Brazil. Tell us that you weren't in Rio," she said challengingly.

The server approached the table with pen and pad in hand ready to take their orders. "Hello, my name is Gina. I'll be servicing your table. Are you ladies ready to order, or do you need a few more minutes?" she asked while simultaneously chewing on some gum. Her blond hair was pulled back in a ponytail and her blue eyes were intently fixed on Justine for some reason.

So Justine directed her gaze toward Viola and said, "Do you know what you are going to order?"

Viola put down her menu and looked up at Justine and said, "I guess I'll have the big salad."

Justine looked up at the waitress whose gaze was still fixed on her and said, "Two shrimp linguini and broccoli with garlic sauce," and pointing to Viola she said, "She'll have the big salad."

Gina scribbled the order onto the pad and before placing the pen back in her hair just above her ear she said, "Would you ladies like to order some appetizers?"

All three replied, "No" in unison. They looked at each other, and began laughing, because these women really watched their weight, and probably wouldn't even eat half of what they ordered. Gina shrugged her shoulders steadily chewing on her gum and scurried off to place their orders.

"Well, go on," Salina said, "you went to Brazil in February on business…"

"Oh, Yes," Viola said. "It all happened so fast. This woman named Nelda came into my Manhattan salon promoting this great hair product that she manufactures. She has her own business and she had only begun to sell her products to specialty salons here in the States. She manufactures her product in Brazil."

"So is this why you went to Brazil?" Justine interrupted impatiently.

"I'm getting to that," Viola said hurriedly.

Viola owned a chain of beauty salons spread out in different borrows in New York. She opened her first shop on Boston Post Rd in the Bronx in 1989. It was so lucrative she opened another one in Harlem in 2000, her third salon opened in lower Manhattan in 2006. Viola began fidgeting with her earring as she went on to say, "So Nelda and I got talking about becoming partners by opening a Salon in Brazil. She doesn't have a license to run a beauty salon, but she would help to back me financially, and this way she could feature her new products there in the salon. She speaks Portuguese and I can understand a little of it, being that I speak Spanish, so when I read her proposal I liked what she had laid out. In effect, we've been interviewing people in Brazil to work in the salon when it opens."

Justine said, "So you went to Brazil to open…?"

"No," Viola cut her off. Originally, I went to Brazil to learn more about Nelda's hair care product and to take a few classes on how to apply the product so I could teach the methods to my stylists here in the States. It was there that Nelda convinced me that it would be lucrative to open a shop in Brazil as well. That's when she hit me with the proposal. She even had her eye on a property that we could buy. Anyway, while I was there I met Claudio."

"Claudio!" Salina exclaimed.

Viola smiled and winked devilishly and said, "Ah huh!"

"Well don't stop there, who is he? What is he? Tell us all about him," Salina said.

"Well don't get your feathers all ruffled up, he's nobody, really. One day after class, I was on the beach in Rio. Everyone was in a titter about the up and coming Carnival and I was all sprawled out taking in the sun, when I heard this voice say, 'Are jou goin to de Carnival?' Girl I looked up into the most gorgeous green eyes and liked to die."

"Go on," Justine urged.

"Well to make a long story short, we became an item during the festivities."

"And that's it?" Justine asked disappointedly.

"Well, no. I guess I better fill you in on a few things."

"Yes, please do," urged Salina.

"Well his name is Claudio Rivera and he is 29 years old, gorgeous, warm golden brown complexion, great body, you know the biceps and triceps, muscular chest with the six pack, the whole nine yards. However, girls the brother is broke," she said, lowering her eyes somewhat.

"Don't tell me you picked up a wretch on the beach?" Salina stated surprised.

"Yep, that's just what I did," answered Viola, staring her directly in the eye.

"Viola, tell me you didn't sleep with him. You know a lot of those people are sick," Justine said, surprised by her friends' casual attitude. She knew that Viola was a free spirit, but she didn't think her to be stupid.

"Now, you know me girl. I wined and dined him and then I marched his ass over to one of the local doctors and had him checked out."

"And you trust that?" Justine asked amazed.

"Justine, don't be an American snob. They have very competent doctors in Brazil. People from all over the world go there for surgery. Anyway I'm bringing him to the States. He'll be here on a work visa in about six months."

"How did he get a work visa, much less a job that fast?"

"Easy darling, I'm his boss, ha, ha."

"I can't believe you!" Justine said exasperated.

"Believe, believe girl he's great. He is like the energizer bunny he takes a licking and keeps on ticking."

"You are something else girl. So when do I get to meet this Mandingo?" asked Salina greedily.

"Gurl," Viola said, raising her voice an octave higher, "I'm not bringing him to the States to merge into my social circle. He is going to be my very own p r i v a t e boy toy," then she threw her head back with her eyes half shut reminiscing. And then they all burst into laughter and afterward Viola looked at both of them and said, "Look I know this little fling is temporary so I'm not tripping; I'm just enjoying the ride until it's over. I'm only telling you guys, because you're my girls and I trust you. I don't really care for anyone else to know that he and I are an item because he'll be working in the salon."

"Well you are certainly investing a lot in this boy toy to be treating it so casually," Justine said.

"Look Justine, I'm forty-four soon to be forty-five years old and he is twenty-nine. I know it's not going anywhere, but he satisfies me, he's a lot of fun and I can afford it so I'm enjoying myself. Anyway, I don't look my age so why should I deprive myself? I need someone who is able to quench my seemingly insatiable desires," she said, running her tongue over her full lips again. "I don't know what happened but when I turned forty my sexual appetite expanded. Men my age just aren't cutting the mustard even when they're in excellent shape, they just don't get the job done. So when I went to Brazil and found Claudio…Well let's just say I am going to enjoy the hell out of him and nothing either of you say can rain on this parade so don't try."

"What can I say? She's gotta have it, pun intended," Salina said, shifting her eyes back and forth and they all began to laugh.

"OK Viola, just be careful," warned Justine.

"I will, so what about you?" asked Viola directing her question at Justine.

"Me, nothing has changed I have my work. I haven't been doing anyone," Justine said with a wicked smile.

Viola stared across the table at Justine in disbelief. She

couldn't believe that Justine hadn't done anything since her break-up with her husband years ago. She must be living a secret life of some sort, she thought. Nobody's was that good. The waitress came to the table with their orders and they said their grace. Viola thought to herself, if my friend isn't holding out on me then I pity the guy that breaks through and starts up that volcano. Salina's eyes met Viola's and Viola smiled and said, "So what has your ass been up to and don't tell me nothing because I know you better than that?"

Salina laughed and said, "You know that's right!" And they all busted into laughter again.

Then Salina looked at them seriously and stated sadly, "Well, I'm still kissing frogs looking for prince charming, but I haven't found him yet." Then she looked at Viola and said, "I sure as heck don't have my own p r i v a t e boy toy. I can tell yah that!"

Justine raised her eyebrow in disapproval and said, "Well that certainly doesn't sound like anything I care to aspire to."

Viola shrugged her shoulders in a devil-may-care manner and said, "Let's all get toasted." Then she waved the waitress over and ordered two bottles of wine with their meal. After dinner, they had a few more drinks as they sat there laughing and talking away the hours catching up on all the gossip. As they started feeling the effects of the alcohol, they began to make fun of some of the sights that passed by the window and whaled with laughter. After a while of this, Viola glanced at her watch and realized that it was later than she thought and blurted out. "Oh look at the time! Girls, I have to get downtown to the shop and pay my employees. The manager is on vacation." Viola waved her hand for the waitress to bring the check. Justine and Salina opened their handbags to get their credit card, but Viola stopped them. "I've got that," she said.

"No," Justine insisted. "We can't let you pay all the time," opening her wallet to pull out the card.

Viola waved her off again and said, "If I can feed Claudio and pave the way for him to come to the States, I can feed my two best friends."

"OK you've twisted my arm," Justine said laughing, "but I'm sure Claudio earned his way!"

Viola nodded her head in agreement and laughingly said, "You better believe it!"

Viola rose to go to the ladies room. She left her credit card on the table for the waitress to collect. She moved across the floor gracefully; her body was that of a ballerina only her breasts were much fuller. A couple of men sitting at a table across the room turned their heads to observe how beautifully sculptured she was as she glided toward the restroom. Viola visited the gym at least four times a week. Her black and white jersey dress clung to her like liquid as she moved fluidly toward the restroom. Justine suspected Viola had her breasts touched up, because she was not wearing a bra and the sisters were firm and erect. Upward pointed nipples were visible beneath the jersey fabric. Minutes later, Viola emerged from the ladies room, signed the receipt, picked up her credit card, and the three ladies left the restaurant.

Out on the sidewalk Justine turned and said, "Well I really enjoyed this long overdue visit, girls."

"Me too," Salina said. "I don't get to see enough of you Vie, I just can't say goodnight just yet. Do you mind if I ride downtown with you?"

"No, I don't mind," Viola said, sounding a little flattered. "I've missed you too, boo."

Justine and Viola did their ritual kiss in the air, hugged

one another and Justine looked at Salina and said, "See you Monday." And they headed off in different directions.

HAND OF FATE

As storm clouds gathered across the weary skies of the Bronx, Keith exits the train station with a euphoric enthusiasm after his workout at the gym. Trotting effortlessly down the elevated stairs, he decides to walk up the street to the supermarket to pick up a few items before the water escaped the clouds and rained down it's fury upon the earth. He pranced purposefully up the block past the park and crossed the street onto the Avenue. People were still bustling about in pursuit of their various endeavors. Street venders, who created a scene of market place as they lined the streets decorating the sidewalks with their draped table offerings, gathered up their wares before the threatening monsoon delivered its promise and lay waste their livelihood. Keith quickens his steps as the sky seemed to darken. He worked for a Home shopping network station as a host. Even though the economy was said to be bad, he was doing rather well. The truth of the matter was everybody wasn't broke and people who had money were buying. He walked along hurriedly past the pharmacy, shoe repair shop, bakery, and the bank, but as he passed the GNC store his phone rang. He reached in his jacket pocket and answered it.

"Hello."

"Hi Keith," Sylvia's high pitched voice rang through the air waves.

"Hi, Baby, what's up?"

"Well, I was hoping to get you up, if you know what I mean, he, he."

"Girl, you're so bad."

"Well I try, he, he. What are you doing tonight, would you like some company?" she asked.

"Ah," he paused in thought then said, "OK I don't mind, but I'm not home yet. I'm headed toward the supermarket."

"Which one?"

"I am going to the one by my house."

"Oh yeah, I know the one. Are you going food shopping?"

"Yeah, but just a little; I just wanted to pick up a few things before I headed home. I'll be home in about thirty minutes."

"Oh OK then, so I'll see you later?"

"Ah," he hesitated again and then he said, "I don't see why not."

"OK then; Smooches!"

"Yeah, OK, bye."

Keith hung up with mixed feelings about seeing Sylvia. He enjoyed her company but wondered if he had done the right thing by agreeing to see her again tonight. He had already seen her three times that week and he didn't want her to get the idea that they were a couple. She was nice and he knew that she liked him and he liked her too, but not enough to commit. He didn't want her to assume that he was her man. She was beginning to leave little things at his apartment. He had packed them into a bag for her to take home, but she kept leaving the bag behind. After she had gone the last time, he noticed that she had left her toothbrush in the bathroom as well. When she comes over tonight, he would have a talk with her. However, he would have to be careful how he worded it, because even though she acted like a ditz, she could be very sensitive and her feelings hurt easily. He didn't want to be cut off because he rather enjoyed their late night sessions. Just thinking about the things she did stirred his member and he had to redirect his thoughts. He turned his thoughts to her beauty. Her cinnamon light brown complexion, big doe like eyes, full pouting lips, shit she's a knock out, he thought. Men couldn't help gawking at her and he couldn't keep his hands off her. He knew in his heart that he really didn't want to mess that up. What was that old saying, he thought to himself. "You can't have your cake and eat it too." Why was that? he pondered as he entered the super market. He grabbed a basket, went down the aisle, and picked up some soda. Doubling back, he approached the bread aisle and threw a loaf of whole wheat into the basket. He walked all the way to the end by the dairy section, picked up a dozen of eggs and a container of orange juice, and headed for the checkout counter when he spotted Justine leaving the store. He hurried over to the express lane and laid his items on the counter. The cashier was texting and she was in no hurry to take on a customer. Her fingers, whose nails were painted black, a dramatic contrast against her pale white skin, traveled across the phone's keyboard in record speed. Rain or no rain she wasn't going anywhere. She would be there until 9:30. She glanced over at Keith; her heavily painted eyes seemed to cut, as she picked up the bread with the speed of a slug and ran it over the scanner. She then picked up the bottle of soda and turned it around in search of the bar code, and finally, in what seemed like forever, ran it over the scanner. If that wasn't bad enough, it wasn't registering. Impatient, Keith shouted, "It's on sale for $1.65!" She ignored him and treated him as though he were a ghost. Scratching her head, whose hair was dyed jet black except for a patch of pink at the nape of her neck, she turned to ask the cashier at the register next to her if he knew how much it cost. The cashier leaned his portly body across the counter, squinting as he looked over the rims of his glasses, and confirmed that it was in fact on sale for a $1.65. She nodded her head and added the sum manually, without so much as looking in Keith's direction, then picked up the eggs and rang them up. When all of his food was finally totaled, Keith paid her for the items, picked them up from the counter, and put them in the bag himself, by passing the little cup she had on the side reserved for tips. Where did they get off thinking that they should be tipped for inadequately performing their jobs? Everyone wanted to get paid, but nobody wanted to work, he thought as he shook his head and scurried out the door, and onto the street.

He spotted Justine exiting the GNC store heading toward the house. He could tell by the way she kept switching the packages from one hand to the other, that the contents were heavy. Her steps were short and quick and one could tell she was trying to get up the block before the Heavens opened up. He skipped and began to trot in order to catch up with her. He slid up alongside her and said, "Hey Justine," as he gently tugged at her bag.

"Oh hi Keith, no, that's alright," holding firmly to her bag. "I can manage," she said.

However, Keith persisted, "I insist let me get this," he said, removing the bag from her hand. Reluctantly she conceded and allowed him to take it. "Now doesn't that feel better?" he asked smiling revealing his pearly whites.

At thirty-nine Keith's hairline had begun to reseed so he shaved it all off which went well with his features, and his Hershey chocolate colored skin. Justine looked up at him and thought to herself, he is a handsome so and so.

She smiled and nodded her head in agreement. She wondered how old he was, she figured that he might be younger than she was, and wondered if he noticed the age difference.

"What are you doing shopping so late?" he asked.

"It's not that late it's only 8 o'clock. I was downtown having a bite to eat with some friends," she said smiling.

"I see. I hope you had a nice time."

"I did," she replied. "And you, why are you shopping so late?"

"Me? Well it's Friday evening, I just came from the gym and I heard it was going to rain tomorrow so I thought I'd pick up some odds and ends so I wouldn't have to come out."

"Me too," she said and laughed. "Only I didn't realize how many odds and ends I needed."

"I see!" he said in agreement. "What do you have in these bags? They weigh a ton," he said laughing.

"I decided I'd cook tomorrow," she said.

"I've smelled some of your food from time to time and I wished that I had been invited for dinner. Your food smells great!"

"Does it?" she said, smiling, looking at him sheepishly.

"You know it does, girl. You could be a chef."

"How would you know that? All you've ever done was smelled it," she said laughing.

"Well that could be remedied if you invited me to dinner." They were actually laughing when they entered the building and Justine was even pondering the idea of inviting him. As if to announce the presence of trouble, thunder sounded and lighting cracked the sky. Justine was about to reply when Sylvia popped up from a bench in the lobby.

"Hi, baby," she said to Keith and nodded a gesture of

hello at Justine.

Justine gave her a nod in response and turned to Keith retrieving her bag and said, "I can handle it from here, thanks," and walked away from him toward the elevator. Sylvia tiptoed upward in order to kiss him on the lips. He turned his face slightly and the kiss landed on his cheek instead. Sylvia looked at Justine and then back at Keith who was looking down.

"What's wrong with you?" she asked demandingly.

"Nothing," he answered annoyed and then added, "What's wrong with you?"

She looked up at him stunned by the tone in his voice. He sounded so cold and harsh. Was it because of that stuck-up bitch over there? she thought. She looked Justine up and down and thought to herself I know I look better than she does. He can't be shunning me because of her. She must think that because she lives next door to him, that she can take him away from me. Huh, I've got news for you sister. I'm going to stop taking my birth control pills. I know Keith loves me. He just needs a nudge in the right direction. It's like a jungle out here, with all of the vultures circling around. A girl has to take extreme measures to secure her goods. Trust me, she thought, I'm fixing to close in on this prey before little miss stuck-up next-door homes in on my pigeon. I haven't been letting him ride me like a horse all this while for him to end up with someone else. Hell to the no! Huh, you're not getting your claws in this. This one belongs to Sylvia Cartier! Huh, when I get him upstairs, I'm going to blow his freaking mind. These thoughts and more were rolling through Sylvia's head as they rode the elevator in silence. Keith kept his head down. He was totally defeated and somewhat embarrassed, because Sylvia was acting as though they were a couple. He could only imagine what

Justine must think of him now, because he had clearly been flirting with her. When they reached the nineteenth floor, they all exited the elevator and headed toward their respective apartments.

Keith felt like he had taken two steps forward and five steps backward all in the course of ten minutes. Was it the hand of fate arranging Sylvia's constant interception of his progress with Justine? Each time it had been his choice to have Sylvia over. He put his key in the door and looked over at Justine who had just turned her key in the lock. He said goodnight, and so did she, but it was so low it was barely audible as she opened her door and quickly went inside without so much as a glance in his direction. Just like that, he thought, I am back to square one. I am going to have to put a stop to the familiarity Sylvia assumes with me.

He opened the door and they entered the apartment. Sylvia had been carrying a bag of groceries that Keith neglected to take out of her hand when they met in the lobby. Without either of them speaking a word, she carried it into the kitchen and placed it on the counter. Then she removed her jacket, went into the main room, and placed it along with her handbag on the love seat. Keith was in the kitchen putting the food he purchased at the supermarket away. Sylvia walked over to the window and cracked it to let in some air. Keith walked into the bathroom and turned on the shower and begun to shed his clothes. Sylvia went into the kitchen and washed her hands. She opened the fridge door and took some green peppers from the veggie bin. She took two steaks out of the bag she had been carrying and laid them in the sink. It's time that Keith sees that I can do more than screw, she thought. She seasoned the meat and put a pot of water on the stove to boil. She took a box of spaghetti from the bag and began dicing the onion, peppers, garlic, and tomatoes. Huh, if Keith thinks he's going to get rid of me just like that he's got another thing coming. I don't want to go psycho on him, but he's not gonna use me! She found a skillet to prepare the steak. Then she took a bottle of olive oil from the bag and poured some into the skillet.

Fifteen minutes later Keith emerged from the shower, grabbed a towel from the rack, and tied it around his waist. His nostrils were permeated with the aroma of spaghetti sauce, steak, and onions. Sylvia smiled and walked out of the kitchen and kissed him softly on the lips. He had been brooding in the shower over his luck with Justine. This was the first time she had given him the time of day. However, before he could give it further thought, Sylvia's new routine caught his attention. He was shocked that she was cooking and it smelled great too. She smiled and winked as she put her arms around his neck and pecked him on the lips. She smells really good, he thought. Was this a new perfume she was wearing? She pulled away from him giggling and said, "You hungry baby?"

"Yeah," he said, grinning from ear to ear. I didn't know you could cook!"

"Well there are a lot of things you don't know about me," she giggled turning her head sideways then tip toed and planted another kiss on his lips. He returned the kiss whole-heartedly. Earlier she had slipped a CD into the DVD player while he was in the shower and it was playing softly in the background. Suddenly Keith didn't feel that this would be the proper night to talk to Sylvia about taking her things home. She pulled away from him gently so she could attend to the food. He went into the main room and pulled some briefs and a tea shirt from a drawer that was built into the side of his bed and put them on.

Then he walked back into the kitchen to see how Sylvia and the food were coming along. She sprinkled fresh oregano into the pot and stirred it. She had a spoon in her hand with some spaghetti sauce in it and she spooned it into his mouth for him to taste. Then she turned to attend her pots. "Umm," he said. "That's good. Baby you can cook!"

She smiled as he was standing behind her holding her around the waist. She let her bottom rub against his man part that was beginning to swell. He pulled her closer to him, but she pulled away giggling and said, "Oh no you don't. I haven't finished cooking and we have to eat first this time." He laughed surprised at how good the food tasted. He was actually amazed at her. Maybe there was more to her than what met the eye? Go figure, he thought, just when you thought you knew everything there was to know about a person, they show you another side. She took two plates out of the cabinet and silverware from the drawer. Then she turned and asked Keith to get the snack tables from the closet so that they wouldn't make a mess by dropping bits of food on the floor. Keith obeyed her commands surprised at how much she knew about his place. With the snack table's set-up in front of the love seat, Sylvia set the food down along with the napkins and utensils and settled down beside Keith who had already seated himself on the sofa behind one of the snack tables. She looked at Keith smiling because he was looking at her in amazement and she flashed him a wink thinking to herself, Baby you don't know it yet, but you're in it for the long haul. Keith smiled back at her, picked up his knife and fork, and began to chow down. Keith hadn't realized it but he was really hungry and was no longer annoyed with Sylvia. He was somewhat intrigued with this side of her; somehow he had never envisioned Sylvia in the kitchen.

Justine had just finished the dishes. She entered the living room to settle down on her white el shaped couch when her phone rang. She went into the bedroom, took the cordless phone from its bed and said, "Hello."

"Hello mom," the voice of her younger daughter Jackie filled the airway.

"Jackie darling, how are you doing?"

"I'm good and how are you?"

"I guess you can say I'm fine."

"You Guess? Now what does that mean, mom?"

"Oh nothing, just a figure of speech; how are the kids?"

"They're good. Natalie has a cold, and Marla is doing just great. In fact, Marla will be graduating from middle school with honors in June!"

"You don't mean it," Justine exclaimed joyfully.

"Yep and you should see her, she's taller than I am now and both girls keep the phone jumping off the hook. If they're not on the phone with some boy, then they're texting some boy. I have to fight just to have a decent conversation with either of them. It seems we only exchange words in passing these days," Jackie said laughingly.

"Yeah well you better put a check on that, because boys and books don't match. Before you know it one or both of them will be in trouble and have to drop out of school."

"Mom, I can't keep them locked up in the house away from boys. That's just the way it is. They're teenagers."

"So what are you saying?" Justine said, sounding perturbed.

"Look mom, I just called to see how you were doing. I don't want to get into a debate on how to rear my children; we all know that you and dad were great parents and I for one know how strict you were. However, your way is not the only way to rear children. We are living in a different age now and frankly I don't think your way is the best way for today's children."

"OK, OK, you're their mother, I was just saying…"

"I know I know mom. Anyway how's your love life?"

"What? Oh please Jackie," Justine said, perturbed again.

"Ha, ha, ha, you don't want to talk about that," Jackie said teasingly.

"How's Greg?" Justine asked changing the subject.

"He's fine; the typical scientist always with his nose in a journal."

"Well does he spend time with you?"

"Mom, Greg is Greg. What can I tell you? I mean I knew what I signed up for in the beginning. Greg has always been honest about his work. I guess I wasn't really hearing him. You know how some of us girls can be. Sell our bodies mind and soul for that one moment in a white dress where we can be queen for a day. Then when the wedding is had and the honeymoon is over, you deal with the reality of what you just did. One thing leads to another and the next thing you know a baby arrives and well, the rest is history"

"Jackie, I don't like the tone of that."

"What tone, mom?"

"The tone of complacency, you sound lonely. Are you happy?"

"Happy? Mommy, happiness is relative. Who is happy?"

"Jackie, there are plenty of people that are happy."

"Really?" she exclaimed. "Do you know any of these happy people? I mean happiness comes in spurts and then it leaves. That's how it is, you deal with it."

"Is that what you really think?" Justine asked warily.

"Mom, I'm just a realist."

"I really don't like the way you are talking," Justine said flatly.

"Listen mom, it is what it is. Are you happy?" Jackie asked sharply.

"Me?"

"Yes you," Jackie asked adamantly.

"Well, yes, I guess I'm OK," Justine stated wanly.

"I didn't ask you if you were OK, I asked if you were happy and you can't even give me a straight answer, because there is no such thing as happiness except in spurts."

"Jackie, that's just not true. I was happy once and it lasted for years. If I knew then what I know now it could have lasted a lifetime. People just have to learn how to communicate with their mates. I'm worried about you and Greg. I think you two should get some counseling. This is a critical time in your relationship. The children are almost grown and will be leaving your house soon. If you and Greg are still in this hum drum place that you speak of so casually, there will be nothing to hold your relationship together," Justine said earnestly.

"You know mom, I think you should spend more time thinking about your own life," Jackie said flatly.

"Now that was not called for, Jackie I was only showing my concern for you."

"I know mom, anyway are you still coming to visit us?"

"Yes, I thought I'd wait until the weather gets hot here. I hate the humidity in New York in the summer. I figure that would be a great time to get away and I really appreciate the coolness in the air in Santa Rosa."

"Well mom, let me know when you're coming and I'll schedule my vacation accordingly."

"OK, I'll let you know. Give everyone a hug and kiss for me."

"I will mom, love you."

"Love you too baby-girl. Goodbye."

"Bye mom."

Justine hung up the phone feeling as though she had been kicked in the stomach. She didn't like Jackie's overall tone. But she had to agree with Jackie on one thing, she really wasn't happy. Jackie was right. It was time she concentrated on her own life and started living. She had been deliberately putting men off for years. At least Jackie was married and she and Greg had two beautiful children together. She just wanted Jackie to be aware and realize that her marriage was well worth working on. However, whatever Jackie did, Justine was smart enough to recognize that it was time for her to back up out of her daughter's affairs and get back into the game herself before it was too late.

Her mind wandered off to Sylvia. What about that little bimbo next door, she thought? Looking me up and down on the elevator as though I was trying to take her man. She was glaring at me so hard. If looks could kill I would be dead, and I didn't even do anything. If I wanted that player, I could have sampled him months ago. OK, I was kind of enjoying our little chat, but it was innocent. She had better watch her step or I'll give her something to worry about. After all I'm right next door she chuckled to herself feeling a little impish. Moreover, she thought, I was minding my own business. He approached me! I wonder how old he is. She thought again. He looks like he's around thirty-five. He could be older cause black don't crack. Not that I would be robbing the cradle if I did decide to take the plunge. After all I don't really look my age, and a ten or twelve year difference really isn't that bad. What am I thinking about, she thought, making a jerk like motion to her head? Keith is a player!

Little Ms. Bubbles is not the only one I have seen coming out of lover boy's apartment. Who cares what Keith does? I wouldn't get involved with him anyway. What happens if it doesn't work out? That's almost always the case these days. I would have to bump into him in the hall, the super market, or anywhere else in the neighborhood. Better to date men away from the homestead. The problem with that is I don't get out much. The only place I go to is work and church. I'm sorry, but I'm not trying to date any of those lame brothers at the church, and I couldn't think of dating anyone at work. God no! I'm sorry Lord, but the choices are not good.

Justine thought about the available men in her church and began to shudder. It's time to go to bed Justine. You're getting silly she told herself and went into the bathroom to draw her bath water. I must be real lonely she thought, because Keith was really starting to get to me today. She poured some bath powder and oil into her bath water. I must always keep it in mind that Keith is a player, she told herself. I must never allow myself to get caught up in his web. After all, I am too old to get mixed up in a mess, she thought. If I do get into a relationship, I want it to be meaningful.

THE BUSINESS TRIP

Viola packed the last of her overstuffed luggage and motioned for Claudio to remove it from her lavish king size bed. She stood in the middle of the floor wondering if she had forgotten anything. It was 3 p.m. and she had a 6:45 p.m. flight to catch. She was giving herself plenty of time to deal with the scrutinizing process connected to international flights. She was going to Brazil to tie up some loose ends concerning her new salon. Nelda, her partner in the Brazilian venture, was already at the job site in Brazil consulting with the contractors. She hated leaving Claudio behind, but she had to concentrate on the business. Claudio would be a distraction. She made sure that he had an endless supply of condoms and her blessings. It was the middle of May and she figured he would be out and about prowling the clubs in her absence. There was only one thing she demanded of him and this was that if he dated other women he would use condoms and not bring any of them to her house. She shuttered to think of some mindless bimbo in her house, sleeping in her bed, and touching her things. The thought was nauseating. Claudio assured her that she need not worry about other women because, she was his only interest. She did not even offer a rebuttal, because she knew he was a young man and in her absence he was bound to seek out other female companionship. The fact that she had brought him home to share her bed did not negate the fact that he was a gigolo and in her mind gigolo did not equate with monogamy. Viola's main concern was that he showed her the proper respect if the urge should hit him while she was away.

Looking around her bedroom her eyes landed on the wall opposite her bed where a hand carved Italian marble fireplace stood in the middle of the room embellished by a handsome antique brass screen. She caught a glimpse of her reflection in the oversized gold frame mirror above the mantle and sighed. She had warned Claudio earlier that if he violated her trust by bringing women into her home it would undoubtedly end their relationship. Viola dearly hoped that he heeded her warning because she was painfully serious. She walked over to the mantle and picked up one of the two Ross-Simons figurines that stood on either side of the mirror. She caressed it lovingly then gently set it back in place. She didn't like to think about him being with another woman, but she wasn't foolish enough to think that he wouldn't. After all, she really didn't know how long she would be gone. Why, she couldn't even speak for herself! If she was gone long enough, she might be the one who would take another lover. Though she doubted that she even would have the time, but one could never tell. One thing she knew for sure, with all of her money love was the one thing that couldn't be bought and she wasn't trying to. All she demanded was loyalty. If she contracted a venereal disease from him or he violated their agreement concerning women in the house, she would toss him out on his ear without a second thought.

Turning around sharply, she said. "Wait a minute Claudio I forgot to put my lap-top in my take-on luggage."

Claudio sat the luggage back down on her bed which was dressed with white silk sheets and pillow cases married with a white on white brocade comforter. Beneath it all a white laced bed skirt draped down onto the plush white carpet. "No problem Babe," he said smiling. She picked the lap-top off of the eighteenth century desk she found in an antique store off Broadway and tried to place it into her overstuffed take on luggage, but it wouldn't fit. Claudio looked at the lab-top and said, "Vie the luggage is very too small. Jou can put it in jour handbag no?"

"I know. I just didn't want to carry it," she said as she stuffed it in her oversized purse.

She turned around to face Claudio once more and said, "Remember Claudio, no women in my house while I'm gone on this business trip!"

Claudio looked at her in dismay, his green eyes denoting a hurt expression. "Honey, how many times jou gonna say me dat. Claudio would no to do des to jou." Claudio stood there feeling helpless. His English was limited and he couldn't express to her how profoundly he respected her. Viola looked at him, she didn't trust him completely and she felt badly about her suspicious nature but he was, after all, a stranger. No matter how you cut it she was taking a chance leaving him in her house while she was out of the country.

Before Claudio met Viola he lived from hand to mouth. He would pick up rich women on the beach in the hopes that they would throw him a few American dollars. He expected to make a living with his conquests. He tried to make enough to buy food for the house, keep a roof over his families head, and keep him in decent outer ware. The scraps these women threw his way meant his very survival. It was hard work because they wanted much for the little they gave. Sometimes they only gave him articles of clothing or a pair of shoes. Sometimes it was much more, it depended on the woman. When he first started he would often wasted his small investments. He would spend way too much money wining and dining, what he jokingly referred to as, counterfeit princesses. His untrained eye led him to women who looked rich to him because they were carrying fake Chanel handbags and wearing knock off designer swim suites. These women had no real money to speak of and they certainly were not financially equipped to afford to deal with a gigolo. In a way they were looking for the same thing he was looking for, a bigger better deal! Such women, for Claudio, were a complete waste of his time. As time went on he learned to figure out how to tell the real deal from the imposters. When he approached Viola he thought that it would be another ordinary encounter with a rich woman from America. However, it turned out to be the best run of his life. She was different from the others. She didn't immediately take him off to her bed. Her eyes glided over him like a scanner taking in every inch of him in a single glance. She asked his name and when he told her a smile magically stole its way across her face, "sit down," she bid him. He proceeded to run his silly little line on her and she let him. Then she laughed and invited him to join her for dinner. She didn't ask him to stay the night but instead instructed him to meet her in the lobby of the hotel for breakfast the next day. Claudio did not know what to expect from Viola. He noticed that her body was perfect as though sculptured from marble and he knew that he wouldn't have any trouble making love to her. However, she wasn't that eager to jump into bed with him. Claudio was very careful himself. He was well aware that sleeping with multiple partners was dangerous. He never went out on the prowl without his condoms. Some of his colleagues were HIV positive because they weren't careful. He remembered how he tried to explain to Vie that he was clean with his limited English. She didn't even try to understand what he was saying. She just insisted that he take a medical exam. Two weeks after he had tested negative on all counts he discovered the joys of being with her. She was not inhibited in any way. She gave pleasure as well as she received it. When it was established that he would be following her to the United States she took him on a shopping spree. She trashed all his other clothes and replaced them with all the top of the line designer names. He had no idea that his encounter with Viola would add up to all of this. She was the next best thing to an angel to him. When her lawyers finished his paperwork, it was not long before he was able to follow her to the United States to a life style that, before, he could only have imagined. He was now working in her shop doing odd jobs for which she generously paid him. Because of Viola, he was able to help his family back in the Favela a Rocinha slum in Rio de Janeiro. Viola had even enrolled him in a barber's school. She wanted him to learn all the current cuts. As soon as he received his certificate she put him to work in the salon under the supervision of her chief stylist, Jose.

When he thought about it he could see how she might think that he would bring other women home while she was away? But Claudio was nobody's fool. He could never be that stupid. One thing he knew about Viola was that she was no dummy and he wasn't going to do anything to jeopardize this relationship and new life. He had gotten lucky and would sooner cut off his hand, at this point, than risk Viola's wrath. He knew she really liked him and though he wasn't in love with her he was extremely devoted to her. He appreciated all that she did for him and he treated her like a princess in return. He doted over her and he enjoyed doing it. He truly cared for her and that was a fact.

They left the apartment and caught the elevators downstairs to the parking lot where he placed her take-on luggage in the back seat of her 2008 Mercedes and went around to the passenger side and opened the door for her. Afterward, the security guard assisted him in putting the rest of the luggage into the trunk. Claudio gave him a five dollar tip and then climbed into the driver's seat and turned the key in the ignition. Facing Viola he said, "Vie Claudio much respect jou, I would no to do dese tings jou say. Jou means too much for Claudio."

Viola looked at him and smiled, she had no intention of debating the matter and just looked through the car windows and said, "Yeah OK Claudio let's get going." Claudio was genuinely wounded and he let her know it.

"Look, Vie, I know how jou meet to me. Claudio is no, how do jou say, the dog for jou. I respect jou!"

Viola made eye contact with him realizing that she had offended him and put her hand on top of his with the appearance of all sincerity and said, "I know you do Claudio, I know," although this did not change her initial convictions concerning him seeking out female companionship. She was, however, giving him benefit of the doubt where bringing the females to her house was concerned. Claudio smiled, satisfied that she believed him, and happily pulled out of the garage. The sun was shining brightly in the sky and they had plenty of time. After their strained start the mood lightened and they were on their way to Kennedy Airport laughing and talking. Viola even allowed herself to feel how much she was going to miss him.

When they arrived at the airport Claudio drove into the parking lot. He wanted to spend time with Viola at the airport before she boarded her flight. He hadn't been consciously aware of how he was feeling until they had actually reached the airport. He was actually anxious about her leaving. Suppose Viola met another guy while she was in Brazil? I mean those guys were very aggressive and Viola reeked of money, he thought. She was a polished woman, and very attractive. Squeaky clean was the first thought that came to mind at first sight. She rarely wore loud color not even on her nails. She mainly wore clear, tan, or white. Her ebony skin was incredibly smooth and soft to the touch. Her hair and make-up was always impeccable. Her teeth, though she was not pleased with them, where white and polished. Why those Brazilian guys were going to zone in on her like buzzards to a corpse and I don't want to lose her, he thought. If she got it into her mind to dump me she could do it without a thought. Where it was true that Viola was capable of taking another lover, she was by no means looking to replacing Claudio for a new model. Her trip to Brazil was strictly business. There would be no playtime on the beach. Besides she had invested far too much in him to start all over again. She wanted to wrap up her business as soon as possible and return to the States.

Viola's first love had always been her salons. The salons were her children. She decided early on that she would bring no babies into the world. She felt that life was complicated enough without having to be responsible for another soul. Viola lived a very free life style and it suited her. Her parents were dead and she had no siblings so she was basically alone in the world.

Claudio knew Viola wasn't in-love with him and he didn't know how to accomplish that; he would have if he could. When it was time for Viola to head toward the gate to board the plane, Claudio pulled her into his arms and kissed her hard on the lips, "Claudio will miss jou," he said.

"I'm really going to miss you too babe," Viola said, looking deeply into his eyes. He actually was beginning to get under her skin. Maybe this trip was a good thing. She didn't want to get emotionally entangled with someone she could never really have. She made herself break free of his grip and heard herself saying "I miss you already." Claudio heard her and smiled and kissed her on her forehead happy to hear her say those words. He made it up in his mind that he would call her every day and every night. He didn't want time, space, or distance to hamper their communication. He knew he would definitely miss her tonight. If he were honest, he couldn't think of another woman who was better in bed. Just thinking about what she would do turned him on that he decided not to change the sheets on their bed until she returned. Carmen, however, had already changed the bed right after they left the house.

Viola arrived at gate twenty five. She reached in her Michael Kors handbag and took out her business class ticket. At that moment she heard the clerk ask the passengers in business class to board. She walked up to the front of the line and boarded the plane along with nine other passengers. It was going to be a ten hour flight. There would be no connecting flight so she hoped that they were serving something good to eat on the plane, because she was hungry and hadn't eaten anything. Claudio acted as though he couldn't let her go before it was time for her to actually board her flight. She chuckled to herself and thought if I didn't know better I'd think he was in love with me. I'm not falling for that though. He's had quite a lot of practice charming women. It would be silly of me to think his feelings were genuine. The flight attendant greeted her as she boarded the plane and she found her seat which was located by the window. She always felt a little uneasy before a flight so she said a small prayer; even though she was not quite sure to whom she was praying. Afterward her mind wondered back to Claudio and she thought to herself get a grip girl. It's not that serious.

CHANCE ENCOUNTER

A fter sweeping the floor, Marcelo Okonedo walked over to the storage room to open the boxes so he could stack the shelves. He had been in the United States for four-and-a-half years now; he arrived in October 2005. When he first arrived he stayed with his friend Kuffee where he slept on the floor in the living-room on a makeshift cot. He now shared an apartment in Brooklyn with a fellow emigrant, Emeka Edo, who came to the States from Nigeria.

Marcelo was what many women would call hand-some. His skin was flawless and his coloring was unusual. It was dark the color of cinnamon. His hair was tightly coiled. Each curl stood separate and individual unto itself spiraling like the springs of a mattress and he twisted them so that they tapered at the ends like cones. He lifted a box from the storeroom and carried it over to the isle where the vegetables were kept. He sat it onto a foot stool and began to unload the contents stacking the cans onto the shelves. When he had completely emptied the carton he carried the empty box back to the storage room and threw it on the floor with the others to be discarded. He unconsciously began to twist the few gray hairs that emerged from his temples but the rest of his hair was black like his goatee which also had a distinguishing grey streak running just slightly off center all the way down to the tip. He was tall and lean with piercing dark brown eyes which were set beneath his brow. His nose was strong and keen and his cheek bones were high. He lifted another box and carried it over to where the bread was kept then opened the box and removed the loaves of bread and quickly began replenishing the shelf, stacking them two at a time. When he had finished he stared off into space considering his next move. His gaze was powerful and somewhat unsettling at times. He could be warm and captivating or cold and menacing. But when he smiled, revealing his even white teeth, his face lit up and you were drawn to a countenance which invoked warmth as well as strength.

Marcelo was from the Ivory Coast, a country formally known as *Republique de Cote d' Ivoire*, in the continent of Africa which is located on the western side of its coast. Countries like Ghana, Liberia, Mali, and Guinea, lined the east and west side of the coast and its boarder. The French occupied the country in the eighteen hundreds and now the primary language spoken in his country is French. English is also taught in their schools and Marcelo was fluent in both languages. Marcelo was charismatic. When he spoke his voice was smooth and calming and it had a raspy quality like the sound of waves crashing up against the rocks. Most people were instantly taken by him, he made them feel safe. When he spoke English, it was impeccable with an ever so slight French accent. He was in this country because he had won a scholarship to study at Fordham University in the Bronx. He graduated from Fordham and obtained his Masters in business administration. He had a masters' degree in Theology as well which he obtained in Nigeria. He had been working at the store now for six months. He was finally able to start saving some money. Marcelo had been married in the Ivory Coast, but was now divorced and was actually hoping to marry an American woman. Fortune had smiled on him when he went to the store to buy some yams and found the owner, sprawled out on the floor. The owner was a Jewish man, named Samuel Shapiro. He had a large gash in his head and the empty cash register was wide open. Food was scattered about on the floor and apparently one of the robbers had hit Mr. Shapiro over the head with a hard object. The gash in his head poured forth blood like a waterfall. Marcelo grabbed a rag from behind the counter and applied pressure to shut off the flow. Marcelo helped him to his feet and seated him in a chair. Samuel was incoherent and dazed. His eyes lazily scanned over the interior of the store as he slowly regained his bearings. Marcelo called 911 and some minutes later an ambulance arrived. The EMS worker said that Mr. Shapiro might not have made it if Marcelo hadn't stopped the bleeding. Mr. Shapiro had lost a lot of blood. Because Marcelo was so caring and attentive to Samuel before the ambulance and police arrived, Mr. Shapiro trusted Marcelo and gave him his wife's number and asked him to contact her and tell her where the ambulance was taking him. He even placed the keys to the store in Marcelo's hands. Marcelo called Arlene Shapiro and waited for her to come to the store and the rest is history. He now manages the store and was making a decent salary for an African who just came to the country to study on a scholarship.

Working in this small store enabled him to execute some of the business skills he acquired in College. Already the sales had picked up due to his great sense of business and the new visual displays the Shapiro's allowed him to put into place. The Shapiro's actually stepped back and allowed him to take the lead. They were an elderly couple with no children and they saw something special in

Marcelo. They even offered to assist him in getting permanent residency. Marcelo appreciated this offer and he didn't turn it down though he was hoping to find an American wife which would reinforce his ability to accomplish his goals in any event. He wanted a mate with similar ambitions, someone who wanted to build something. But he wanted someone that he could care for, and he wanted her to be smart with a good work ethic. He was not looking for a young woman because he didn't want any more children. He was looking for a woman in her mid-to-late forty's. He already had two children from his first marriage back in Africa. Children were expensive. He wanted to send for his children in Africa so they too could go to school in the United States.

Marcelo finished stacking all the shelves and when everything was in its place, removed his apron, locked the front door and closed the blinds so that no one would see him counting the money. When he had finished, he placed it into the safe which was located in the back room of the store so that Mr. Shapiro would be able to take it to the bank in the morning. He walked to the side of the store and used the toilet. After washing his hands he looked into the small dingy little mirror above the sink, twisted a few of the screw like curls on his head, and then took a small comb from his pocket and combed his mustache and goatee. Then he slipped the comb back in his pocket, and headed for the door to set the alarm. After locking the door he pulled the gates together and inserted a pad lock. Then he headed for the subways.

He lived in Brooklyn, but he was on his way up town to Union Square to visit one of his countrymen, Chide, who just arrived in the States and was living on 14th Street in Manhattan. He had not seen him since he left the Ivory Coast. As he walked down the street past the stores toward the station he looked forward to the reunion. He caught the J train at Essex Street and got off at Chambers' to catch the four or five express train whichever came first. He was approaching the top of the stairs leading to the up-town trains and was about to descend when he saw the number five train pulling out of the station, "Shit," he said, annoyed that he had just missed his train. Then he descended the stairs and saw that the number six was still waiting in the station. Crowds of people were waiting for an express train on the other side of the platform. Since he didn't know how long the wait would be for an express he decided to take the number six local up-town. He stepped inside the car and took an empty seat near the door. People were seated on both sides of the train and there were a few people inside who were standing and reading the newspapers. A couple of people were leaning up against the closed doors on the other side of the train. He heard the chime signaling that the doors, on the side where he was sitting, were about to close then he heard the number 4 train pulling into the station across the platform. He sprung up out of his seat and hopped off the train just as the door was closing. The number four train spilled into the station with a rage and the sound of its metal wheels screeched as they came to a halt.

Passengers poured out of the train like cattle. Marcelo stood to the side with other passengers who were waiting to board the train when it cleared. As he stepped in the doorway of the train, he was herded into the middle of the car by a crowd of inpatient New Yorkers behind him. When the train finally pulled into Union Square, Marcelo had to make his way to the door pushing past strap hangers holding onto the bars above the heads of the seated passengers. As he was stepping off the train, a strikingly attractive woman was boarding. Their eyes met and he was suddenly spellbound. He could tell that she was feeling something too, because she actually turned around in the doorway so as not to break eye contact. All the while, they both were being shoved about by boarding passengers hungrily scrambling to win the seats that were abandoned by passengers who had just exited the train.

The chime signaled that the doors were about to close and Marcelo, who was now standing on the platform, made a split second decision and stepped back onto the crowded train. Both their eyes never relinquished their connection. He cupped her elbow, and meandered through the crowd until he won them a spot near a pole where they could hold on as they stood. "Hi," he said.

She flashed him a beautiful smile and returned his salutation.

"I don't know what to say," Marcelo said shyly. "You wouldn't believe me if I told you that I have never done anything like this before."

"Oh, but I would believe you," she said. "This is a new experience for me as well. I'm a native New Yorker and I don't readily engage in conversations with strangers."

"May I have your name?" he asked sheepishly.

"My name is Justine, and yours?"

"My name is Marcelo."

"Hum, Marcelo, that's French, isn't it?"

Marcelo smiled and said, "It's Latin. There are a lot of Spaniard, Brazilian and Italian Marcelo's as well."

Justine extended her hand and he took her hand in his and kissed it. "Oh!" she said and actually giggled. Smiling broadly she injected, "how chic!"

"I could do no less," he said, staring deeply into her eyes. Justine couldn't turn her gaze away from his. They stood there awkwardly for a moment. Her heart pounding so rapidly she felt she might faint. His lips were so perfectly sculptured so full and inviting she had an overwhelming desire to kiss this perfect stranger. Usually Marcelo was able to hold someone's gaze until they shifted their eyes away, but he knew that if he didn't turn his eyes away from hers he would kiss her right there on the moving train in front of everyone and possibly scare her away. He turned his gaze away from the magnetic hold her eyes had on him and looked down at her hand which he was still holding in his.

Then he spoke, "Are you going to work or coming from work?" His voice was so calming she was momentarily unaware of the people around them or even the noise of the roaring train as it raced toward the 42nd street station.

"I just got off work. Actually, this is quite early for me. I usually work much later," she said, surprised at how freely she had offered up the information. It was then that she became aware that he was still holding her hand. She started the action of pulling it away, but he would not let it go.

He raised her hand to his lips and kissed it again; "I can't let you get away. Listen," he said, smiling broadly. "The train is pulling into the station. Let us get off there so we can go to Starbucks and talk."

Justine couldn't believe it, but she heard her voice saying, "Sounds like a plan to me."

"You," they both said simultaneously.

"Go, ahead," he said.

"No, no what were you going to say?" Justine asked anxiously.

"There's a bar restaurant on Park Avenue and 42nd I can't remember the name, but I've always wanted to go in there," he said.

"I'm game," Justine said smiling. What had come over

her? He made her feel so giddy. Maybe it was because it was summer, or maybe it was because of his strange magnetism or, maybe it was just the right time in her life. Whatever it was she knew that something was happening between them and she didn't want it to get away. Marcelo lied when he said that nothing like this had ever happened to him before. Now that he thought about it he realized that it had happened to him several years before. Only then he didn't act on it and he promised himself that if he was ever struck by anyone else in that way again, he would not allow the opportunity to evade him. He had not been consciously aware when he jumped back onto the train. However, he was sure that his unconscious mind was in operation and had taken the decision to re-board the train.

They exited the train together and instantly began laughing and talking just like they were old friends. He discovered that she was Operations Manager for an advertising company in the city and that she loved to dabble in art in her spare time. He told her that he was into business, but loved to engage in photography. He shared that he recently obtained his masters in business and was presently working at a grocery store in lower Manhattan. They exited the station on the Lexington Avenue side and headed over to Park and 42nd Street on the South side of the street. The Bar restaurant was on the north corner and a sign in the window stated, *Wednesday & Thursday Night's "Happy Hour" from 6 p.m. to 8 p.m.* Music greeted them at the door. The place was already beginning to fill up. The bar was stationed at the far corner of the room. People were seated around it while others were standing laughing and talking. Servers' dressed in short black skirts and white peasant blouses where weaving in and out and to and fro the bar like worker bees in and out of a hive. They were carrying drinks on trays which rested in the palms of their hands and they delivered them to tables where their perspective customers awaited. Marcelo saw an empty table in the back so he took Justine's hand and led the way meandering through couples who were headed in the opposite direction. He forged ahead and grabbed a cozy little table which was situated in the corner of the room.

A server approached them shortly after they were settled.

"Hi, my name is Sal and I'm your server for tonight. What are you drinking?" Marcelo waved his hand at Justine and said, "After you."

"OK," Justine said. "I'll have a Mojito." Looking over at Marcelo she smiled devilishly.

"I'll have vodka and orange juice," he said and reached over the table and took both her hands in his.

"We have a buffet table on the other side by the mirrors for the happy hour," said the server, her soft brown eyes shifting from Marcelo to Justine as she set two small plates on the table.

"Feel free to help yourselves." Then she scurried off into the crowd to get their drinks.

"Shall we check out the buffet table?" asked Marcelo."

Justine stood to her feet and said, "Don't mind if I do."

Marcelo stood up and they took their plates and went over to the buffet table and filled them with broccoli, Buffalo wings, and little potato thingies.

"I'm really happy I met you," he said, gazing into her eyes.

"I don't know what's come over me, but I'm pretty happy that I met you too," Justine said, drinking in the magic of his eyes.

"You might not believe this," Justine said laughing,

"but I have never, ever in my life, not even when I was teenager, met someone on the train and gone off with them. This is like something that you see happening in a movie. I never really imagined real people doing something like this."

"Sure they do," Marcelo said. "Where do you think the writers get their information, they take it from life experience. Anything that you see in the movies has happened to someone in real life."

"You think so?" asked Justine.

"I know so," Marcelo said confidently. They went back to their table.

"Ooh, so I guess now it's our turn to have one of these life experiences," Justine said, looking at him sideways and biting her bottom lip as she smiled.

Marcelo leaned forward flashing her one of his breathtaking smiles and said, "Yes, it's our turn." And they both laughed, then the server came over with their drinks. "Thank you," Marcelo said. Then he turned to Justine and said, "This is my lucky day." He lifted his glass and toasted her saying, "To us." Then he touched her glass with his.

"To us," she replied, and by their third drink they were throwing back their heads and laughing loud really having a great time like two old friends. Later Justine had to use the ladies room and when she stood up she realized that she was feeling woozy.

"Woo, I think I had too much to drink," she said.

"Are you OK?" Marcelo asked, sounding genuinely concerned.

"Yeah, I think I can make it, but I, woo, I feel wobbly."

"Be careful," Marcelo said, looking worried. "Wait a minute I'll go with you. I think you have to go down a couple of steps before you reach the restroom and I don't want you to fall." He could see that she was not steady on her feet and took hold of her arm. Now Justine was embarrassed. She thought what must he think of me? When they had made their way through the crowd he held her around the waist and led her down the few steps that lead to the restroom. She opened the Ladies Room door still a little wobbly and went inside. He stood by the door and waited for her to come out. When she exited the restroom she put both arms around his neck. She was feeling no pain and as she leaned in her lips touched his ear and she whispered, "Can we go to Starbucks?"

Marcelo laughed and said, "Yes we can go to Starbucks." Then he gently guided her up the few steps and they went back to their table. He signaled for the server to give him the check. After a few moments the server approached their table and scribbled out the check. He put sixty dollars in the little black leather folder that housed the check and handed it to the server. They put on their jackets readying themselves to leave. When the server returned with his change, he waived for her to keep it and they left. They stepped out onto the streets. It was dark now and the cool air blew gently over their faces. The moon was out and the night was clear Justine felt safe as they headed toward Madison Avenue for Starbucks. The mild cool breeze of June's night air helped to clear Justine's head. As they strolled Marcelo put his arm around her shoulder and they appeared to all eyes a seasoned couple.

Leaving the coffee shop Justine was feeling much better. Marcelo wanted to ride up-town with her, but she assured him that she would be alright. As taken as she was with him she didn't want him to escort her to her door. There was, just a little bit, too much chemistry between them and she couldn't trust herself in her condition should he kiss her good night. With all that chemistry between them, if he walked her to her door a kiss was certain. Besides it was a straight ride and the train station was only a block away from her house. Better to end it here. He had her phone number. She was certain that they would see each other again and when they did she surely would not drink nearly as much as she had tonight. Though they were headed in different directions, Marcelo insisted on escorting her to the up-town train platform and waited there with her until she had boarded the train. Justine found a seat in the center of the car. Spotting Marcelo on the outside of the car she waved as the train pulled out of the station. Marcelo waved back then climbed up the stairs taking two steps at a time and ran over to the down-town side just in time to catch the number five, which was pulling into the station.

This was his lucky day he thought again. She was American and he really liked her and he knew that she liked him as well. He would have to see Chide another day. He'd call him tonight and tell him what happened. Chide would surely understand. After all, Chide had stood him up many a time for the sake of a woman. He chuckled feeling quite pleased with himself, everything was falling into place. He had graduated with honors, he had a fairly decent job; though he knew that he wouldn't be working there long after he obtained permanent residency. He wanted to go into business for himself; he was determined to do so.

How lucky could one man be, he thought. He knew that he was being a bit presumptuous, but he felt a real connection with this woman and it would be great if this chance encounter actually lead to something. He couldn't believe how she made his heart race. How great would it be if she turned out to be the one! Let me not get too overjoyed, he cautioned himself. Let's see how it all plays out, after all I only just met her. Nevertheless, he couldn't help thinking that they were destined for each other and they would make a distinguished couple. The chemistry was amazing! Wow, they seemed to be a perfect match, him with the streak of white hair running through his beard and her with the patch of white hair on one side of her head. That was part of what attracted him to her. He couldn't get over that whole scene on the train. It was really spelledbinding. Why, it was even crazy. He knew that he would be calling her tonight after he spoke with Chide. He hoped that his roommate Emeka would be asleep when he reached the house.

Marcelo didn't feel like going over tonight's encounter with him. He would tell Chide, because Justine was the reason that he had stood him up and that was something he would not ordinarily have done. However, he would be careful not to go into too much detail. Maybe he was being silly, but he didn't want to jinx it. She was the first woman who sparked his interest since he'd been in this country. She was quite intelligent. He would have to play his cards right. He had to show her what he was bringing to the table, because ultimately he was looking for a wife. Most of these American women were different from African women, their customs where certainly not the same. In Africa the man is almost always the aggressor. Not so here, these women are bold, very aggressive, and difficult. However, Justine didn't appear to be like that. In the Ivory Coast the man is the head of the household. It is as the Bible teaches, he thought. Therefore his way was most definitely the right way. It was crazy the way these American women behaved with their men. Some of them were out right disrespectful. But Justine didn't seem to be like that. She was a lady, though, she couldn't hold her liquor. I could take care of that later, he thought. If we become serious I would not allow her to drink. I must tolerate it for now, because drinking will help break down the barriers. Justine, however, does not appear to be a drinker and that's a good thing, he thought as he twisted on the grey hairs at his temple.

Marcelo was very tired and mellowed by the alcohol. He was about to drift off when he heard the chime signaling that the doors of the train were about to close. It was then that he noticed he was at Fulton Street. He jumped up barely making it off the train. The doors closed in on him, and had to re-open so he that he could get off. That would've been awful if he hadn't realized that he'd reached his stop. He would have had to ride all the way to Wall Street before he could get off. Then he would have to cross over and ride back up to Fulton Street in order to get the A train. Marcelo wasn't really a drinker either. He did it to be social. He would keep beers in the fridge in case some of his friends stopped by. But if it were left up to him, he wouldn't bother with hard drink at all.

He made his way down the stairs and walked down the long corridors to the platform where you catch the A, C, and F trains. There were not many people in the subway at this hour. There was a young couple sitting on the bench caressing each other, a man pacing back and forth on the platform, and a few other people at the other end of the station. It was really complicated underground when one was sober, but when you've had a few drinks, it was a bit of a challenge. And if you didn't really know where you were going, being tipsy in New York, you could ride the trains all night.

In a way he was glad that Justine didn't want him to ride up-town with her to the Bronx, because he was really feeling the alcohol now and just wanted to get home to his bed. Had he gone with Justine he would have had to ride all the way back downtown, because there was no way she could have allowed him to spend the night in her house. After all, they were strangers who met on the subway. If he had gone uptown and she had invited him to sleep over night, he would have done so, but that would have put her out of the running of becoming a serious partner in his mind. He had specific expectations of the woman that he would call his own. He preferred to think that the reason Justine didn't want him to escort her home was, because she wanted to spare him the long train ride home from the Bronx. Marcelo savored the thought and took a seat on the other side of the wooden bench opposite the young couple and waited for the train. No matter how he went over it in his mind, though, he felt badly about not being physically able to escort Justine home. He would have to get a car. But then, he thought, if he were driving a car tonight they would never have met. Then he wondered how much it would have cost to take a cab from the Bronx to 42nd Street. He had just met her and amazingly he couldn't get her out of his mind. He hoped that she reached home safely. As for him, he was overcome with fatigue, but he dare not close his eyes for fear of falling asleep and missing the train altogether. Perhaps he would wait to call Justine in the morning.

AN EVENING OF SURPRISE

I t was a moon lit night crisp and clear and the stars adorned the heavens illuminating the skies with cosmic splendor. Keith glided into the parking lot of his residence on the wheels of a shiny new 2009 Nissan Maxima, inundated with feelings of joy having just purchased the burgundy coach that graced the parking garage in all its brilliance. He was returning from a weekend get-a-way with a hot little number he met that Friday at a barbeque party. He arrived at the party that night generating charisma likened unto a prince. The instant he laid eyes on Chichi a thirst developed that only she could quench. Quickly she recognized it, and teased him unmercifully all night, until even she herself could not deny the primal urge which consumed them both directing their paths to the Holiday End. They had breakfast in bed, that Saturday morning, and decided to spend the balance of their weekend dancing to the tune of the horizontal mambo. Normally Keith would have counted himself lucky and taken her home, that Sunday night, with a promise that he would call. Then he would neatly file her number away in his little black book along with a host of others. However, since Keith was off for the 4th of July and didn't have to work Monday, he decided to bring the party home. He hopped out of the car, ran around to the passenger side, and opened the door. Chichi Wang stepped out. Her long straight hair fell forward creating a veil like covering over her face. She flung her head back casting the hair away revealing beautifully almond shaped eyes. Tiptoeing in order to get her arms around Keith's neck, she pressed her perfectly sculptured lips on his and gently kissed him. She was maybe five feet tall if that. Petite would be an accurate description. Keith was amazed at how flexible she was in bed. He just couldn't get enough of her. After the kiss she walked around him and headed toward the entrance of the building. Playfully she swayed her hips seductively while Keith eyed the show she performed, for him, from behind. She was a compact little ball of fire. She was wearing a cream colored blouse with a v neckline that ended just above the waistline exposing the sides of her breasts. Her short, tight, satin skirt clung to her curvaceous little body like the peal clings to an apple. It had a split on one side accentuating her shapely legs, and she was sporting seven inch stiletto platform heels. Keith whistled, and made some whopping noise as he caught up with her, and put his arm around her tiny waist. Plus, he thought, she needed some help navigating in those ridiculously high heels. Joe, the doorman, came from behind his counter to open the door for them. He was a tall and portly African American with skin so fair he appeared to be an albino. His face was speckled with freckles and his eyes were small and set far apart burrowing deep beneath his protruding brow.

"Mr. Huston," he said. His large mouth spread out across his face into a toothy grin thus causing his wide flat nose to flare at the nostrils.

"You the man!" he said, eyeing Chichi thirstily.

"Hey man, how's it going?" Keith replied coolly. Keith put his arms around Chichi's shoulders and led her toward the elevator banks. The doorman watched them until they disappeared into one of the cars. Wow! he thought, how does he do it? He is the man. Each one is better than the last and they ALL are FINE! Man he can send me his leftovers any day, any time, and anywhere. He even had that cold fish in 19A smiling the other day and that's something, because she doesn't socialize with any of the men in the building. It's impossible to befriend her...she's so damn stuck-up. But Mr. Huston had her smiling from ear to ear, that is, until that little Cajun spit fire jumped up off the bench and made her presence known. I thought she was gonna lasso him and place a "SOLD" sign on his chest or something. Man if I could only be him for a day! While he was deep in thought Sylvia, the Cajun spit fire, approached the desk.

"Hey Joe, I'm here to see Keith." Sylvia knew he was home, because she spotted the burgundy Maxima pull into the driveway when she was pulling up in the cab. She had been calling him all weekend but Keith wasn't picking up her calls so she decided to come over and see why he was avoiding her. If she could have finished up her transaction with the cabby sooner, she would have actually caught up with Keith in the Lobby.

"Ms. Sylvia, le-let me call him an-and tell him you're here," Joe stammered as he picked up the phone to ring Keith's apartment.

"Oh he's expecting me," Sylvia lied.

Somehow, Joe didn't quite believe that could be the true. "I know but I have to check it out first," Joe said, gaining his composer.

"Since when?" Sylvia demanded, because Joe had allowed her to go straight up on several occasions. However, Keith didn't appreciate it and spoke to Joe about it so he was certain Mr. Huston wouldn't be happy to see her walking up on him now.

"Management is cracking down," Joe said, removing

his hat and scratching his curly red hair, then replacing it back on his head nervously. "I have to announce all guests before allowing them to go in." He dialed Keith's number but the phone just rang. Pick up the phone, he thought to no avail. Keith had stopped in the hall to converse with one of his neighbors, who was waiting for the elevator, when he and Chichi were getting off on his floor. While Joe was ringing Keith's apartment, three visitors approached the desk.

"Welcome to the Gin-gum Towers," he said with the receiver still in his hand. One of the visitors, a elderly woman in her 70's, said, "We come to see Ronald Fox, in 19C."

"OK let me call him for you," Joe said, hanging up the phone. He motioned with one finger for Sylvia to wait as he dialed Mr. Fox's apartment. After a few rings, Mr. Fox answered the phone. While Joe was on the phone two residents were exiting the building and Sylvia slipped through the door as they were coming out. Joe turned around just in time to see her entering and called after her to halt, but Sylvia proceeded to the elevator banks and boarded an open car.

Joe was still calling after her and Mr. Fox said, "What's going on Joe?"

"Ooh, Mr. Fox, some visitors are here to see you."

"Yes, have them come up, I'm expecting them."

"OK sir." He had them sign the book and when they finished signing, he pressed the buzzer so that they could enter. Picking up the phone, he tried Keith's apartment again but there was still no answer.

Keith and Chichi had just reached his door and Chichi was fondling him, standing on her toes, trying to kiss him while he fumbled for his keys. Keith could hear his phone ringing inside his apartment and thought, I'm going to have to turn the phone off when I get inside because I don't want to be disturbed. Finally Keith located his keys and inserted one into the lock and opened the door, at that precise moment, the elevator bell chimed, the doors of the elevator opened and Sylvia stepped off just as he was about to enter his apartment. He turned when he heard Sylvia's sing song voice shouting, "So this is why you haven't been picking up my calls!"

Keith turned around in shock! "Sylvia, What the... why are you here?"

"Are you talking to me like that because of that thing over there?" she screeched as she pointed her finger toward Chichi. Keith stepped away from the door and walked over to Sylvia grabbing her by the elbow and ushered her over toward the elevators.

"You can't just waltz up here anytime you feel like it. Go home I'll call you tomorrow," he said.

Sylvia quickly maneuvered her way free of his grip and like a cat she sprung around and jumped on Chichi who was completely caught off guard. Before she could react, Sylvia had grabbed a hand full of her hair and flung her up against Justine's door and commenced to pound her face with her closed fist. She was wearing a ring which cut the delicate tissue of Chichi's face opening a waterfall of blood. By the time Keith was able to get over to where she was to break it up, Sylvia had struck Chichi five consecutive times about the face and head. Keith literally had to pick Sylvia up off the ground, by her waist, in order to pull her away. Chichi lost her balance because of the extremely high heels she was wearing. One of her knees was dragging the ground while she was attempting to regain her footage, when she fell, the other shoe came off. Sylvia was kicking and thrashing her legs about, trying to get Keith to put her down. She had still managed to maintain her hold on Chichi's hair. Justine opened her door because of the commotion when the elevator chimed and Mr. Fox's visitors exited the elevator. Mr. Fox had also heard the noise and opened his door as well. Keith was finally able to pry Sylvia's hand open to release her grip on Chichi's hair. Chichi was then able to scramble to her feet.

"Shall I call the police?" Justine asked amazed and astonished at what she was seeing. Thinking to herself my mind never leads me wrong, glad I stayed away from this player!

"No, no," Keith said. "I've got it under control."

He was so angry and embarrassed he flung Sylvia up against the wall holding her there and yelled, "What the hell is wrong with you? Are you crazy?"

Chichi picked up her shoe and handbag that was scattered on the floor and limped on one heel toward the elevator bank. Keith released Sylvia to go after Chichi and Sylvia took that opportunity to enter Keith's apartment.

"Chichi don't leave. I'll get rid of her," Keith said.

"No, no, let go of me," Chichi sobbed. Her face was beginning to swell, her lip was cut, and her nose was bleeding. She pressed the button for the elevator and opened her purse to get some tissues for her nose.

"Here let me help you," Keith said, trying to assist her. She pulled away from him. She was crying hysterically and everyone in the hall looked on astonished. The bell chimed and the elevator doors opened and Chichi stepped on. Keith followed leaving behind the blatant stares of his neighbors and the visitors who were still standing in the hallway. Keith tried to apologize, but Chichi was having none of it. Keith looked at her face and shuttered. Her left eye was closing up.

"I'll take you home," he said.

She didn't respond. She just put on the other ridiculously high heel so she wouldn't have to continue limping. He wanted to console her and wondered how Sylvia was able to get into the building. He felt angry, embarrassed, helpless, and badly for Chichi all at the same time. Finally they reached the lobby. Keith marched straight over to Joe.

"How in the hell did you let this happen?"

Joe threw his hands up and exclaimed, "I'm sorry, she ran in when tenants were leaving the building and I was attending to visitors…"

"I don't give a damn about all that. You should not have allowed this to happen. You get paid to protect the residents and their guests. I'm going to report this shit to management."

Chichi shouted, "Keith, are you going to take me home?" Keith walked over to her and ushered her through the door, when he suddenly realized that he had left his car keys upstairs in the door.

Then he said, "I just have to run upstairs and get my car keys. Wait here I'll be right back."

This was the last straw for Chichi as she turned to him pointing at her distorted face and screamed. "Look what you're crazy girlfriend did to me. Do you think I'm going to wait down here for her to come back? I don't need you to take me home. Just get me a cab."

Joe leaped from behind the desk and took to the street to hail a cab. He knew that there would be repercussions behind all of this. It was all because of Huston and that crazy nut Ms. Cartier. And to think, that he was actually envying him. The grass always looks greener on the other side, he thought. He saw a cab coming down the street and hailed it and brought it over to the building. Joe opened the door so that Chichi could enter. Keith accompanied Chichi to the cab and attempted to get in, but she put up her hand to stop him.

"I don't need you and I don't need all of your trouble. You know what Keith, I never want to see you again." She pulled the door shut and gave the cabby her address and they pulled off down the street. Keith stood there watching the cab until it reached the corner and turned out of sight. Then scratching his head he walked back over to the building. Joe tried to apologize again, but Keith pointed to the door for him to open it and when he did Keith stepped inside and walked over to the elevator banks without as much as a glance back. An elevator was waiting with its doors open and he went inside and pressed for his floor and the door shut.

Stepping off the elevator he was grateful to see that his neighbors were no longer in the hall. The keys were still dangling in the lock and the door to his apartment was opened. He removed the keys from the lock and entered. To his utter disbelief, Sylvia was sitting on the loveseat wearing one of her nightgowns that she'd left behind. She was actually drinking a glass of orange juice as though nothing had taken place. She turned to look at him standing in the small foyer and said, "I bet we won't be seeing her again." Keith could not believe her gall, who in the hell did she think she was, he thought. He was furious as he approached her and snatched her off of the loveseat holding her arm firmly this time.

"You're hurting me!" she yelled.

"I'll do more than that if you don't get the hell out of my house!" He pulled at the nightgown tearing it off of her shoulder which knocked the glass of juice out of her hand onto the parquet floor. It splattered into pieces spilling juice all around.

"Put your clothes on. I want you out of my house. I can't stand the sight of you," he shouted. She wheeled around and spit in his face. He released her instantly astonished as he wiped the spittle off.

"Did you think you could use my body, over and over again, and then just push me aside whenever it suited you?" she squealed. Then she walked back over to the love seat, stepping over the juice and broken glass, and sat down. She looked ridiculous sitting there half naked in a torn gown. Keith who was blind with rage slapped her so hard it knocked her off the seat and landed her onto the broken glass and juice that was splattered on the floor. The impact was so hard that she was unable to utter a sound. Her knees were bleeding from the broken glass, and her mouth was gaped wide open as she knelt there in the mess holding the side of her face. After a few seconds, sound was able to escape as she exhaled and her scream filled the room, "Aaaaaaah!"

Keith still furious grabbed her by the hair dragging her across the floor causing the glass to cut her legs and thighs. He was about to strike her again when she cried out, "I'm pregnant! Please, Keith, don't hurt me." Keith's open hand was suspended in mid air and as the meaning of her words registered in his mind, he was shocked for the second time that night.

"What did you – say?" he asked, not quite sure of what he had heard.

"I'm pregnant," she said, sobbing hysterically. Keith returned from that dark place of rage and released his hold on her as he sunk down to the floor completely deflated.

Sylvia was a small woman, not as small as Chichi, but she could also be considered petite. Shame stole its way into the corridors of his mind. No matter what she had done, he knew he should have exercised more control. He had lost it. Maybe she was right. He hadn't taken her feelings into consideration. All he did was follow his own lust and now she was pregnant and He knew it belonged to him. Even though she wore tight clothes and sometimes acted like a ditz, he knew she really wasn't a loose woman. He was completely aware that her feelings for him were strong. Normally when he didn't return a woman's feelings, he just broke it off. Why was he playing this game with Sylvia? She must have called him two dozen times. Why didn't he just pick up the call and tell her to buzz off? What had he been afraid of? He looked over at her on the floor sitting in the mess sobbing. Then he rose to his feet and helped her to hers and took her into his arms and began to stroke her hair as she sobbed. Why had he been so angry with her? It wasn't because of Chichi. He didn't even really know Chichi. Maybe it was her gall that had angered him. She was a spitfire with balls and he knew this.

"Shush," he said in a soft voice "don't cry, I'm sorry." Keith had never actually hit a woman in his life and the shame of it fostered the fact that he never would again. He knew that Sylvia was wrong in what she had done, but at the same time he had to own some of the responsibility for what had happened tonight. It wouldn't have come to this if he had answered his phone or, better still, stayed where he was, he thought. This caused him to ask himself the question of why he hadn't answered Sylvia's calls. Did he not want to talk to Sylvia, because he knew that she would question him on his whereabouts and he was afraid to tell her? When had she acquired that kind of power over him? And she did have a power over him. It was quite simple actually. Deep down, he was afraid of losing her. He was still very angry with her, because of what she had done tonight. But it was more than that. He was angry because she actually felt she could get away with it, and better still, she had. Why hadn't he called security to get rid of her and insist that Chichi stay? He could have done that if he really wanted to. He could have won Chichi over if he really cared to. He knew how to beg when he wanted something from a woman. But, he hadn't done that, because if he had done that it would have ended the relationship he had with Sylvia for good. He would have been forced to take a stand. He had to face a simple fact. He didn't want his relationship with Sylvia to end. He couldn't imagine her being escorted out of the building by security or worse the police. No matter what he told himself, he wasn't ready to end it with her. She had once asked him when they were in bed together if he would mind if she dated other men and it angered him.

"Do you want to see other men?" he had asked angrily. Before she could answer, he shouted, "Go ahead, if that's what you want to do. See if I care."

Sylvia giggled and rubbed her leg against his and said "I was only kidding, Keith." Then she kissed him on the cheek and after that he had made love to her with a passion that seemed to come from nowhere. This was something that he had never experienced before. He never cared what the women he dated did once they left his house. She knew he had feelings for her or she wouldn't have had the nerve to come to his house tonight. She knew that she'd acquired a certain status of worth to him even if he wouldn't confirm it verbally. She was intuitive, he himself was not aware of how much he felt for her until now. Why, he had even stopped trying to date Justine next door. And he really liked Justine, but Sylvia had somehow gotten under his skin somewhere along the way. She became more than just a lay and she had more in common with him than he first thought. She was alone in New York away from her family and no real friends to speak of. Keith was alone too. Miss Sylvia was actually much smarter than he initially thought also. She fooled a lot of people with her demeanor and that squeaky voice. The truth of the matter is she was probably much smarter than Keith!

Tonight everything happened so fast it was like a dream or more accurate a nightmare. However, something changed tonight. Tonight he had knowledge that he did not possess before. Tonight he discovered Sylvia was going to be the mother of his unborn child. More than that, he discovered that he wanted it! She had told him that she was pregnant and he didn't feel like running for the hills. He welcomed it; he savored it. The truth was Keith had been lonely, but he didn't know it. It was time he grew up, he thought. Women were not toys and Sylvia certainly was no joke. But what was he going to do? Did he really know Sylvia? Had he ever really listened to anything she said? He certainly heard what she had to say tonight! If it wasn't so serious he would have to laugh. She accused him of using her body, but that was not exactly true. They had been using each other, he thought. Maybe he had started out to use her in the beginning, but it changed somewhere along the way. He had to admit that he enjoyed her company. She could be pretty funny and he was beginning to like having her around.

As he stood there holding her in his arms he realized how much she mattered to him. He had never really been in a serious relationship before. His father had left his mother long before he was born and he just didn't know how to be anybody's man. What he was feeling now was strange, but he was going to try. Maybe that was why he let his relationship with Sylvia go on so long. He had told himself Sylvia leaving her clothes in his house bothered him. However, he never got around to telling her to take them home. Why hadn't he sent her away a long time ago? Keith was asking himself a lot of questions. Even why he had gone to that party on Friday without her? Maybe he was running from what he was feeling all along. Maybe he had been afraid. Keith has had a lot of women in his life and he knew how to get rid of them when he wanted to, so why was Sylvia still around? Maybe he really wasn't a player. Maybe he just hadn't met the one! Keith honestly didn't know the answer to these questions. He was tired and just wanted some peace and order in his life. He gently took her face in his hands and noticed that the side of her face had red marks, and was beginning to swell where he had slapped her. He felt badly about it. He wasn't the kind of monster who knocked women around. He kissed her tenderly on her forehead and said, "Let me put some ice on that. I'm really sorry. I've never hit a woman before in my life. Please believe me. You caught me off guard. I lost my temper after you spit in my face. Not to mention everything else you did tonight."

"I'm sorry too, Keith. I don't know what came over me."

"Well, I'd like to think it's your hormones and that you won't go off on me like that again."

"Keith, I love you so much I just went crazy when I saw her all over you like that."

"What did you say?" Keith's head was beginning to spin. This was just too much to sort out in one night. This had certainly been an evening of surprise.

"Oh Keith you know I love you. I've never said it, because I didn't want to scare you."

"Yeah, well you're scaring me plenty right now. This whole thing is a little scary for me."

"Keith, do you love me?"

"Do you really want to know the truth?"

"Yes, I do, tell me the truth," Sylvia said, looking at him earnestly.

"Well the truth is you are going to have to cut me some slack. I don't know exactly what this is I'm feeling. But I know that I'm not trying to let you go. And it's not, because you beat up my friend," he said with laughter in his voice, a smirk on his face, as he cut his eye at her causing them both to chuckle.

"But, seriously the fight has nothing to do with this. You didn't win anything! The fact that you're carrying my baby is what ignited my train of thought. Sylvia, I really want to be here for both you and the baby. I never had my father around when I was growing up and I don't want any child of mine to have to experience what I did."

"Keith, I think you do love me," Sylvia said. "I would do anything for you, but you have to know I'm no fool."

"I know that, but I can't say that I approve of the way you chose to express yourself. What you did tonight was unacceptable. I have to tell you that if you ever do anything like that again it will be the end of us."

"Keith, everyone loses it once in a while."

"No, Sylvia, not like that."

"Well what was that you did to me tonight?" she asked.

He stopped and pondered over that for a moment and then said, "OK I lost it, but I didn't continue to assault you like you did my little friend. You may even be in trouble! Anyway let me get some ice to put on your face," he said, kissing her on the forehead again before heading toward the kitchen to get the ice.

While Keith was getting the ice Sylvia took her cell phone out of her purse that was resting on the love seat, and took a picture of her face and the cuts on her legs. Smiling she placed the cell phone back in her purse. You never know when this could come in handy, she thought. People take me for a fool, well there's nothing foolish about Sylvia Cartier. I took a risk tonight coming here, and, I'm not letting anyone take my man from me. So I hope the word goes out to all the bitches. She smiled to herself as she stroked the side of her face where Keith had struck her. She was very pleased with what she had accomplished tonight. Minutes later Keith returned with an ice bag and placed it on her face and told her to go lie down so he could clean up the mess. An hour later, Keith climbed into the bed next to Sylvia. She had fallen asleep but was still holding the mostly melted ice bag to her face. Keith had brought a wet cloth with him which he used to wipe at the small cuts on her legs. She flinched and he pulled her close to him and kissed her tenderly on the side of her face where he had slapped her. She turned her face toward him and their lips met and he kissed Sylvia for the first time without lust. This was a loving kiss and it made him feel as though he was a part of something. As crazy as it seemed this was somehow better than sex to him. He took the ice pack away from her and placed it on the stand beside the bed along with the wet cloth. He laid his head on the pillow and put his arm around her and they remained like that until the morning.

EGUSI SOUP

J ustine surveyed the room to make sure that everything was in order. Her apartment had an open floor plan. The dining room flowed into the living area lending depth and continuity to the space. A life size painting of a woman seated on a blue velvet chair wearing a white evening gown hung from the wall in the dining area. The wall to wall mirrors on the opposite side reflected the glass dinette set in the dining space. A white el shaped couch was stationed directly in front of the mirrored wall and spoke elegance to the décor. It semi-surrounded a square chrome and glass coffee table which held a sphere resting on a block of crystal serving as centerpiece and the sphere was covered with mosaic mirrored tiles flickering light from every direction. The dining table was set with Waterford crystal stemware and fine white china. A silver candelabra stood dead center on the table causing the objects to glisten as the light bounced off of them shimmering like diamonds. The chandelier hung above the dining table and its' light was dimmed lending a sense of romance to the setting. Smooth jazz emanated the airwaves and in the kitchen a special fish and meat dish agusi (a-goo-see) soup simmered which she would serve with fufu. It was an African dish commonly eaten in West Africa. She had eaten it once when she attended her girlfriend Grace's baby shower. She heard Marcelo say that he missed having it so she labored to surprise him by making the dish. She had no idea that the fufu was so difficult to prepare. It was made from ground cassava that her girlfriend Grace purchased for her from the African grocery store. Grace, a tall and graceful woman with creamy smooth ebony skin, was from Ghana and knew just how to prepare it. It was definitely a hands on project that had to be manned until it reached the right consistency. Grace stayed with her to supervise the project. Justine was grateful because she doubted she would have been able to pull it off alone. Justine perused the room with her eyes, one last time, to make sure she didn't miss anything. She had been dating Marcelo for three months since that magical evening, in June, when she met him on the train. Tonight was the first time he would visit her home and she wanted everything to be perfect. She glanced in the mirror for the hundredth time to make certain that her head wrap was in place. She was wearing a beautiful silk afghan with an African print of purple and yellows. Yellow, she knew, was Marcelo's favorite color and purple was hers. She had gotten Grace to wrap her head with the left over fabric from the afghan so as to create the perfect mood for the evening she had planned. Justine was so excited she really did like this man and hadn't felt this way about a man in years. She had been hurt in the past and was apprehensive about letting her guard down. Nevertheless, she felt that she had reached a place with Marcelo where she could trust him. He made her feel safe and this was important to her. Although he was a serious individual, surprisingly enough, it was one of the things she loved about him. In his own way, he was able to make her laugh and despite his serious nature, he did appreciate humor and could be quite funny. However, he was a focused individual for the most part.

Marcelo was extremely intelligent and was kind and

thoughtful. However, he could be somewhat judgmental at times, and wasn't shy in noting the differences in their cultures. He never blatantly stated that he thought his culture was better, but Justine knew that he did. Surprisingly, this didn't bother her. Justine believed that one should be proud of one's own culture and so she appreciated this about him, though she knew that every culture had their pros and cons and she was equally as proud to be an African American. Marcelo was a man with a purpose and in little time, she knew, he would be quite successful and she admired his drive. She loved everything about him, even his occasional moodiness. This gave her the time she needed to focus on herself. He wasn't one to laugh a lot, he was a thinker, but whenever he did laugh it took her breath away. When she could do something that would win her his nod of approval, it was magical. Justine was not the type of woman who needed a man to be underfoot every moment in her life to know that she was loved. She felt that she could be faithful to this man and even withstand separation, for long periods of time, because she knew that in the line of business he was pursuing he would be doing a great deal of traveling. Marcelo hoped to get into the import and export business. She suspected that he was a bit nomadic and that he might not even be aware of it. Oddly enough, this didn't frighten her. Justine measured a man's love by the way he treated her. It was the quality of time that mattered to her not the quantity. She didn't need to have him around all the time. He was a doer, and in the short time that she knew him, he proved to be a man of integrity. You could count on him and nothing was more attractive to Justine as that. She knew that when she needed him, he would be there for her whether he was in the States or thousands of miles away. That was why she was a little nervous. He said that he would be there at seven and she knew he would be ringing the buzzer any second and she wanted everything to be perfect when he arrived.

What impressed Justine most about Marcelo was his honesty. He made no qualms about his desire to live in the United States. He was very forthcoming about his plan to marry an American woman in order to establish himself here in the States. He assured her that while this was his objective, he would put no pressure on her in that regard, because if they decided to marry he wanted their union to be one derived from true and mutual caring. He candidly spoke about foreigners who made financial arrangements with American women to establish their residency, and how he didn't feel marriage was a business and couldn't and wouldn't go that route. If this relationship did not lead to marriage then he would take the Shapiro's up on their offer to assist him in getting his papers and afterward he would apply for citizenship. He confided in her about the money he was able to save, and how he wanted to use that money to invest in his business. He felt that in a year or two he would be in a position to put his plans into action. Justine believed in him and she believed him when he said that the way he felt about her, at this point, could not be measured by anything he hoped to accomplish. Justine was comfortable with all of this because she didn't want to be pressured into marriage. She just wanted to enjoy their relationship and really get to know him.

They spent every free moment together even to the detriment of their relationships with other friends. Marcelo's friend Chide, a tall, black, lean individual who exuded the arrogance of a Zulu warrior, was not pleased with Marcelo's failure to keep him in the loop. And Justine's friends were tired of her calling to cancel their plans and had quite obviously stopped asking her to join them. But, at this time in Justine's life, she couldn't spare a moment for anyone else. She needed time to really get into him. They were still exploring one another and she knew that Marcelo had invested a great deal of money courting her. They had seen several plays, dined in fine restaurants, and went out dancing. They also walked in the rain, spent time at the beach, visited museums, and strolled through Central Park.

It seemed they had lived a lifetime in the few months that they had known each other. During that time, Marcelo told her about his first marriage. He told her how it ended because of his ambitions which kept him out of the country and away from home a great deal of the time. During one of his many trips to England, his wife Mercy took a lover. The remarkable part of his story was that he didn't blame her. The reason he divorced Mercy wasn't that he no longer loved her. It was because he could no longer trust her and he felt that people looked down on him because he forgave her after what she had done. He became exceedingly jealous and the jealousy alone caused undo discord in their marriage. Marcelo had truly forgiven her and bore her no ill will. However, because of her infidelity, he suffered badly from trust issues and shame. He knew that their living situation was not about to change, he couldn't afford to bring her and the children with him to the States, so he thought it best to give her her freedom. He admitted that he was deeply hurt by it all, and how he had spent a lot of his time thinking about her. He actually shared in the blame of her infidelity. He felt that she was too young of a woman to have been left alone for such long periods of time. He realized now that women today are quite different from women of yester-year, even African women had changed in that regard. Or maybe not; perhaps he was just a hopeless romantic. If he could have accomplished what he needed to do in his own country, maybe things would have turned out differently. He wished that he could have had the foresight to see the hand writing on the wall before they had children. When he spoke of his children his eyes welled with tears and he'd have to blink to hold them back. He said that after leaving the Ivory Coast, he hoped to eventually bring his children to the States to be educated. He looked so serious when he talked about his children, and Justine could see that he loved them very much. She was also aware that he was not entirely over Mercy, but he had come to terms with the fact that their marriage was over and had put it behind him. His daughter, Eny, was only nine, but his son, Jon Paul, was thirteen. Marcelo had been on the go for five years now. He had lived in England, Germany, and now the United States. When he and Mercy had their first child, they weren't married and perhaps they married for the wrong reasons. Now his children lived with his mother and father. The last time he spoke to Mercy, she was making plans to marry the man with whom she had the affair. Justine wondered how she could leave her children and Marcelo explained that in most countries in West Africa the children remained with their father unless there was an agreement that they stay with their mother. Mercy was a beautiful woman and he had never doubted she would remarry though he admitted it angered him to think of her with that particular man. He would have felt better about it if she had met someone else. Nevertheless, it wasn't about him, he wished her well, because when it was all said and done he knew she was not a bad person. Justine was impressed. This spoke volumes about who he was as a person. Justine shared with Marcelo about her divorce and how it had been ten years now. She too had been hurt deeply by infidelity. She was thankful that her children were grown now and not too deeply affected by the divorce. She confessed that she had resolved herself to being alone and was totally taken off guard by their meeting. She didn't however tell him how deeply he affected her. She still felt vulnerable where it came to romance. However, when she was feeling anxious she would remember the time Marcelo had looked deep into her eyes and said, "Though I've been hurt, Justine you have renewed my joy. I use to think about Mercy all the time and was unable to feel joy like this. Now, I find myself thinking about you and wanting to be with you." Then he kissed her gently on the lips. She had never wanted a man as badly as she wanted him at that moment. It wasn't just sexual. She wanted to be with him body and soul. He stirred something inside her that had been dormant for years. She was ready and she felt that, quite possibly, tonight would be the night.

Justine was on her way to the kitchen to check on her dish when the door bell rang. She went into the kitchen and lowered the flame after which she scurried to the door. She took one last glance at her reflection in the hall mirror and then opened the door. Marcelo stood at the doorway of her apartment for the first time. He wore a Khaki jacket and a colorful printed shirt peeked out from beneath it. It reminded her of shirts worn in the Caribbean's and oddly enough the colors yellow and purple were present in the print. It went well with his Khaki Levi jeans. His shirt was unbuttoned to mid chest showing off a gold chain which glistened richly against his dark brown skin and mingled handsomely amongst the soft curly hairs on his chest. He was carrying a bottle of Dom Perignon. Justine stood back in the doorway and made a gesture with her hand to bid him welcome. He flashed her one of his breathtaking smiles and said, "You look beautiful." He entered the apartment looking around pleased with what he observed, and handed her the Champaign as he kissed her on the lips. She shut the door and told him to have a seat in the living room while she checked on the food.

"Hum, something smells delicious and familiar," he said. "Yeah Its egusi soup and fufu."

"What?" He laughed heartily and said, "What do you know about egusi soup and fufu?" He followed her to the kitchen to see if she was kidding him. Justine sat the Champaign on the counter and began placing the food in serving dishes and Marcelo was truly taken aback.

"Hey!" he exclaimed, "I can't believe this." He was grinning from ear to ear. "I can't believe you fixed this." He was truly amazed and quite impressed. He looked at Justine beaming with delight and said, "I must be dreaming. Oh my God, this woman is special."

"Oh Stop, Marcelo," Justine said blushing.

"No, I can't stop. You are too much. I would have never dreamed this in a million years. This is wonderful." He took her into his arms gently touching the head wrap she was wearing and kissed her softly on the lips. Afterwards he looked into her eyes. If he had any doubts before, he now knew that she was the one. "I'm blessed," he said softly and kissed her again. Justine returned his kiss feeling as though she were the happiest woman in the world. She had not spoken the words; however, she was aware that she was falling in love with this man.

"Now you go in the dining room and sit down so I can get this food on the table," she ordered him.

"Where is the bathroom? I have to wash my hands."

"Straight through the living room through the small corridor on the left, you can't miss it," she said as she carried the food over to the table.

After washing his hands Marcelo came out of the bathroom and stood in the doorway and watched Justine setting the food out on the table. All he could think was that she had actually prepared egusi soup from his homeland. This woman was special. He didn't really want to fall in love again, because women had the ability to cut into the core of a man. However, Justine was truly knocking on the doors of his heart. She was everything he had hoped for in a woman and more. He had grown deep feelings for her and it was scaring him a little. He felt as though their fate had been sealed from the moment he set eyes on her. It was kismet. He would be happy to spend the rest of his life with this woman. He thought about her all the time. He had been particularly excited about visiting her in her home today. He was pleased to see how neat and clean she was, and now all of this, cooking of his native food. She never ceases to amaze me, he thought. Marcelo couldn't believe that his feelings were stirred to this extent. He wanted to make love to her that very moment. He had been with many women before, and during his marriage to Mercy or even after the divorce, he had never felt anything more than release. Mercy had been the only woman he had ever truly loved. "Justine, Justine who are you?" he said. Justine looked up and saw him standing there, and beckoned him to come to the table.

After blessing the table Justine poured them each a flute of Champaign, then they began to sample the food that she had prepared. To Marcelo's delight, it was very tasty and though there were subtle differences, it very much reminded him of egusi soup from home. If she could spend some time with his mother, she would have it down to perfection. But he would never tell her that. He knew that this meal was difficult to prepare and at this moment he would not have accepted food made by any other hands. Even if it were prepared by the most experienced woman in his village, he would push it to the side and eat the food prepared by Justine's hands. He must take her back to his country and let his people meet her, especially his mother. He knew that she would love her. Justine was a woman of class and it showed. Who would ever think that I would find such a jewel in America? he thought. Justine was so proud that Marcelo was enjoying the meal that she had prepared, even if she did require help. It still gave her much joy watching him eat. Marcelo leaned in and kissed her on the cheek. Their eyes met. He picked up the Champaign flute and took a sip. He pushed away from the table and pulled Justine to her feet and into his arms. Their lips met and she felt as though her heart would burst through her chest it was pounding so hard. In the background, Marion Meadow's saxophone radiated the airwave with "Wishing on a Star." They swayed slowly to its melody and Justine inhaled taking in his scent which was totally intoxicating. His hands found the opening in her afghan and their eyes met, they knew instantly that tonight they would know each other. Justine took his hand and led him toward the bedroom. They stopped at the entrance of her bedroom and he kissed her again. This would be a day she would always remember, because this was more than just the entrance to her bedroom. It was the beginning of something that she both feared and desired. She was not just surrendering her body to this man. She was surrendering her heart and though she felt it was all happening too fast, there was nothing she could do to stop it.

FATAL WORDS

The low rumbling in the distant night gave conformation to the promise of the upcoming storm. Claudio angrily paced back and forth in the guest room of Viola's condo. Viola's maid had reported an incident that had been totally taken out of context. However, that was not the main thing stirring the anger within him. Viola had engaged her maid to spy on him. He was totally unaware and taken aback by the level of distrust she had displayed tonight. Oh he was aware of the way they met, the differences in their ages and what she had to lose. But he thought she knew him better than that. She didn't even try to hear him out. Carmen's word was gold! He was not out to get her. And the differences in their ages didn't matter to him. He was OK with that. Viola obviously had a problem with it all. In Claudio's mind Viola was this amazing woman with an amazing body that could put many younger women to shame. When he was with her, age never entered into the equation. She had been his savior. He thought that she really cared for him. Now it was clear what she really thought of him and he was hurt. He didn't believe that he could ever get past what she had said to him tonight, or if he could ever forgive her. He didn't hate her, he owed her a lot, she had done a lot for his family and he would always be grateful to her for that. Nevertheless, it didn't change what she said to him. He was ashamed of his past life and just wanted to go somewhere and hide. His poverty had stolen his dignity and now it seemed Viola wished to emasculate him as well. She had made it clear that she had absolutely no respect for him as a man at all.

About two weeks prior to Viola's return from Brazil, Claudio had gone to a club where he ran into some old buddies from Rio and partied with them all night. Viola had been gone for four months, and he drank far too much because he missed her. He decided to leave Viola's car in the parking garage and take a cab home. He didn't want to chance driving her Mercedes in his drunken state. Marco, one of his Brazilian buddies, offered to drive him home. Marco was the designated driver for the group, because he didn't drink, and he was headed in the direction of Viola's condo. Claudio accepted the offer of the ride and when they reached the condo complex, one of the ladies in the car needed to use the rest room. Claudio didn't see any harm in allowing her to use the toilet so he let her and her friend come up. It never occurred to him that Viola's maid was watching him, neither did he believe he was doing anything wrong. The ladies were in and out in less than five minutes. It was so inconsequential that he had totally forgotten all about it.

When he'd picked Viola up from the airport this morning he did so with a clear conscience. Carmen had breakfast ready for them when they returned but he hardly ate. He couldn't wait to be alone with Viola. He was all over her, giving her pecks on the check and stroking her hair, and just doting on her in general. She in turn told him that she couldn't wait for them to be together and how she had been daydreaming about him on the long twelve hour flight home. She asked him to wait for her in the bedroom while she went over a few things with Carmen. He thought nothing of it and when Viola entered the bedroom she seemed to be her normal self. They made love all morning and slept all afternoon. Later, they went out and dined in a lovely Italian restaurant on 79th Street. When they returned home they made love again. Claudio was happy and thought all was right with them. The weather had been threatening a storm all day and he relished the thought of being curled up next to her with the sound of the rain beating up against the window.

As they lay there in bed literally spent and reveling in the moment, Viola suddenly turned over, looked him in the eyes, and calmly asked him if he had another woman in her house while she was away.

He said, "No," without hesitation and was totally unprepared for what was to follow.

This is when the nightmare began. Viola sat up and got out of bed, her eyes were cold and her face without expression. When she spoke her tone was that of an attorney cross examining a witness in a court of law. She was calm and precise as she posed the question again in a different manner.

"So what you are telling me is that the entire time of my absence, there was no one other than yourself and the maid on the premises." Claudio, who was baffled as to why she was posing these questions, was offended by her tone, because he actually didn't understand every word, but he got the gist of her accusations. He answered her showing his full annoyance.

"Jess, I say no one come for here just de maid and Claudio."

Viola retrieved her robe from the foot of the bed, and slipped into it as she walked over to the bedroom door and shouted. "Carmen, Carmeeen!"

"Jess madam, a voice sounded from outside the bedroom. Come here please." "Jess Madam." Claudio was shocked as he sat up in bed pulling the covers up over his nakedness. Viola waited for a few moments for Carmen to reach the door of the bedroom. Then she proceeded as though she was calling a witness to the stand. "Carmen," she said, "When I asked you if anyone had been in my house in my absence did you or did you not tell me that Claudio brought two women here one night?"

Carmen, a short stout Mexican woman who appeared to have no neck, stood in the doorway nervously stealing glances at Claudio twirling her stringy hair around her finger as she spoke, "Jess, Madam two ladies come for here." Like a bolt of lightning Claudio's memory was jolted.

"Ooh," he said as a mental picture of the two women flashed before him. He chuckled nervously, "Jess de two lady." He chuckled again as he recalled the incident.

"Des eh happen maybe eh two weeks pass. Dey come for to usey de toilet. Dey no stay longa only five eh minutes. Jess, Carmen?" He looked to Carmen for support, but Carmen wasn't taking sides with the accused.

"Ooh, I don know how longa dey stay," Carmen said defensively. "I open door, I see two lady dat's all. I close door, I go to de bed."

"Thank you Carmen," Viola said curtly. "That will be all."

Claudio got out of bed, his naked body glistening as he approached Viola to offer her his explanation, "Listen Vie," he began, "I forget des eh happen."

He tried to explain, but Viola put up her hand to block out his words and said, "I don't want to hear it, Claudio. The one thing I asked you not to do you did, and then you lied about it, twice. I left condoms and you have money. You could have taken the whores to a hotel. If Carmen had not been here, your lies would have gone undetected."

"Undetected," he repeated. He knew exactly what that meant and he was furious. "Wha is eh des?" "Now I am as eh liar?"

"Yes, you're a dirty liar," Viola shouted. "Do you think I'm a fool? Did you think I'd leave you in my house not knowing what was going on? A bum I picked up off the beach in Brazil! When I told you not to have women in my house I also told Carmen to watch you."

Claudio was looking at her, but he couldn't see. All he could see was red. As if adding insult to injury she walked closer to him, her face was less than an inch from his, when she screamed as loudly as she could, spittle splattering in his face. "YOU WHORE, I TOOK YOU OUT OF THE GUTTER AND SHOWED YOU A LIFE YOU COULD ONLY DREAM ABOUT AND THIS IS WHAT YOU DO TO ME? I knew I couldn't stop you from whoring, but I thought you'd have the decency to keep it outside." Her face was flush and distorted and her eyes filled with tears.

Claudio was livid and now had no desire to explain. He was tired of behaving like a child. He was a man and now he knew what she really thought of him. He had bent over backwards to show this woman how much he cared, and what made it maddening is, he had been faithful to her for four months. The whore, as she put it, had touched no one in her absence. Not in or out of her bed, and he could have. As she so pointed out, he could have gone to any hotel. However, the truth of the matter was, without even knowing it, he had fallen for Viola and just didn't want to be with anyone else. Was it love? He honestly didn't know. It probably was a variety of things. Viola, he felt, had rescued him from what he saw as a lifetime of wretchedness and self loathing. Who as a little boy says, to himself, when I grow up I want to be a gigolo?

Now she reminds him of what he was. It was comical, because he thought they had a real relationship. He had just finished making love to her, he thought to himself angrily. Now here she stands cross-examining him as though he were a criminal. Viola's face was still inches away from his. She glared at him and he pushed her away. If a man had spoken to him in such a manner, he would have belted him.

Claudio pointed to his chest as he shouted, "I' AM EH WHORE FROM GUTTER? OK, OK. IF EH DES IS AH TRUE WHA KIND DEE WOMAN ARE JOU?"

Viola was shocked. Claudio had never spoken to her in that tone before. More than that, he had even put his hands on her.

"YOU PUSHED ME," she shouted.

"JOU CALL EH ME DE WHORE," he shouted back. IF EH I AM DE WHORE, WHA ARE JOU? TELL EH ME. ARE JOU DE JOHN?"

"How dare you," she hissed.

"AND ME, I DARE JOU," he shouted.

Viola laughed contemptuously and said, "Just who the hell do you think you are? Huh?"

"No, no Viola, who do jou thin I am?"

The insolence, she thought. She laughed and looked at him as though he were putrid and vile, and her voice trembled as she hissed, "You're nothing, nothing but dirt that I scraped from the bottom of my shoe when I stepped in the gutter to pull you out. That's what I think you are!" She stepped back and glared at him. "Ha," she chuckled contemptuously, "You're not even good enough to be in the same room with me. You should be kissing my feet. I can't believe I lowered myself to get with you."

He couldn't speak English well, but he understood her words and they connected like punches. He was learning the language rapidly and the very tone of her voice cut. What she had said was horrible but it wasn't as horrid, as was her delivery. Viola was angry and not aware of the impact behind the words, words that after all was said and done, she would live to regret. She had taken the fire out of him. He stood there deflated, cored like a pitted apple. Hurt to epitome of his sole.

Here was a woman who he had dared to allow himself to have genuine feelings for. Feelings that were slowly changing with every word that came out of her mouth. It was like a light had come on in a dark room. All this time, he had not been aware that when they made love he was working. She was right, he thought. I am filth! His life had been hard. There were days that he and his family had gone hungry. A low rumbling of thunder echoed from somewhere far off in the distance and a flash of lightening flickered through the window. His voice was barely audible when he spoke.

"Jou're right Vie I no should be in room with jou. We be different jou and me. My papa died from de pneumonia," he stated staring off oddly into space as though he were reaching back into some long ago memory he had tucked away in the pockets of his mind.

"We no can by de medicine. Claudio's bad, Viola, bad because I am eh poor." What he was trying to say was that he had done a lot of bad things for money. He looked at her and Viola felt ashamed. Instantly she was sorry about what she had said to him. She could see the pain in his eyes and she remembered the pain of losing one's parents for she had lost both of hers at a young age. The difference was that her parents had money. They were killed in an auto accident but they had left behind a great deal of money for her to have a decent start in life. Viola was truly sorry and wanted to take back her words.

"Look Claudio," she said, touching his arm, but he gently pulled away.

"No," he said. "I want for to say jou sometsing," he continued. "I am eh no good for jou. When I live in my country, I try to make job, but job money too small. I have some school, but no too much. I not can get good job. My sister, Alisa, she was too sick. I'm feel eh bad. One guy he say to me rich ladies come eh to Rio for to have good fun. He say me dey pay too much money. So I start to be the whore. I get money for to buy medicine for to give my sister. All de time I do dis for eh my family, but I stop to do des when I meet jou. In Rio des is my life, Vie."

Then he paused, because he didn't want to cry. Viola reached out to touch him, but he pulled away again and put up his hand to put her off.

When he had gained composure, he began again, "I wan to say jou des," he said. "I thin jou was my lady." Damn-it he thought as more tears invaded his eyes, he lowered his head in order not to look directly into Viola's eyes. He did not want her to see his tears. He tried to smile, but it was a dead sad smile and he let the tear run down his cheek. Speaking softly he said, "I thin when I come to live in jour house I was no more the whore. I thin," he paused again then said. "I thin in jour mind, Claudio always be de whore."

His whole body vibrated from the sudden rush of emotion he was trying to compress it but the tears came. However, it was brief. He quickly regained composure and said with a new resolve, "No more. After tonight no more will Claudio be de whore again."

Thunder clapped as though to underline his statement. He stiffened his lip and said, "I am eh sorry, Vie. I'm eh sorry to let my friends to use to jour toilet, but I don to fuck nobody in jour house," he said with force.

"Listen Claudio, let's just forget about it," Viola interjected.

But Claudio shook his head and said, "No, it's eh too late." He looked directly into her eyes and said, "I no can forget. I sleep now in guest room, tomorrow Claudio leave eh jou house." He went to the closet and removed his robe and put it on his naked body.

Violas' furry had completely dissipated and she realized that she may have gone too far. All she felt now was regret. She walked over to him and touched his arm again. Her voice was soft when she said, "Look Claudio things have gotten a little out of hand. You don't have to sleep in the guest room. We just had our first quarrel is, all." He looked at her and gently touched her face he had so much feelings for this woman. Even in all his anger and hurt he still wanted to take her in his arms and pretend that all of this never happened. Maybe he could have if she hadn't involved the maid. Maybe if nobody else knew. He smiled that little sad and empty smile then said softly, "Jess Viola, Claudio must sleep in guest room. We no more can be together. I know dat jou no can respect me. In jour heart I no can be jour man. Jou thin Viola," he said, looking at her earnestly as he pointed to his head.

"How can I forgot wha jou say me? Des thin to jou was, how do jou say? Fake. But not for Claudio, I feel eh my heart for jou."

Then Claudio left the room and walked down the hall and entered the guest bedroom. Lightning flashed through the window momentarily illuminating the darkened room. He walked across the floor and switched on the lamp. Multiple claps of thunder sounded into the night and Claudio braced himself against its furry. This was going to be a long and lonely night. This was nothing like the night he earlier envisioned. He sat down on the side of the bed, stinging tears form tightness at the back of his throat, as the water gathered and flowed from his eyes. It loosened the mucus in his nostrils and he reached for a tissue from the night stand and blew his nose.

The room was beautifully decorated with colors of brown, beige, and muted blues which spoke cheer to a room where sorrow now dwelled. Three rounds of loud thunder volts trumpeted into the night followed by a flash of lightning flickering through the sheer chocolate brown linen drapes. Claudio jumped at the sound of thunder and sunk his toes into the thick beige carpet. His body slumped forward and he placed his head in his hands.

He felt as though something had died. It was a feeling of profound loss likened unto his father's death. He was sick to his stomach and his head throbbed. Before he met Viola, he had been in a constant mode of survival. He neither had the time or the luxury to feel anything, much less contemplate a serious relationship. He had dared to believe that he shared a life with Viola. He accepted everything at face value and attributed it all to luck or fate if you will. She had been his world. Now he could see that he had been very naïve. He was her toy, a means to satisfy her sexual urges. That's all! Why even after the maid told her all about his so called sins, she was able to come into the room and have sex with him before she told him what she really thought of him. The thought sickened him because all this time he had been stupid enough to think he was in a loving relationship. That was part of the reason the sex was so damn good! As hurt as he was he had to laugh. He thought she was different, but she was just like all the rest. All this time he had been in denial. What a fool he was. He had never truly given himself to any women until he met her. All the others were meaningless acts of sex. Most of the time there was no real pleasure in it for him. They had all been a blurred collage of faces that merged together day after day doling out the paper of life he needed for survival. He had allowed Viola to touch a virginal part of him. A part he, himself, never knew existed. What he felt for her had been pure. He had totally misread her. When he looked in her eyes, he thought that he saw love there, but what he actually saw was lust. I was just a gigolo! he laughed, someone to help her get off. What had she called me? he thought. Was it garbage? No it was dirt. Dirt she scraped of the bottom off her shoe when she lifted me out of the gutter. There is no way she could expect him to forget those words.

He could hear the thunder crackling off in the distance as he reentered the bedroom. It promised to bring the rain that was still imprisoned deep within the bowls of the clouds. I will buy a plane ticket and go back to Brazil in the morning, he thought. Claudio had not followed Viola this far to live in America as a gigolo. He followed her, because in her he saw promise of a brighter future. When in reality all he had done was become a different kind of whore. The difference was that he had upgraded his status to a live-in whore, when he thought about the letters he wrote home to his family he laughed out loud. He had to admit one thing, there was some good that had come out of the whole experience. He knew that he no longer wished to live his former lifestyle. In him now stirred an unquenchable thirst for a deeper connection which, ironically, was born out of what he thought he had with Viola.

He drank from the cup of hope in the form of Viola only to discover that her wine had been vinegar. He would not allow himself to indulge in such feelings with her again. In the future he would guard his feelings jealously and never involve himself emotionally with a woman of her status. His mind was full of thoughts. He thought about how he was actually employed in her salon for which she paid him handsomely. It had all been fake. The clients in Manhattan were mostly wealthy women like herself and their tips had been generous as they perused him with greedy eyes. Maybe they were sizing him up for the ultimate proposition when Viola was finished with him.

Viola really hurt him tonight, but he couldn't hate Viola. He had been fooling himself she had never spoken of love. No matter, he told himself, his life was changed for the better even if he had misunderstood. The mere act of living with Viola had given him a taste of another side of life. There is no way he would allow himself to go back to his former lifestyle of poverty and shame.

He had managed to save a great deal of money, money that would triple in value in Brazil, and even though he was sending money home to his family every week, he was still able to save the majority of what he made. Viola provided everything he needed so there was no real need for him to spend his own money. He had planned to buy Viola something expensive for Christmas to show her how much he cared for her. He thought they would spend the Christmas holidays together. But now that he thought about it, she had never really included him in her social life. He had never been introduced to any of her close friends. He heard her speak of them, but had never actually met any of them.

He now realized that all this time he had been providing a service. She was just like all the women in his past. She was just a customer. How naive of him to have believed himself to be more. Now that he could look at it realistically, what had he to offer a woman like her other than his body? Surely she didn't need his love. Who in their right mind loves the gigolo? Tears welled up in his eyes and it both frustrated and angered him. He was still a man and this behavior was totally unacceptable. He stood up and punched the wall, managing to bust a hole in the sheetrock and hurt his hand.

Viola entered the room in time to witness the scene. She had hurt him deeply and wished that she could erase everything that was said. She realized that the whole bad episode was born out of her own insecurities. She was so afraid until she had been unable to allow herself the luxury of just loving him, and she did love him. She had no idea how to humble herself and let him know. So she did the only thing she knew how to do.

"Claudio," she said, "stop being so silly. It was just a quarrel is, all. Everyone says things they don't mean when they are angry."

She should have told him she was sorry and that everything she said to him was due to her own fears. She should have told him that she loved him with all her heart and didn't care about his age or his past or whether or not he had money. She should have told him that she really didn't look upon him as dirt and that she was only trying to hurt him, because she thought he had betrayed her. Maybe if Viola could have taken the chance and expose her true feelings, right then and there, she might have been able to repair some of the damage she had done to his already damaged ego. But, that was something that Viola didn't know how to do. At that moment, she just didn't have a clue.

Without realizing it, she had ripped this man apart all in an effort to protect her own feelings. Not knowing her fatal words would kill everything that he felt for her.

Claudio stared blankly at the wall holding his hand which was bleeding and had begun to swell. He heard her enter the room and said, "Claudio will pay for de wall."

Viola approached him from behind and gently took hold of his hand, put it into her mouth, and sucked the blood away. This was her way of letting him know she cared. But Claudio was unable to read it as such. It angered him.

"Come on," she said. "Come back to our bedroom."

Claudio laughed, but it was harsh and sinister, full of venom and sarcasm. "I thin jou make de joke," he said and chuckled. "Claudio has no bedroom. It is jour bedroom, jour house. Everysing is jours." And then he snatched his hand away from her. "If jou wan I fuck jou again, no? Jou already pay me, jess? But, I no can sleep together with jou. Tomorrow I go to Brazil."

Viola backed away from his cutting words. Her throat closed and she swallowed as tears filled her eyes. Her emotions were causing her to breathe rapidly. She felt as though she was chocking. Touching her chest she backed away toward the open door.

Thunder roared through out the house and lightening lit the darken hall. The very thing she had feared was happening, but not in the way she had imagined. God she didn't want to lose him, but she had lost him, hadn't she. Not to another woman, but she had pushed him away with her words. She reproached herself. Why had she order Carmen to watch him. Carmen wasn't the brightest star and her report was obviously inaccurate. Who knows, she may even have embellished a little out of jealousy taking the entire incident out of context. But she, Viola, could not blame Carmen for her inability to trust and she couldn't blame herself either. She couldn't just trust a man whom she met on the beach in Brazil. He should understand that, things like trust take time. Viola knew only too well that trusting Claudio was not the issue here. Even

Claudio would have been able to accept the fact that she didn't trust him. After all they hadn't known each other that long, and when they met he was, after all, a gigolo. No, that was not the issue. She had said things to him tonight that no one should say to another person. One should never put another person down especially if one professes to care.

Claudio still had his back to her. He wouldn't allow himself to face her he didn't want to look at her. His body was stiff and his jaw clinched tight. He had closed himself off from her emotionally. A menacingly loud clap of thunder jolted them both causing each of them to jump and finally the rain began to fall. They could hear the tap, tap, tapping as it beat up against the window. Exhausted from her flight and the time change Viola crossed the threshold into the hall. A chain of thunder volts trumpeted into the night, the wind howled and sheets of rain clung to the pains of the windows. Viola totally drained walked back to her bedroom alone. She was scared though, because she had never seen Claudio like this before. She had been cross with him in the past, but he had never taken it this seriously. Perhaps this time she had gone too far. Even she had to admit, she was very disrespectful. I didn't even give him a chance to explain, she thought. She could see now how he might think that she meant the things that were said, especially when taking into consideration the way they met and the fact that she had given him so much. Naturally he could misconstrue the gifts as payment after what was just said. But this was ridiculous, she thought. She couldn't help but share what she had with him. She had so much and didn't he say some unkind things to her as well? Why couldn't he just forget it? She was trying to convince, herself but she knew she had overstepped her bounds tonight.

The truth of the matter was, Viola did bring Claudio here to satisfy her physical needs. She as much as said so to her friends. No matter what she tried to tell herself, she had thought of him as her personal play thing, right up until the moment that Claudio made her look at how she was behaving. She had dehumanized him. Even a dog had feelings what was she thinking? She shouldn't have said those things to him. She didn't feel that way about him, at least not anymore. Maybe she never did. Maybe she had been lying to herself all along about how she really felt. Whatever the case may have been she had never really considered him her equal.

She had never formally introduced him to her friends, and most certainly not as her man. They had seen him working around the salon, the same way they had all her other employees. Truthfully speaking he was not her equal and she had treated him like a servant. She hadn't realized it and he hadn't realized it either. But tonight, she had made it crystal clear. There was no doubt about it. No wonder he said those awful things to her in the guess room. He had been tried and judged and treated like a discarded employee. He must have felt terrible having the maid report him as though he were just another servant, a sex slave at that. Oh Claudio, I'm so sorry, thought Viola. She hadn't meant to treat him that way. She hadn't taken his feelings into account until now. Viola had behaved with pure narcissism. And to think she had actually believed she was being good to him. Viola felt badly now. She only now realized what he meant to her. She knew now and still was unable to bring herself to tell him.

Viola threw herself on the bed. A low moan from somewhere deep within escaped her throat. And then the tears came, they were like the rain that was falling outside her window. Lighting flash and thunder sounded like great boulders crashing together into the night and Viola could hear the cars below as they glided through the wet streets making their slushy, watery sounds.

Claudio heard her sobbing from down the hall. He couldn't understand why she was making such a big deal out of the whole thing. All she has to do is find herself another whore. One whore is as good as the other, it wasn't as if she were in love with me, he thought. Viola finally fell to sleep, fitfully tossing and turning throughout the night. Intervals of sleep were so brief that she was unaware that it had taken place at all. Viola tossed and turned until the grey light of dawn took over the night and stole its way through the window. When she woke, it was still pouring rain from the heavens.

Claudio had called the airline and purchased a one way ticket to Brazil. Unable to sleep he decided to pack so that he would be ready to leave at first light. Viola had such an extensive wardrobe that most of his things were located in the hall closet so he was nearly finish packing when he noticed Viola standing in the doorway of the guestroom. She looked frightful. She must have had little to no sleep, he thought. "Sorry to wake jou," he said.

"You didn't wake me. I don't think I ever got to sleep. "Claudio please don't do this." she said. She spoke softly, and there was pleading in her voice. Viola was holding back tears though she had been crying most of the night. Her eyes were puffy and red. Her head was pounding.

Claudio looked at her and said, "Look Vie, I'm no mad for jou. I have to leave for to fix my life. For us, it is over."

Viola, an emotional wreck became infuriated.

"Over, what do you mean it's over?" Her rage returned. It's over when I say it's over, she yelled. She was really not accustomed to being denied and she was not handling it well.

Claudio looked at her and chuckled. He resented her talking to him as though he were a slave. He walked over to her putting his hands on her shoulder he leaned into her so that their faces were inches apart so close that Viola thought that he was about to kiss her. Instead he whispered in her ear almost hissing, "Wha's wrong huh, jou want me fuck jou one last time? Get jour money worth? Hum?"

He sounded nasty and vile. Then he laughed and pushed her away. Viola flew into a rage, she was livid. She made one last desperate attempt to force him to stay. She ran over to the bed where his close lay neatly packed. They were expensive clothes, clothes that he would not easily replace, and began to pull them out of the luggage and casting them about the room. Tears streamed down her face as she shouted "You didn't buy these clothes and you are not taking them out of this house. If you leave then you leave the clothes behind." Claudio smiled, but he was not amused. He reached for the twenty thousand dollar white gold chain that she had given him after he received his certificate from barber school. She had purchased it from Tiffany's. He removed it and threw it on the bed. Then he removed the Rolex watch she had given him for his birthday and tossed it alongside the chain. Viola stood there looking from him to the objects. She was completely caught off guard. Her body was shacking, she was standing there observing his face which was hard his eyes were void of emotion they seemed to look right through her as though he had nothing left for her not even hate. "Now jou have eh everysing," he said. He didn't bother to pick up the luggage that was already packed and resting on the floor. He just left it there and brushed past her and headed for the front door. He opened it walked out into the hall to catch the elevator. She screamed after him "You'll be sorry, if you leave now. If you leave now, don't come back." Viola didn't know what else to say. She had never really wanted anything that she could not have. Then she cried out, "I'm sorry Claudio, please don't go."

The chime signaled that the elevator had arrived and the doors opened. Claudio stepped into the car, and the door closed.

Viola stood in the doorway to her condo sobbing and feeling as though her heart had been ripped from her chest. Slowly she slid down the side of the door frame until she was stooped in the door way sobbing uncontrollably.

Claudio stepped out of the building into the rain. A cab was waiting outside to take him to the airport. After what seemed like an eternity, Carmen came to the door where Viola had slumped into a ball crying. Carmen felt badly about how thing had turned out. She heard them arguing last night as well and she knew that she had not been completely truthful in her report. She had actually lied. She knew that the women had used the toilet and left. She had made it seem as though they might have stayed the night. She resented Claudio's position. Who was he that she, Carmen, should have to wait on him. She knew that Madam had brought him back from Brazil and sent him to school so he could work in her salon. Yet she Carmen had to clean up after him make his meals. She didn't figure he would actually leave. She just wanted to get him into a little trouble, take him down a peg. It seemed that everything backfired on Madam. She hadn't thought that it would turn out this way. She hoped that Madame was not angry with her. This is the best job she ever had. She made pretty fair money working for Viola. Viola had even sponsored her and got her permanent residence. She hadn't left because she was paid well. Viola even paid her health insurance. Carmen didn't want to lose this job.

Carmen helped Viola to her feet and closed the door. Viola stumbled back to her room it was 5:45 a.m. She went over and sat on the edge of the bed and picked up the phone. Carmen went into the kitchen and put on a pot of coffee. Viola let the phone ring three times and she was about to hang up when she heard Justine's sleepy voice, "Hello." Viola tried to return the greeting but her voice cracked.

"Hello, hello. Who is this?" Viola took a deep breath and projected her voice as best she could. "It's Vie," she raddled into the phone.

"Vie, what's the matter? You sound awful!"

"He's left me," she blurted and began to cry uncontrollably.

"Hey!" Justine said, sitting up in bed. Marcelo turned over and put his arm around her waist.

"Vie, I can't understand you. Is everything all right?"

Viola continued to cry, she couldn't talk.

"Look, I'm coming over just give me some time to get on some clothes."

Justine got out of bed and Marcelo, now fully awake, sat up.

"What's going on?" he said.

"I don't know. That was Vie and she was crying and I couldn't understand a word she was saying. She never calls this early in the morning on a Saturday. Something is wrong she needs me."

"Do you want me to go with you?"

"No, whatever it is I'm guessing it's personal and she wouldn't want me to bring anyone with me."

Marcelo was not happy about Justine jumping out of bed so early and leaving. It was Saturday morning and he normally worked in the store, but he had taken the day off specifically to be with her. Now she was trekking off to the aid of this Viola and who knows how long she would be gone? She probably had a fight with her boyfriend is, all. Did she have to involve Justine? He thought. He knew that Justine and Viola had been friends for years and it wouldn't do for him to make a big deal about her leaving, but that didn't dismiss the fact that he was annoyed. Justine sensing that Marcelo was less than pleased turned to him and said, "I know that you took today off to be with me. Baby, believe me I'm not loving this either. But, I can't just turn my back on my friend. If I see it's going to take a long time, I'll call you. OK? You have to know that I wouldn't be running out into a storm if it wasn't an emergency."

"What can I say? Do I have a choice?"

"No you do not," Justine said.

Wearing a smile, she leaned over and kissed him on the lips. "I'll be back as soon as I can."

"Yeah, sure what ever," he said sullenly. It was not as if he didn't understand that Justine really didn't have a choice. This is what friends do. He didn't fault Justine. Her caring was one of the reasons he loved her. But, he didn't have to like the fact that his Saturday had been foiled and he wasn't going to pretend to like it. However, he did say, "Hurry back, I'll be waiting." He reached out and took her hand and kissed it. Justine squeezed his hand then went into the bathroom and took a shower.

An hour later she was pulling up in front of Viola's building in a yellow cab. She paid the fair and exited the cab. The wind was howling and the rain was in full force. Her umbrella was useless against this storm. Justine pulled her rain coat over her head and ran toward the entrance of the building. When she got off the elevator, Viola was standing in her doorway and came out to meet her. They embraced and then Justine stepped back and said, "Damn, girl you look awful! What is going on?"

Viola busted into tears again and sobbed, "H-He l-left me, Justine, ooh ho, ho, ho Claudio left me."

"Claudio left you?"

"Yes, and I don't know what to do."

"Well what happened? Why did he leave?"

Viola let loose another flood of tears she was talking in such a way that Justine couldn't make out a word she was saying. Justine led her back into the apartment before they attracted an audience in the hall and ushered her into the living room. In all the years that she had known Viola, she had never seen her so disheveled. She must have dropped her guard and fallen in love with this one.

Carmen came to the door and said, "I made some coffee."

"Thanks bring it in the living room," Justine said. Justine glanced into the open door of the guest room and saw all the clothes strung about the room and wondered just what took place there.

"What did Claudio do?" She asked.

Viola looked at Justine pitifully, her voice raspy from all the crying.

"He didn't do anything. Justine it was me ooh, ho, ho," she began to cry again. Carmen came into the room with a tray Justine took it from her hands and placed it on the coffee table and said, "Thank you. That will be all. You can leave us." Justine sat down on the couch she poured a cup of coffee and handed it to the sobbing Viola then she poured a cup for herself. Viola took a sib and then sobbingly went over the whole horrible episode. When she was finished, she sat there looking at Justine as though Justine would magically have the solution to all of her problems.

Justine digested everything she had been told. She stood up and began pacing the floor. Suddenly she turned to Viola who was hanging on her every motion and said, "You love him don't you?"

Viola shook her head indicating that she did.

"Then off to the shower with you, and make it snappy. We're going to the airport."

"He's gone," Viola said hopelessly.

"He's not gone," Justine said with confidence. "The weather has been storming all morning. I bet you anything that his flight has been delayed." Just then two thunder blots sounded as if to underscore her statement.

"Do you know which air line he took?"

"No," Viola said fretfully. "When I woke he was packing his things."

"You mean those things in the room all over the floor?" Justine asked nodding in the direction of the guestroom.

Viola shook her head signifying that those were his clothes.

"He stayed in the guest room last night?"

"Yes, I told you!"

"OK," Justine said, summing up all she had been told. "Then he must have used the phone in the guestroom to make his reservations and call a cab." Viola looked at her suddenly understanding where Justine was going with her line of questions. "Yes, yes, he used the phone in the guestroom." Viola hugged Justine and said, "You are a genius."

They went into the guestroom and Justine picked up the phone and pressed redial. The phone rang three times and a voice said, "Tri-borough Cabs" Justine gave the address of their location and explained that her friend had called a cab from that address this morning and that he inadvertently left a piece of important luggage at the house and she needed to know what airline he took because she was unable to contact him on his cell. The dispatcher told her to wait while he checked his log. He returned shortly and said, they went to Kennedy Air-port and he was dropped off at the Delta airlines. Justine thanked him and hung up the phone.

"OK Vie," she said. "Get a move on it he's at Kennedy airport." Viola showered and pulled herself together in record time. By 7:47 a.m. they were scurrying out the door. By 7:50 a.m. they were on the road and headed for Kennedy airport.

After parking the car, Viola and Justine approached the ticket booth and inquired about the Delta flights to Brazil. The agent informed her that all flights to Brazil had been delayed due to the inclement weather. Viola exhaled knowing that they had got there in time. She knew that they would not allow her to inter the terminal to the gate without a ticket. She asked if the flight was full and when they told her that it was not, she purchased a one way ticket to Brazil.

"Please wait for me here," she told Justine. "I have to go it alone from here" She hugged Justine and hurried off to the check point. Justine called after her, "Remember what I told you, swallow your pride, and let him know how much you love him."

"What if he doesn't believe me?"

"You have to do everything in your power to make him believe you."

Viola gathered all of her courage and scurried off.

Claudio went over to the coffee shop to get something to eat. He should have been up in the air by now. The storm was tapering down now. They should be posting flight schedules on the board soon. He was feeling awful. He had had no sleep last night and was hoping to get some sleep on the plane. He had a tight feeling in his chest not anything like the oncoming of a heart attack it was more like heartache. He missed Vie and it felt as though a part of him had been ripped away. He was beginning to regret the things he had said to her before they parted. He never wanted them to part that way. He purchased a cup of coffee and a cinnamon bun and was headed back toward his gate to sit down when he heard a familiar voice. "Claudio, wait." He turned around and saw Viola running toward him. He couldn't believe his eyes. How was she able to get through the check point without a ticket, he thought.

"Vie," he said, astonished, "what are jou doing here?"

"Claudio," she began, "I'm so sorry for everything I said. Darling I didn't mean any of it, please come back home."

"Vie, I no can live dis way."

"Claudio I know it will take time for me to prove to you how much I love you." "What?" Vie I no can believe jou." He turned and started walking away when Viola cried out his name again, "Claudio." He turned around to ask her to please leave when all of a sudden she fell to her knees. He placed his food down on one of the tables in the food area and rushed over to lift her up off of the ground, because people were beginning to notice them. Viola was quietly sobbing she didn't know what else to do.

"Claudio please, I'm so sorry!" In all the time he had known her, he had never known Viola to lower herself to anyone. This was utterly shocking and he felt badly for her. "Please Claudio I love you, she went on. I-I don't think I can go on without you. Please find it in your heart to forgive me."

Claudio lifted her off of the ground and took her into his arms and began to stroke her hair. "Shush, don cry" he said, kissing her on the head and trying his best to comfort her.

She looked dreadful she wasn't wearing any make up. Her hair was disheveled and she was wearing dark shades, because her eyes were swollen. He felt really bad for her, she didn't even seem to care that people were staring. But, then again, he thought, this was Viola she wouldn't care about what other people thought. All that she cared about now was getting back together. Viola Banks was undeniably in love and she wanted her man back.

Claudio, himself, could see that Viola truly believed herself to be sincere. He was miserable and tired needed sleep. Who knew how long his flight would be delayed. When he thought about everything perhaps he had over reacted, booking a flight and running away early in the morning.

Viola looked up into his eyes. Her eyes were pleading with him. "I meant none of the things I said to you at the house. I should never have said those things to you, especially, because of the way we met. I should have trusted you. I don't want to have to live without you. I know I haven't shown you the proper respect, but if you give me the chance, I promise to make it up to you. I need you, Claudio, please give me another chance, darling, please! I'm begging you."

She started to say more, but Claudio put one finger over her mouth to shush her and put his arms around her shoulders and kissed her forehead, and said, "Come on babe, I'm eh tired. Let's eh go home!"

They walked away from the gate and past the concession stands and through the check points as people walked by them headed in the opposite direction. They turned the corner where Justine was waiting.

Justine looked up and saw Viola walking toward her with Claudio at her side and her face lit up.

Viola looked up at Claudio smiling and said to Justine, "I want you to meet the love of my life. Claudio Rivera, this is one of my closest friends Justine Parker."

Justine directed her gaze toward Claudio. She hadn't been to the shop in a few months now she was so taken with Marcelo she was doing her own hair. She looked at Claudio and thought, he is amazingly handsome and his eyes are gorgeous. No wonder Viola was tripping.

She extended her hand and said, "I am so happy to meet you. I'm glad my friend was able to find you, because she really loves you."

Claudio smiled and hugged Viola with one arm as he extended the other arm to shake Justine's hand. "I am eh happy to meet jou," he said, and they all began to walk over to the parking lot to get the car.

TIME IS ON MY SIDE

I t was getting dark earlier now and the air was much cooler. It was Sylvia's favorite time of the year, when the leaves fall from the trees carpeting the ground with their colorful array of yellows, greens, oranges and reds. Squirrels scurried about gathering their nuts to store them, in secret places, to be retrieved later upon winter's famine. The stores exhibited lavish displays of Halloween decadence and jack-o-lanterns with their sinister smiles. A time of year that reminded her of her childhood, pumpkin pie, hot apple cider, and the carefree laughter of play.

Sylvia was an only child and her parents doted on her giving her whatever her heart desired. I guess you can say that Sylvia was spoiled. Because, for all intent and purpose, when it came to Keith, Sylvia accomplished her goal, yet she was not satisfied. It was evident by the bulge in her belly that life was flourishing within her. Keith openly showered her with affection both privately and publicly. He was constantly chattering about the baby and had even purchased a crib which was stationed in her bedroom. Nevertheless, Sylvia was not pleased about the fact that he absolutely avoided any subject leading to marriage. Whenever she posed the subject he was evasive and noncommittal. But, it was her consistent nagging that was putting Keith off.

She tried moping about the house so that he would inquire about her mood. However, he seemed to sense the purpose of her trap and evaded it. If Sylvia outwardly brought up the subject of marriage, it would anger him. If he was at her house he would leave and not return. If she was at his house, he'd leave and return in the wee hours of the morning after she had fallen asleep. The subject was just taboo. Keith once told her that when he was ready for marriage that she would be the first to know. Since she was the only woman in his life, it should be enough for her. But it was not enough for Sylvia. She wanted the security that came along with marriage, and she was used to getting what she wanted. She didn't want her baby to be born out of wedlock.

However, she decided for the time being not to push the issue any further and run the risk of pushing him away completely.

She walked across the floor of her spacious one bedroom apartment and sat down by the window in a chair which she borrowed from her dinette set. She loved to sit there, because it gave her a view of the courtyard. She was able to see everyone coming and going. She lived on the 14th floor of a large high rise complex in Queens. The courtyard's landscape resembled a mini park with trees, flowers, bushes, and benches which encompassed the oval shaped garden. There was a flag pole in the middle of the island were the American flag stood majestically flapping proudly in the wind.

Sylvia knew a lot of the people who resided in the complex and she wondered if they were whispering about her unmarried state now that her pregnancy was apparent.

The last time they quarreled concerning marriage she tried to use her neighbors as a form of leverage to bring her point across. However, that proved ineffective. Keith angrily and belligerently proclaimed that he could care less what any of her neighbors had to say and that she shouldn't care either. She rebottled with the fact that she was the one who had to bear the brunt of their stares and whispers. His answer to that was none of her neighbors did anything for him or her, and that he wasn't going to live his life worrying about what people thought about their marital status. At which point she resorted to tears saying that it wasn't just the neighbors that concerned her, but she didn't want her parents to know that she was pregnant and unmarried. His argument for this was that her parents lived in St Louis and if she was so sensitive about having a baby out of wedlock, then she should have waited until she was married before she got pregnant. She then argued that she had been taking the pill and that something must have gone wrong. To which he would always look at her and smile and shake his head. It was almost as if he knew what she had done, so then, she would challenge his unusual response and asked him why he was smiling. That's when he would end the discussion by saying that he wasn't going to spend his day off battling about the subject. By the tone in his voice she knew what that meant he was through with the subject so she would drop the issue, because she knew if she pursued it that he would grab his belongings and leave. It was a sore spot with him and no manner of manipulation was effective. As a matter of fact, if she had been in need of a tactic to get him out of the house, all she need do was bring up the subject of marriage. She was at a loss as to what to do about it.

As she sat by the window pondering over her predicament she saw Keith entering the courtyard carrying a bag of groceries. He hadn't told her he was coming over today. It was Saturday and she wasn't expecting him until Tuesday. Keith's job's, head quarters was stationed way out in Jersey. Most times he just stayed in Jersey until his shift was over; because of the show host's irregular hours the company arranged accommodations for them near the studio. She hoped everything was alright. With jobs being the way they were today, one could never tell. One day you're working and the next day you're unemployed. Several minutes later, she heard the key in the door and Keith entered the apartment.

The door to Sylvia's apartment opened directly into the living room which was el shaped with an area designated to accommodate a dinette set. Her furniture was traditional. The couch was positioned in the middle of the floor facing an electric fire place she had purchased on sale at Raymore and Flanagan. A life size picture of Sylvia wearing a black evening gown decorated the wall directly over the fireplace. There was about twelve feet separating the couch from the dining area.

Keith walked across the floor and set the groceries on the round mahogany dining table and proceeded over to where Sylvia was seated and planted a kiss on her lips. He put his hands on her belly and greeted the baby, "Hey baby," Keith said in a high pitched voice, "daddy is here." He knelt down on one knee and planted a kiss on her belly as well. Then he gently laid his head on her belly in order to be closer to her and the baby. When he folded his arms around her, she felt a sudden rush of love for him.

"How are you honey?" he said, looking up into her eyes lovingly.

"I'm fine," she said, stroking his bold head gently.

"What are you doing here today? I thought you were coming over on Tuesday?" Keith rose to his feet, "Oh."

He had deliberately made no effort to inform her of his early arrival. It was his way of demonstrating his machismo. He never said it, but he felt that since they had gone exclusive, there wasn't any need for him to announce his visits.

"I exchanged days with one of the other hosts," he said casually.

"It was unexpected," he injected. "One of my co-workers needed to be off Tuesday through Thursday. No biggie, I just exchanged tours with her. So I'm off until Wednesday. What's the matter, are you not glad to see me?" he asked quizzically. "Of course I'm glad to see you," Sylvia said as she kissed him on his forehead. A soft moan of delight escaped her as he folded his arms around her squeezing her gently, "Hum girl you feel so good."

"I do?" she asked taking in his scent and loving the feel of his arms around her. "Yeah, you do?

"Really?"

"Yeah!"

"You silly boy," Sylvia said laughing.

"I brought a few things for us to eat and guess what?" Keith said beaming. "What?" she answered happily.

"I'm going to fix you a wonderful dinner," he said, and gently rubbed her belly. Sylvia swooned in his arms and couldn't understand why he wouldn't marry her. It was obvious that he loved her. He treated her so well. He was thoughtful, kind, and caring, so what was his problem?

What Sylvia didn't know was that Keith had reservations concerning marriage to her. She was right, of course, he did love her. However, he had some serious trust issues stemming from his childhood, and her performance in the court room with Chichi a few months back which gave him cause for pause. Sylvia had out and out lied and put him in a very precarious situation. Sylvia told the judge that she and Chichi had a fight over Keith and that Chichi had started it, and simply lost. If that wasn't bad enough, she produced pictures of her face which was badly swollen where he, Keith, had struck her. She even had pictures of the cuts on her legs.

Chichi was baffled and so was he for that matter, because in truth, they both knew that Chichi did not lay a finger on her. To add insult to injury Sylvia called Keith as her witness and he had to perjure himself in order to support Sylvia's claim. She had tricked him into accompanying her. She claimed she needed his moral support. So there he was standing beside her in a court of law. He had a choice, collaborate her story or incriminate himself by admitting that he inflicted the damage to Sylvia's face thus exposing Sylvia as a liar. He was paralyzed with shock and when the judge began to question him he was in a quandary, the judge had to insist he answer the question and Sylvia's eyes were burning into him like hot coals. He made a quick decision to perjure himself under the pressure. He couldn't even look in Chichi's direction.

He was angry with himself for allowing Sylvia to put him in that position, and after he and Sylvia left the court that day, they quarreled. Sylvia was one slick cookie and Keith was amazed how she had plotted everything down to the smallest detail. It was frightening to think, but she anticipated all of the judge's questions and planned her testimony. She even had pictures to back up her story, pictures that could only have been taken after he slapped her. Now that in particular, he thought, was scary.

Chichi was livid, she looked to Keith for vindication. But, Keith looked away. He didn't really know Chichi and felt he had too much to lose. Chichi couldn't believe his and Sylvia's egregious act of deception and she lost all control. She continually interrupted their testimonies calling them liars which irritated the judge who repeatedly instructed her not to speak out of turn. Finally, when the judge asked Keith if Chichi threw the first blow and he said yes, Chichi flew into a rage insisting that Keith and

Sylvia were lying on her. The judge, fed up with Chichi's constant outburst, dismissed her case.

Chichi was incensed and looked at Keith as though he were the scum of the earth. "I hate you!" she shouted at him. "I wish to God that I never met you!" she shrilled as she came toward him with balled fists and the bailiff intercepted her and literally carried her outside. This angered the judge who was about to step down off the bench but instead cited Chichi with contempt of court and affixed a fine of $500.00.

When Keith looked over at Sylvia, he was astonished to see that she was actually standing there with a smirk on her face. Sylvia had calmly and quietly watched Chichi being ushered out of the courtroom. He couldn't place Sylvia's expression then, but in hindsight, he would have to say she looked smug. It was then that he realized how shrewd and calculating Sylvia was. She was no joke and was certainly no bimbo as he had initially thought. Sylvia was actually dangerous.

Sylvia threw people off guard with her Marilyn Monroe like mannerisms. She was very sexy. Even with her baby bump her body was exquisite. Her doe like eyes gave her face a child like quality, innocence, if you will. The judge was hooked from the start. Sylvia knew how to behave in a courtroom. She answered all the questions posed her without adding any flair. When Chichi presented her case, Sylvia was quiet and demure. She never flinched when Chichi painted her in an unkind light. When the judge questioned Sylvia as to whether or not the testimony against her was true, she simply denied that it happened in the manner in which the plaintiff presented it. Chichi had subpoenaed Justine Parker and Raymond Fox to testify on her behalf. However, Justine and Raymond were unable to collaborate her story, because they only witnessed the fight after it had commenced and when questioned, it was discovered that, they didn't really know who actually threw the first blow. Keith was the only eye witness to the incident and he had testified on Sylvia's behalf. So Chichi's case was weak at best. Poor Chichi, he thought.

When Sylvia was asked to give her version of the incident she negated everything Chichi said. She presented her photo to establish that it was a fight and not an assault as was Chichi's claim. Chichi's witnesses could not collaborate her story that Sylvia struck her first which gravely angered Chichi. When the judge cross examined her, she exhibited her frustration with exaggerated facial expressions and hand movements. On the other hand, when the judge asked Sylvia how it was that she had taken pictures of her injuries right after the fight. Sylvia spoke calmly and softly in her squeaky little girl voice and stated that she initially had planned to sue Chichi but later changed her mind since they had injured each other. After that, the case heavily leaned in Sylvia's favor. Chichi was behaving so poorly that it convinced the judge that Chichi was most likely at fault.

The object of the fight had just testified on behalf of the defendant. And to add insult to injury, the judge looked at Chichi and stated, "Whenever there is a fight, one side wins and the other side loses." Then cautioned Chichi to consider this the next time she was so inclined to start a fight. He dismissed the case, slamming his gavel on the podium and started to leave the bench. That's when Chichi lost her mind lunging across the aisle toward Keith. Sylvia was a pro and Keith knew that he wouldn't want to be on the other side of a court battle with her.

Keith also suspected that he too had been manipulated by Sylvia as well. Oh he wasn't planning on leaving her or anything, he was hooked and he knew it. Keith was convinced that her pregnancy was no accident. She was too smart to have missed taking her birth control pills. It was true that he loved her, but he was reluctant to give her the legal leverage of marriage.

Keith had accumulated quite a bit of money over the last few years, and he had worked very hard to accumulate what he had. The only thing he had purchased in the past few years was a car. He was hoping to eventually go back to California and buy a house. His sister, Joyce, lived in Glendale with her husband Carlos and their sons, Jaden and Miles. In California, your spouse automatically got half of everything you owned. If children were involved a woman with Sylvia's cunning could actually wipe a man out if the marriage didn't work out. He shuddered to think of what could happen if he got on the wrong side of Sylvia if he were married to her. Sylvia could be mean when crossed. Mean enough to take him to the cleaners. With his investments, he had well over a million dollars on paper. Now Keith knew in his heart that no matter what happened between them that he would always take care of his child, this was not an issue. As it were he now considered Sylvia and the baby to be family and he genuinely loved Sylvia. He was in it for the long-haul, but marriage was a big step and he couldn't bring himself to take that step yet. Keith feared Sylvia as much as he loved her, she was a scary lady!

Keith was recently offered a major television network position as a host on a game show and his agent was in the process of that negotiation. He hadn't told Sylvia about it yet, he wanted to wait until the negotiations were final.

It was interesting how Keith got into the business. He had been a back-up singer in this little group which called themselves the "Kings." They had signed up to perform at a Jon Bon Jovie concert. The group was booked to precede the main act. There was a portion in their routine where Keith had to speak. A talent scout was in the audience and liked the sound of Keith's speaking voice and approached him later on after the show and asked him if he would be interested in hosting a TV Game show.

The scout felt that the group was lousy and he was only interested in Keith. The truth of the matter was Keith's group wasn't exactly booking gigs on a regular basis. They had actually gotten the gig on a fluke. The band that was originally booked to work the gig was unable to make it and they got the gig by default. So when this scout offered Keith the chance to host a game show he accepted it, and it was a good thing too, because shortly after the concert gig, his group broke up.

Had he not been offered the job, he would have had to take a job as an intern in an advertising company in New York. He had a bachelor's degree in journalism and it would have been good experience, but there was little to no money involved. Keith was trying to get paid. Experience was nice, but Keith didn't have any family he could fall back on while he was obtaining this experience. Being a TV host was the best job offer he had heard since he started out in show business. The pay was good, it was steady and he enjoyed what he was doing.

The ladies were plentiful and he wasn't wanting for anything. Everything was working out well for him. He worked at that job for several years and then the show ratings dropped and they went off the air. He was out of steady work for about two years. He did some TV commercials, but Keith was struggling to keep his head above water. Then he was offered the position as a shopping network host which he accepted and he's been doing that for the past five years.

Keith didn't know exactly what to do about Sylvia. He experienced extreme anxiety whenever the subject of marriage was posed. He knew he was trying Sylvia's patience's and he didn't want to lose her. He once thought about popping the question after the baby was born with a stipulation of a prenuptial. Keith didn't know how he would present something like that to Sylvia. He knew without a doubt that it would upset her and he wasn't looking forward to the drama that was sure to follow. He was just barely a millionaire. He just didn't want to get hurt financially if it didn't work out. Sylvia's people had money, but he had struggled hard for everything that he had. There was no one to cushion the blow if he should fall.

The idea of a family made him feel like he belonged and in a way he needed Sylvia. She and this baby was his family. She was the mother of his child. Sylvia had very much gotten under his skin.

Keith never really had much of a family life. His mother, Gail Huston, was a hippy type. She was one quarter Cherokee, one quarter French and half African American. She was beautiful in a quiet way. It was like you didn't really notice her beauty at first and then after a while it crept up on you, sort of like the hiccups. You didn't quite know where it came from and suddenly it was upon you. She was tall and slim with high cheek bones. She possessed the most beautiful smile. Keith could be so angry with her, but when she flashed her smile at him, it was as calming as a lullaby. Gail had trekked him and his sister, Joyce, all over California partying and getting high with her friends. They lived in various trailer parks and dingy apartment complexes in Crenshaw, Inglewood, and East L.A. to name a few.

He and his sister migrated from one school to another never really having close friends. There was no real stability in their lives aside from each other. Keith had a photographic memory and despite the fact that they were never in one place very long, he still was able to get good grades. His sister, on the other hand, struggled all through middle school and eventually dropped out altogether and ran away when she was seventeen. Luckily for her she met Carlos, an older man. Carlos had invested in a couple of those fast food restaurant chains and was quite well off. She happened to be employed in one of his stores. Keith's sister Joyce was a true beauty. The kind that stood out in a crowd, her skin was flawless.

Keith had nick-named her peaches. Her eyes were large with thick dark eyebrows and fan like lashes. Her cheekbones were high like their mother's, with full pouted lips and her teeth were like fine pearls, uniformed and even, as though she had worn braces as a child. That was so far from the truth it was laughable. They were lucky as children to be able to get three square meals a day, a few pieces of clothing, and a place to lay their heads. Dentistry was definitely not a part of their reality. Their mother had great teeth as well so it must have been genetics coupled with the fact that he and his sister both brushed their teeth after every meal. Their mother insisted on it. Keith suspected that they had different fathers, because of their mother's life style coupled with the fact that they did not have a strong family resemblance. The only thing that tied them together was their teeth and the way they held their mouth when they smiled. She had a peachy complexion. He was chocolate. Her eyes were light brown and extremely large, his were dark brown and slightly slanted. However, they both had high sculptured cheek bones and they were both very good looking children.

Keith loved his sister dearly and they were very close. There was not a week that went by that he did not call her. She, as far as he was concerned, was all the family he had in the world, that is, until Sylvia told him of her pregnancy.

Keith had lived with his mother long enough to graduate high school. After high school, he moved away and worked his way through college. The last time he saw Gail was at his college graduation. She had left his current stepfather, at that time, and was headed to Colorado with yet another new found love right after his graduation ceremony. Why she had bothered to come to his graduation was a mystery. He guessed it was an all out effort on her part to act like a parent.

Keith guessed he should be thankful that she kept him and his sister around until they were big enough to fend for themselves. Many women who lived life the way she did just dropped their children off on other people. She could have abandoned them, but for better or worse she didn't. He once heard one of her boyfriends say to her, "Don't you have any folk where you can drop these kids off?" That was the last time he asked her that. Gail flew into a rage. Her eyes narrowed and her teeth were clinched shut as she spoke, "Don't you ever, speak about dropping my kids off" she hissed. "If they bother you, get the Hell out." Keith had never seen her that way and, in spite of the way they lived, he had never heard her use profanity before either. The tone in her voice was more of a growl than it was anything else and her face conveyed the message she was sending louder than the words coming out of her mouth. It was kind of scary! She wasn't the hugging kissing kind of a mother, but he guessed she must have loved them in her own way and he loved her too in his.

One thing she did do was to make sure they had food and that they were clean. Another thing to her credit, she often boasted about how she never smoked pot during any of her pregnancies. She also surrounded him and his sister with music and Keith loved music so much he joined a rock band in everyplace they landed. After graduation he hopped in the back of a beat up old van and followed a band to New York. Deep in his heart, Keith always wanted a family. He spoke to Gail from time to time when she called, but had never made it out to Colorado to visit her. He probably couldn't have found her if he wanted to, she moved around so much. Since he and his sister where more stationary, Gail usually contacted them. The only thing that had changed about her was that she once was a young hippy and now she was an old one.

Keith had never told Sylvia about his past. Had he done so, he felt, she would know how important the life inside her was to him and she would surely use that information to her advantage. He already loved the baby and was very excited about its pending birth. He didn't need to be pressured into marriage.

After stealing another kiss from Sylvia, Keith released her, got up and walked to the dining area and picked up the groceries and went into the kitchen. Sylvia made up her mind that she would not bring up the subject of marriage this weekend. She was just going to enjoy the weekend and Keith without drama. Maybe after his baby was born he would want to do the right thing without her having to pressure him. Keith loved R&B music so Sylvia slipped in a DVD and "Sunshine" by Baby face filled the house with its message of love. Then she got Keith a Budweiser which she always kept stocked in the fridge, because she knew he liked them.

She handed it to him and said, "Why don't you let me do the cooking? You know I love to prepare your food and watch you eat."

Keith put the bottle to his mouth and guzzled down half of it and then he said, "No, no, no I have this recipe and I already tried it out the other day. It's delicious! I brought shrimp and they're already clean. All I have to do is rinse them off. Now you get out of the kitchen and give me room. I'm going to make you something that's going to knock your socks off."

"But, I don't have any socks on," she said jokingly.

He gave her a little spank on her bottom and said smiling, "Well go put some socks on so I can knock them off." They laughed and Sylvia left the kitchen.

Keith stuck his head out the door and said, "Hey, did you miss me while I was away?"

"You silly boy, I miss you when you walk into another room." She meant it too, she had never been this wild about anyone in her life.

"Ooh, girl, see now you're trying to blow up my head," he said.

"Yah think?" she asked looking at him smiling seductively and winked.

"Girl, you better stop that or we're not going to get anything to eat." She laughed and walked over to the window and sat down in what she liked to call her spy corner.

There were a few men in and out of the complex who would have loved to be in Keith's shoes. There was this guy named Robert that lived on the 19th floor who was actually heart broken when he saw that she was pregnant. He had done everything he could to get a date with her, but she would only flirt with him. Sylvia enjoyed the attention she received from other men, but she rarely went beyond flirtations. Because of Sylvia's playful flirtations,

Robert had been hopeful, but he was never able to get her to date him no matter how hard he tried. The closest he ever came to a date was when he spotted her in the neighborhood coffee shop and she let him purchase a cup of coffee for her. They sat at the same table. They laughed and talked for about an hour or more that afternoon. Then she had to run off and finish her shopping. He was never able to get her number so it could go no further.

It was just as well, because he wasn't her type. Robert was a plain looking man of average height with an average personality. He was not really obese, but he could stand to lose a few pounds. Had she allowed him to spend any real time with her, she would have used him up and tossed him aside at her earliest convenience. Sylvia had done similar to a lot of guys in the area. She loved the attention and she delighted in the fact that they thought she was easy, because she knew all along that no matter what they did, it would never progress beyond the flirts. This kept her suitors wanting and won her plenty of favors. Miss Cartier was on the take, she wasn't about giving up much of anything. She used her looks as part of her scheme to get whatever she wanted and she had a nice personality as well. She could be very funny.

But when she met Keith, she knew, at once, he was the one for her. Oh, she teased him the same way she had done the others for as long as she dared. She knew from the moment she laid eyes on him, that he would be the one warming her bed and she was going to make the experience worth his while. Her objective, from the very beginning, was to make him hers. Sylvia knew that Keith was a playboy, but Sylvia had no plans on being his play thing. Sylvia was no virgin. She knew what to do. If she decided to go to bed with a man, she always left him wanting more.

She knew Keith was slippery, but not unobtainable. A girl just had to know how to play her cards, she thought. She didn't really want to play the baby card, but she could smell something brewing between him and Justine and she had to put a stop to it before it got out of hand. It was a dangerous game, the baby card could go either way, and she hadn't even been aware of Chichi. The baby came along right on time, because she almost lost control of him that night.

Sylvia was happy to see that Justine was fully occupied with her new African boy friend. Sylvia had to give it to her, Justine really had good taste. If she wasn't in love with Keith she might have given a guy like Marcelo a chance herself. He was strikingly handsome and classy as well. When the four of them met in the hallway, he only glanced at Sylvia long enough for the introductions. Afterwards his eyes where properly glued to Justine. It was kind of unsettling to Sylvia, because she was used to men stealing extra glances her way even when they were with their, as she liked to put it, insignificant others. But not Mr. Okonedo, he only had eyes for Justine. Sylvia wondered what Justine's angle was? How had she managed to hook that one? She also wondered what Keith found so captivating about Justine? She wasn't bad looking, but she knew it wasn't her looks. She had something else going for her and whatever it was, it was working well for her. As long as her attention was no longer focused on Keith, Sylvia was happy. As far as that little Asian chick, Chichi was concerned, she now hated Keith and that was fine by Sylvia. Chichi didn't know who she was messing with, Sylvia thought to herself.

Now that the baby was on the way she didn't believe that she would have to worry about Keith straying. She had sensed a longing in Keith and perceived that he needed something solid in his life, that's why she dared to allow herself to get pregnant. She could see that he was afraid and that is why she decided not to push for marriage so hard. Sylvia's perceptions were correct. She knew how to read people.

As far as Keith was concerned, marriage or no marriage, there was no turning back for him at this point. It didn't matter, because Sylvia was going to stick to him like a tick. There'd be no drama so long as Keith understood the program. Sylvia was a master of deception. No one could figure her out, because she knew how to cloak her intelligence when necessary. In fact her little ditz act was her most powerful weapon. She had ciao a lot of folk with that.

As quiet as it was kept, Sylvia was the best paralegal in the law firm where she worked in Manhattan. She was like one of those beautiful meat eating plants in the rain forest of Brazil, pleasing to the eyes, seemingly harmless, and extremely inviting. But when the unsuspecting insect is lured by what it perceives to be a free meal, and crawls inside the beautiful flower to have a sip of its nectar, without warning, the flower snaps shut and it is devoured. That was Sylvia. She was a predator and that's why Keith was reluctant to drop his guard. He could feel it and he was at a crossroad. Should he simply marry Sylvia and throw all caution to the wind? Or should he just string her along in order to raise his child. Truth be told, he didn't really believe that the latter was even possible. However, he would not have to make that decision this weekend, but he knew his time was running out, the birthing was near.

Sylvia, seeing that he was almost finished preparing the meal, took the dinnerware out of the cabinet and began to set the table. Keith stood in the doorway to the kitchen and observed her from behind. Despite his fears, he loved her. Who was he kidding? He was in deep. Sylvia looked up in time to see the look of love in his eyes and blew him a kiss. Clearly this stalling game would soon be over, she thought. He was like a big fish on the hook, she couldn't yank him into the boat just yet. She would have to be patient, give him a little more rope, let him splash in the water a bit and, when he was sufficiently tired, she could reel him on in.

She began to hum to the music that was playing ♪ ♫ "Time is on my side, yes it is Tiiiime is on my side, ♪ ♫" as she considered the chess game they were playing. It was just a matter of time before the baby arrived and between the two of them … just a matter of time before wedding bells were going to chime.

"♪ ♫Time is on my side…Oh yes it is…♪ ♫"

VIOLA'S DILEMMA

Marcelo was very happy. He had purchased a beautiful engagement ring and was taking Justine out to dine at Tavern on the Green. Viola, Claudio, Chide, and a few other friends were scheduled to join them later on that evening. He arranged it so that they would arrive after he proposed to Justine. He wanted everything to be perfect. He would first take her to a Broadway play and then they would go to Tavern on the Green where he would propose to her around 8:30 p.m., then around 9:00p.m., his party should arrive.

He was hopeful that he and Justine would be announcing their engagement to their closest friends. He was nervous. Even though he knew Justine was crazy about him, he was not entirely sure what she felt about marriage. Justine once told him that she had been married before and wasn't in any hurry to go down that road again. However, a lot had transpired between the two of them since that conversation. He stayed at her house at least three nights a week for the last four months.

The way he figured it, Justine seemed to be ready for a husband now, because she never wanted him to go home. It was comical the way she would do all kinds of laughable things to get him to stay over. She once pretended to accidentally spill tomato juice on his shirt and had him take it off so that she could wash it and of course he'd end up staying the night. Other times she would find all sorts of chores for him to perform whenever he was about to go home and the chores would always be time consuming. So much so that he'd end up spending the night. He was at her house so often, now half of his of clothing was in her wardrobe.

There was no reason for them to continue playing this ridicules game. They obviously enjoyed each other's company and wanted to be together. They were certainly in love. So they should just get married. To Marcelo it was simple.

Now Marcelo had sworn Viola, Salina, and her friend Grace to secrecy, though he was aware that Viola thought this to be a potentially explosive situation. Viola felt that everything he was doing was sweet and extremely romantic, but she didn't believe that this was the right time for him to propose to Justine. Knowing that Viola and Justine were close it did give him some pause for concern.

Viola was home pondering over the conversation she had with Marcelo concerning his little surprise. She had told Marcelo, that she knew for a fact that Justine had reservation concerning marriage. She and Justine had actually discussed the possibility of her marrying Marcelo on numerous occasions and the conversation always ended the same way. Justine liked things the way they were. They got along so well together. She feared things might change if they married.

One of the things that concerned Justine was the fact that Marcelo was African. She felt African's had all these cultural differences and traditions, and Justine just didn't know if she would fit in. More than that, she didn't know if she even wanted to fit in.

Viola was conflicted. She didn't know if she should allow her friend to venture out on this date tonight with no knowledge of what it entailed. Here it is Marcelo had actually planned a party to which she and Claudio are to be a part of, and it is all based on the hope that Justine would accept his proposal. If Viola had to guess the outcome of Marcelo's proposal based on the conversations that she and Justine had in the past, she'd predict that his proposal would more than likely be turned down. Viola felt that it was her duty as a friend to tell Justine what was in store. However, before she did that, she would consult Claudio on the matter.

Claudio was sitting on the terrace enjoying the beautiful spring weather. It was May and the trees and flowers were in bloom. From where he sat on the twenty-third floor, he was able to look out over the city blocks and see for miles. He looked up just in time to see Viola approaching the door way with a tray. She was bringing them some cocktails to drink out on the terrace.

"Hi Baby, what are you doing out here, day dreaming?" she asked smiling.

"Nah, not really, just enjoying the beautiful weather," he said as he reached out to take the tray out of her hand. She handed the tray to him and he rested it on the little table.

He looked at her and asked, "What's on jour mind, Baby?"

"I'm worried about tonight's event," she said.

Claudio looked at her puzzled and said, "Why?"

She pulled up a chair next to his and said, "I know my friend Justine loves Marcelo very much, however, I'm not sure that this proposal thing is going to turn out well". "Why do jou say dat?" Claudio asked.

"Well, Justine and I have discussed marriage on several occasions and she always says that she didn't think she ever wanted to get married again."

"Jeah, well maybe dat's how she felt before she met

Marcelo," Claudio said.

"No, we discussed it recently, at least two months ago. In fact, she stated that she liked her relationship with Marcelo just the way it was. I asked her what she would do if he asked her to marry him and she said she wasn't sure she would say yes."

"Well, there jou are, she told jou a couple of months ago dat if he asked her to marry him dat she was not sure she would say jes, however, she din't say she would say no."

"I know, Claudio, but there are other things. We have talked about marriage in depth and I don't think that's what she wants. I don't want her to be put on the spot. Even worse I don't want her to jeopardize her relationship with Marcelo, by allowing him to propose and then turn him down before his friends. You know these Africans are very proud people and he might not take kindly to a public refusal of marriage, especially when he has gone through all this trouble."

"I don know Viola, Marcelo is the one who has made it public. I don thin dat jou should interfere. I know wha she may have told jou, but jou don know dat she's going to refuse him."

"I know but..."

"Viola," Claudio interrupted. "Knowing the right time to propose has always been a mystery. I thin jou should stay out of it," he said flatly. "Jou don know wha Justine will do when faced with an actual proposal. It's very easy to speculate about wha she would or would not do when she hadn't actually been presented with a proposal. When speculating, people often say they would do one ting and den surprisingly dey do another. Des is serious," he went on to say. "If jou tell her about it and she is open to his proposal, den, jou will spoil a wonderful surprise. Don't interfere," he urged. "Just do jour part. Jou show up tonight and wish them well."

Viola was amazed at the wisdom of her young man, and she told him so. Claudio's English had greatly improved over the last two years. Not only was he picking up different phrases during the day to day conversations, he had actually enrolled in a class the year before last to learn English. He could now read and write English exceptionally well. It was amazing what the human mind could accomplish. Viola's compliment was not well received by Claudio. Though, he did not verbalize his feelings to her, he couldn't understand why Viola should be so surprised that he had the ability to think. He felt most American's had the tendency to judge non English speaking people as though they lacked intelligence. Which he thought was absurd, because they would face the same obstacles if they went to a country where they had no understanding of the language. Nevertheless, he was better able to communicate with her which gave her a greater window into his mind.

He was wrong to think that Viola thought he lacked intelligence. Nothing could be further from the truth. Viola felt lucky to have found him and was proud to have him as her man. Secretly she thought he had a really cute accent, and that he was extremely handsome, very intelligent and a really great lover. Why, she had even started using the love word. Though she noticed that he never reciprocated when she said it and this did concern her.

Viola was learning Portuguese as well, partially because of her business in Brazil. However, she also enjoyed engaging Claudio in his language. Viola felt that she and Claudio really complimented each other. She would marry him in a heartbeat if he asked her. And this was major for her, but Viola was head over hills in love with him.

CLAUDIO'S TRUTH

Claudio cared for Viola, but he had never fully recovered from that awful quarrel that they had the year before last that almost broke them up. He tried to push it to the back of his mind. He didn't really relish the thought of breaking it off with Viola. However, he felt that somewhere on an unconscious level, Viola thought he was beneath her. He was wrong about her feelings, of course, as a matter of fact, he was far off track. Viola loved and respected him. She had completely abandoned the idea of telling Justine about Marcelo's planned proposal solely based on the advice that he had just given her. She thought very highly of him and after that dreaded night that she almost lost him, she had come to believe that he was the best thing that ever happened to her.

She had totally dismissed any doubts she once had about him. She rationalized that he, the person, was not his circumstance. She felt that the person she had met on the beach was someone who was simply trying to survive in a harsh environment. Who was she to judge him? she thought. What might she have done given the same circumstances? The way he lived in Brazil was his past, and the individual he was now, was a totally different person.

This however was not entirely true. Claudio was very much a victim of his past and those demons haunted him.

She had forgiven him his past in ways that he had not been able to do himself. However, Claudio still had a great many of those demons to cast out. Where she had come to trust him completely, he no longer trusted her or himself for that matter. He felt that if she even came close to knowing all he had done for money, she would want nothing to do with him.

Claudio was so troubled by the events that took place in his past it had damaged his self esteem. Though Viola had never said or done anything to attack his character since her performance on that awful night, she had unwittingly opened Pandora's Box, and it ate away at his soul. As a matter a fact, it was her delivery of the assault that continued to haunt his thoughts, and sometimes he even revisited the scene in his dreams. It never really left him. Even though she had retracted her statements over and over again, it just wouldn't go away.

On an intellectual level, Claudio knew and understood that Viola had only wanted to cause him pain. He understood that she genuinely wished that she had never uttered the words, but she had uttered them. And it was on an emotional level that he perceived she meant what she said on some muted unconscious level. He felt that her thought process had to have originated somewhere in the corridors of her mind long before that episode. It was like an ovules, but of thought waiting for the fertilization of a basic concept and was brought to the surface when triggered by, what she believed to be, an aspect of betrayal. He was convinced that she now was suppressing what she really believed to be the actual truth. And that truth is that he, Claudio, is and will always be a male whore. Claudio, himself believed that he had emerged from the gutter and that there would always be some traces of the stench that would forever cling to him.

Now, he knew that he had changed in many ways and there were no words he could say to express his gratitude for the many wonderful things Viola had done for him. In truth, she had saved him from a life of poverty. She gave him hope for a viable future and the medical care she provided for his sister, Alisa, could not be measured on any scale. He knew that she thought she was in love with him and he wished he could just let loose and love her. However, emotionally, he was not up to the task. There were certain aspects of his life she knew nothing about. If she knew…well he didn't even want to venture to think that far.

He certainly couldn't do what Marcelo was about to do tonight. How could he, Claudio, ever think of asking Viola to be his wife? He did not feel worthy of her. He believed without a doubt that her closest friends would think that he only wanted her for her money, because it did start out that way in the beginning. In addition to that there was that fifteen year difference in their ages. Claudio felt he might want to have children some day. Plus he believed that the only reason she didn't get rid of him was, because she herself, was not ready to bare the pain of a break-up. He didn't mean that she had no feelings for him, he knew better. He just didn't believe it was true love she was feeling. Love that was unconditional and all forgiving especially since she didn't have all the facts.

Claudio was deeply disturbed by his past. There was a lot of repair that needed to be done. It went far deeper than where Viola's words had gone. Her words only brought to the surface feelings that had been brewing in his psyche for years. These feelings of degradation and self loathing were there long before, Viola spoke the fatal words. The words only awakened his demons. And after tonight's festivities, he and Viola would be facing quite a few bumps in the road ahead.

It was actually kind of sad, because he had once adored her. Now there was a wall between them that he had erected after that fight. Only now Viola had completely fallen in love with him and Claudio was unable to reciprocate.

His perception of Viola's view of him was so off. They were untrue. Claudio was just projecting his own clouded view of himself onto her and this would be the source of their problems in the future. Claudio knew that he had done things to survive that nobody should have to do. He had suppressed all of these things, because he couldn't justify them in his own mind. It was all too painful. Claudio was strictly heterosexual yet he had even given himself to men. His prostitution of himself did not stop with women. He felt that if she knew this she would not want to be with him. Claudio felt that everyone was above him, especially his friend Marcelo whom he had begun to look up to. Claudio had met with Marcelo on several occasions and Marcelo talked in depth about his quest to get ahead. Claudio very much admired Marcelo. He wished that he had known someone like him when the stumbling blocks of life had befallen him back in Brazil. Maybe he would have taken a different path. He hated all of the things he had done. He even hated the way he initially met Viola. Justine had a good man, a man she could be proud of. Viola was a good person, who unfortunately, received the short end of the stick when she ended up with him, he thought. Claudio had greatly underestimated Viola's love. This would prove to be most unfortunate later on down the line.

Claudio was in a great deal of pain, maybe he had too much time on his hands to think. His life was not nearly as hard as it had been in the past. He liked working with

Vie, but he needed to do his own thing, pave his own way the way Marcelo was doing. Something Viola never allowed him to do because she had so much more than he did. She always provided everything for him. She didn't understand he needed to spend his own money some- times just to have a feeling of self worth. Claudio's truth was that he was his own worst enemy.

THE LEAP OF FAITH

J ustine had just finished showering and she walked over to the mirror to examine herself more closely. She smiled back at her reflection; it was exactly one year to the date that she had met Marcelo. She had been working out at the Gym and was very pleased with the results. There were notable changes in the way her body looked. Even her breasts seemed to be perkier, and she had secret plans to do something more to them. She walked over to the bed and slipped into her black lace panties and bra set. Then she went back over to model them in front of the mirror.

She had been to Viola's salon in Manhattan earlier and had her hair done for her date with Marcelo tonight. He is so cute, she thought, always doing little things to please me. Justine couldn't imagine her life without him and wondered how she had managed before she met him. God I loved that man, she thought. Even when he made her angry, and they did have their little quarrels, she was forever conscious of the fact of how much she adored him. Even in anger, she could not bring herself to say anything that she thought would badly offend him. And if by chance she did offend him, she was quick to rectify it; and he is just as considerate of her feelings.

She felt she could not have designed a better companion if she tried. If she had to name a fault, she would say he was a little chauvinistic. Some of his viewpoints con-

cerning the genders were a bit archaic. They would sometimes debate about, what she felt was, his outrageous
point of view in relationship to women, and the unfair
advantages he afforded the male gender. They would
playfully argue their view points while generously allowing their own gender the upper hand in the debate. She
knew that he really believed himself to be right, but didn't
think that he actually thought that his archaic beliefs
could reasonably play a part, or even could be executed in
today's modern society. She believed it was simply his
personal views and that it could in no way affect their
relationship in the real sense, at least she hoped that to be
the case. At any rate it hadn't affected their relationship to
date.

She wondered, however, what it would be like if they
were to take their relationship to the next level. Would his
dated view of the sexes interfere with the harmony that
they now shared? If she were honest, she would have to
admit that the thought posed a question in the back of her
mind as to whether they could make it as a married
couple. She believed that African men often waited until
marriage to impose their demands on their wives, or so
she had been told by some of her friends. She had tried to
raise the subject with Marcelo once or twice in the past,
but he would jokingly say, "Aw, you must cross that
bridge when we get there." They would laugh it off while
she tried to get him to state his position, but he was rather
slippery when it came to stating anything concrete concerning his views on marriage. To tell the truth it was this,
little underlining factor, which gnawed away at the back of
her mind.

Justine enjoyed her freedom and guarded it jealously.
This was one of the reasons, up until now, that she had
avoided getting into a serious relationship. She knew there

were a lot of sacrifices in marriage and felt that often time those sacrifices were made by the woman. And the woman, more often than not, was rewarded for her effort by betrayal and infidelity. Before Marcelo, she had been perfectly content to remain single for the rest of her life. Now here she was enjoying the companionship of a man she absolutely adored. This whole thing caught her off guard.

Life was amazing. Tonight they would be celebrating their one year anniversary. She slipped into the little black dress, zipped it up and slid her feet into her red pumps, and walked back over to the mirror. Marcelo came out of the bathroom at that point and said, "Justine you really look awesome!"

She was wearing her hair up and the grey streak in her hair was fashioned into a swirl like design. She did look lovely. She smiled and crossed the room and put her arms around his neck and kissed him softly on the lips. He pulled her closer to him prolonging the kiss which started to bring about an erection. She quickly pulled away from him and said, "Oh no you don't, I just got my hair done. I paid a lot of money for this do and you're not going to mess it up."

"Oh come on," he begged. "Let's just get a little quick one."

"Nope."

"I won't mess up your hair," he promised

"Nope," she insisted.

"Justine, you can put a scarf on your hair."

"Nope, nope, no, Marcelo, you have to get dressed. We don't have that much time anyway. We have a schedule and we can't be late. Remember you made reservations," she said as she maneuvered herself out of his embrace over to her dressing table.

"Besides, I have to finish putting on my make-up." Marcelo laughed and walked over to the bed where she had laid out his clothes and started to get dressed.

Justine was glowing, she really enjoyed plays. Marcelo had taken her to see "The Lion King." She was chatting away about it as they exited the theatre and Marcelo was beaming with pride, because he had managed to delight her fancy. He hailed a cab and ushered her inside and gave the cab driver instructions to take them to Tavern on the Green. It wasn't everyday that they splurged this way and Justine was really enjoying every moment of it.

They arrived at Tavern on the Green and the waiter escorted them to the garden room that Marcelo had requested they be seated. When they arrived at their table Marcelo pulled the chair out for Justine to assist her in seating. Afterwards he sat down across the table from her. He smiled at her lovingly and Justine blew him a kiss. "Why such a large table?" Justine asked.

"Maybe we should tell them to give us a smaller table?"

"This table is fine, sweetheart."

"No it isn't;" she persisted. "It's much too large for just the two of us. Waiter," she shouted waving her hand in the air and when the waiter looked up she waved him over. The waiter approached the table and Justine said, "This is such a large table for two people. Is it possible to get us a smaller table?"

The waiter immediately shot his gaze toward Marcelo and Marcelo overruled Justine's request by saying, "it's OK, it's OK. Look I'll move over and sit closer to you. Don't make such a fuss, Babe." The waiter quickly disappeared before Justine could respond. Marcelo had to convince Justine to settle for the large table, so that by the time the waiter returned to take their orders, Justine was resigned to remaining at that table.

Marcelo insisted on ordering for the two of them. He was so old school, Justine thought to herself, and just had to shake her head and laugh. Later, the waiter returned to the table with a bottle of Dom Perignon.

"Oh my God, Marcelo, this is too much," she exclaimed. She leaned in close and whispered, "Honey I appreciate this, but Dom Perignon must cost a small fortune in a place like this."

"Don't worry about it, honey, I've got it covered," he said. After the waiter had poured them each a glass, he left the bottle on the table. Marcelo lifted his glass and said, "To us." Justine immediately responded in kind. Marcelo took a sip of the champagne and put his glass down and took Justine's hands. He looked into her eyes and asked her, "Are you enjoying our little date?"

Justine looked at him and said, "Yes, yes this is the best anniversary I've ever had." "I'm glad," he said. "Because I brought you here tonight to ask you to be my wife." Then he went into his pocket and produced a small box. In it was a two and a half carat diamond solitaire round, with two quarter carat round diamonds set on either side of the solitaire. Justine was taken aback; her head was in a whirl spin. Marcelo had completely sideswiped her with this move.

"Will you marry me?" he asked looking deep into her eyes.

Justine didn't know what to say, she didn't know what to do. She knew that she loved him with all her heart and that tonight was simply enchanting, but marriage? Was she ready to just throw all caution to the wind and marry a second time? This was too much, she was completely overwhelmed.

Marcelo grew worried. He leaned closer to her and

said, "Babe, please say yes. You will make me the happiest man in the world."

Justine couldn't collect her thoughts. Everything seemed to be happening so fast and closing in on her.

Seeing her perplexity Marcelo didn't know what to do. Justine was not responding the way that he anticipated. He had taken a leap of faith. It would be a great embarrassment if she turned him down after he had invited a party of their friends to celebrate the occasion. Maybe Viola was right and it was a bad idea for him to have presented it to her in this manner. Perhaps he should have asked her in a more private setting and then celebrated after she had accepted, if indeed, she did accept. Justine looked at him and could see the anxiety on his face.

She knew that she had to say something.

"Marcelo," she said. "I'm overwhelmed. I had no idea that you were going to ask me to marry you. What a surprise." She took the box that contained the ring out of his hand and examined it more closely.

"It's beautiful," she said.

"As are you," he responded.

"Marcelo," she said, handing the box back to him, "You know that I love you, I'm never happier than when I'm with you, but to be honest, your proposal has completely thrown me off guard. I don't know what to say."

"Say yes," he said. "Honey what are you afraid of?"

She looked into his eyes and said, "I'm-I'm afraid that things will change. Darling, the past year has been amazing. I have never been happier in my life. I guess I just don't want that to change." She looked away from him.

He gently put his hand on her chin and turned her face back around to face him and said, "What makes you think that things will change if we get married, Justine?" Though Marcelo had forced her to face him straight on

Justine managed to cast her eyes downward when she said, "Marcelo, I've seen it happen time without number, hell, it has happened to me." Then she met his gaze, "People get married and then things began to change. Sometime people date for years, but after they get married they break up. I know a couple who were together for ten years, Marcelo, and after they got married they broke up two years later. As soon as they were married, the game plan changed and things that were never an issue before became issues after they got married. I just don't want that to happen to us."

Marcelo was quiet. He listened to every word she said. When she was finished talking, there was an awkward period of silence. Marcelo was carefully digesting what Justine had said to him. Justine had never seen him look more serious. Then he leaned forward laying the box that contained the ring on the table. He took both her hands and looked deeply into her eyes.

"Justine," he said. "In order for a marriage to last, both people have to believe in it. They have to believe in each other." He paused and then he said, "Justine, I believe in us. I don't know about other people and how their marriages fared, quite frankly, Justine, I don't care about any other person, but us. You and I are important to me. I believe that what you and I have is solid. I know that we will have some challenges, but I am willing to weather any storm that comes up during our marriage to keep us together. Honey, I love you. I want to be with you for the rest of my life. I want you to be my wife." With that he leaned forward and he kissed her. Then he looked into her eyes and said, "Will you marry me? Will you trust that our love is worth sanctifying before God, before our families and before our friends?

Justine's eyes welled up with tears and then she began

to speak, "Darling that was the most beautiful proposal I have ever heard. I guess sometimes you just have to take a leap of faith. Yes, I will marry you." Marcelo took the ring from the box and slipped it on her finger.

The timing could not have been more perfect, because at that moment the waiter ushered in the rest of the dining party, it was exactly 9:05 p.m. Marcelo stood up and greeted everyone as they approached. Justine was in a state of shock.

"Viola, Salina, oh my goodness, Grace" she shouted, "How long have you people known about this?"

Viola leaned in and kissed her friend on the cheek and whispered in her ear,

"We've known for a while and I see by the rock on your finger you've accepted. I must say, I am surprised.

"Congratulations, girl," Salina said, leaning in to kiss her as well. Salina was wearing seven inch knee-high silver metallic colored boots and a very short sparkled metallic colored dress. She turned and introduced her date, who resembled a Greek god. His hair was blond, he had abs of steal, and he was wearing a metallic blazer with no shirt. It was buttoned at the waist and a white gold chain with a cross nestled into the wavy blond hairs on his chest.

"This is my friend Hans, Hans this is Justine."

Justine smiled and said, "Hello." And Marcelo shook his hand. Grace made her way over to Justine to give her hugs and kisses and her husband, Majeed followed waving at Justine shyly. Marcelo's roommate Emeka and his date Margie were the last to enter the dining room. Marcelo invited him because Emeka was his roommate and he overheard him talking to Chide on the phone about the party. Justine stood up alongside Marcelo and greeted the rest of their friends. She looked at Marcelo and said, "You really know how to surprise a girl." Afterwards the waiter started to bring out the food. Marcelo had actually ordered for everyone weeks in advance. The only reason Marcelo and Justine were presented with menus was to throw Justine off guard. Everyone was in a jovial mood.

Chide announced that he and Patience had also gotten engaged two weeks prior. Marcelo was surprised that his friend was getting married. Chide had been a big time playboy. Patience must be a special lady, he thought. Patience touched Justine's hand and said, smilingly shyly, "We will both be two married ladies together."

Grace interjected, jokingly saying, "Yes Justine we will all have to get together and discuss our marital woes," and then she laughed. Then all three ladies began laughing. Viola caught Salina's eye and rolled her eyes in discuss. Salina gave Viola a quick wink and turned to say something to her date.

Patience took Justine's hand in hers in order to get a closer look at her engagement ring. "It is beautiful," she said.

Justine then admired Patience's ring.

"Your ring is beautiful as well." It was a large marquees emerald cut stone with two sizable diamonds on either side of the stone. "Have you guys set a date yet or are you still basting in the afterglow?"

"Oh, yes, we have a date," Patience said happily. "We will be married in exactly one year from the date of the proposal. How about you, have you set a date as well?" she asked.

"Gosh, no," answered Justine laughingly. I haven't even rapped my head around the engagement. I was truly taken by surprise. I had no idea that Marcelo was going to propose tonight."

"Wonders shall never cease," Viola said. Claudio gave her a nudge of disapproval.

"So what else do you have in store for us after dinner?" asked Chide.

"Hey, you know me, now," boasted Marcelo, "You know me!"

"Marcelo, Marcelo," Chide chanted his name. "I know you! I know you!" he shouted jovially.

Then Marcelo said, "There is a club on the west side, it's really hard to get in this club, but you know me Chide. You know when I want something I find a way."

"A hen, I know you, you are the man!" Chide said, and the two began to laugh.

"You are not talking about that club called Windows on the West side?" asked Claudio.

Marcelo gently tapped himself on the chest proudly and said, "Yes, I'm talking about Windows on the West side."

"Hey," exclaimed Chide.

Claudio stood up and gave Marcelo a bow and sat back in his seat.

"Hey, I've always wanted to go there," Majeed said.

"I too," Emeka said gleefully.

"Well, this is your lucky night," exclaimed Marcelo.

Never had Justine seen Marcelo behave this way. This, she guessed was a side of him that she had yet to discover. Of course, this was the first time she had seen him partying with his friends. Marcelo was a happy man and it showed in his every gesture. The other men seemed to really be impressed. It was interesting how they openly praised Marcelo and complemented him on his presentation of the engagement. Hans, Salina's date was rather quiet, probably because he didn't really know anyone except for Salina and seemed to be communicating with her mostly in Spanish. He smiled a lot, but his conversation was mainly directed at Salina. The other men were using their own dialect; it was a slang that Justine heard Marcelo use before. Claudio seemed to fall right in even though he was from a different country. Claudio had been hanging around Marcelo a lot these days. It was amazing. Justine wondered how many sides there were to Marcelo. She felt like she was in a dream, it was all so surreal. When she got up this morning, she had no idea that she would be an engaged woman by the end of the day. She had actually been swept off her feet. Everyone knew except for her. She thought to herself, it just goes to show you that you really don't know people. I would have never guessed that Viola would be capable of keeping such a secret from me. She really must be changing, because the Viola I knew would have given me the head's up.

It had been a very interesting evening and Justine was exhausted as she left the shower and walked into the bedroom. Marcelo waited patiently until she reached the bed before pulling her down on top of him. "Oh Marcelo I'm so tired," she protested. But, Marcelo bombarded her with an onslaught of kisses; his hands were rubbing and probing her passionately. Justine could tell he was determined to have her, as he ravaged her with an endless attack of kisses; reaching her breast, he took her nipple into his mouth, invoking in her, feelings of desire. In the heat of his passion his lips found hers and she was quick to respond. Fully erect he mounted her and began to suckle her breast, then slowly descending he kissed her belly. His tongue and lips were in unison as they made their way down, down, down to her soft spot. Justine pushed her hips forward relishing each stroke of his tongue and lips, she gently caressed his head as he feverishly foraged his way deep inside her.

"Oooh, she cried out as she was gripped by thunderous orgasmic waves; every fiber of her being was quickened. Hungrily he kissed the inside of her thighs, then upward to the softness of her belly as he made his way up, up, upward until he reached her lips; and she eagerly returned his kisses as she wrapped her legs around him. He entered her and piston rhythmically within her; Justine imploded with endless delight, with each thrust of his hip she called out his name over and over.

Afterward they lay there, her wrapped in his arms for what seemed like a long time and then Marcelo broke the silence. "Thank you," he said, and gave her a peck on her shoulder.

"What are you thanking me for?" she asked.

"For being my wife," he said.

"I'm not your wife yet," she said jokingly.

"In my mind you became my wife the moment you said yes," he said, looking down at her, and peered deeply into her eyes.

"We learn to say fiancé and fiancée from the Western world. In my village when a man asks for a woman's hand in marriage and she accepts, she becomes his wife. Her father is presented with gifts and she cannot go out with another man after that. The ceremony is just a formality, mainly for the friends and families' sake. To break that engagement is a very serious thing. One would have to go before the counsel and have a very good reason. It could cause feuding between the families. I have made love to you many times, but tonight, for me, it was different. Tonight I made love to my wife, bone of my bone, flesh of my flesh."

"Wow, Marcelo that is amazing. I have a lot to learn about your customs."

"You are everything to me, Justine. There is no one that means as much to me except for my children and my parents. You can believe this. You will come first in my life." He kissed her gently and said, "All I ask is that you love me. I need your love and your loyalty."

"What are you talking about Marcelo? Of course I love you."

He smiled and said, "People speak of love when they are happy and feeling good about everything, but I want you to love me even when I'm not at my best and you are not so happy with me. If you can do that, nothing can come between us. That is the way I feel about you, Justine. I will love you no matter what and I will be loyal to you and if you love me that way too, then nothing but death can separate us,."

"Marcelo, you are scaring me. You are too deep, really! Now I'm very tired, we have had a long day and much too much to drink. I love you, I do Marcelo, but I think we need to go to sleep."

Then she turned her back poking her bum against him and reaching back, she took his hand and pulled his arm around her waist and shortly thereafter fell off to sleep. Marcelo lay quietly in the dark caressing her and listening to the sound of her breathing softly into the night. He was utterly and completely happier than he had been in a long time. He kissed her shoulder gently as she lay there sleeping peacefully and after a while he joined her in slumber.

The night however could not have been more different for Viola and Claudio. Viola snuggled up to Claudio. His back was facing her and she slipped her hands under the covers and into his pajamas, but he caught her hand before she could touch him and said, "I'm really very tired."

"Being tired has never stopped you before, so what really is the matter, Claudio? Viola asked a little annoyed.

"Nothing is the matter I'm just not in the mood. Is

that OK with you?

Am I allowed to say no? You don't seem to have any trouble saying no when you're not in the mood."

"Claudio," Viola said, surprised at his tone. "Did I do something to make you angry?"

"No, you didn't and I'm not angry, however, if you persist in this, you're going to make me question some things," he said flatly.

"What?" she said, shocked at his words. He didn't respond and Viola was hurt, but thought it best to just leave it alone.

She lay beside him in the dark locked in utter confusion. Tears worked their way to the corner of her eyes and trickled down the side of her face onto her pillow in silence. Is he growing tired of me? she thought. Did Justine's engagement make him feel pressured in some way? She didn't know what to think. She lay there in the darkness her mind riddled with questions. After a while she could tell that Claudio had fallen asleep, because of the snoring. But she would not find sleep until much later when the light of dawn slipped in and the darkness faded away.

If Claudio had trusted Viola enough to tell her how he felt about his past he could have saved them both a whole lot of heart ache. Viola was an experienced woman of the world. She was the one who had him thoroughly checked out by a doctor before she would bed him. What he didn't know was she also had a private eye investigate him way before she brought him to the States. There was nothing in his past that he had done that would have shocked her. Nothing for which she would have judged him at this point.

BIRTHING SURPRISE

The cold March air and the rumbling of thunder announced the coming of the last storm of the winter. It was 6 a.m., but the sky was dark and menacing. Sylvia was big with child and it had become difficult for her to get around. It seemed as though she had actually blown up over night. Her feet were swollen to the point that her ankles were no longer visible, her blood pressure was high and she suffered from excruciating back pain. Her mood swings caused her to fly off the handle given the slightest provocation due her hormonal imbalance. Keith was literally going crazy. However, in spite of her sometimes unreasonable behavior, he resigned himself to staying at her house in Queens even though commuting to Jersey for work was tiresome and extremely inconvenient. On the flip side, Keith just didn't feel comfortable leaving her alone in her house, because she didn't have any family here in New York where she could go.

Keith reluctantly left Sylvia's apartment in the early mornings in order to make it to work by 7 a.m. She had had a false alarm the day before and he knew that her time was near. When he got to work he would put in for some vacation time so that he would not have to leave her alone any more. Sylvia lay in bed trying hard to get comfortable to no avail. She had an urge to go to the bathroom and tried to maneuver her way off the bed, when her water broke. She almost slipped and fell, but managed to steady herself grabbing hold of the night stand.

Pain began to grip her body as she picked up the phone and dialed 911. Keith had only been able to secure four hours of sleep, because Sylvia was having a hard time and kept waking him up each time she would get in or out of bed to go to the bathroom.

Keith had just reached his job when the receptionist informed him that he had a phone call. He braced himself, because he was worried it might be about Sylvia. He never received phone calls on his job. He rushed to take the call, and when the voice of an E.M.S. worker informed him that they were on course for the hospital, he hung up the phone and arranged for coverage with one of his co-workers. Keith was back on the highway within minutes when the snowflakes began to fall. He was tired and very nervous about this pregnancy. He couldn't understand why they hadn't admitted her into the hospital when he brought her there the day before.

As he pulled up in front of the hospital the snow was in full force. He decided to park the car in the garage. He went up to the reception desk to inquire as to where they had taken her. He discovered that she was already in the delivery room.

He rushed to delivery and said to the clerk at the desk, "I'm Keith Huston the father of the Cartier baby." Keith realized how poorly that sounded. It announced to the world that Sylvia was his baby's mama, not his wife. If they had been married he would have been told that Mrs. Huston is in delivery. He suddenly realized what Sylvia was trying to convey to him for months now.

Keith had no desire to be like his parents. Hopping around from lover to lover with no care of what their behavior did to their children. Yet, that was the pattern that he had set. If he didn't plant his feet on solid ground and settle down now, then such would be the order of his life. In his heart of hearts, Keith desired stability. He wanted his own family, he wanted to be whole. Every action he had taken from the very beginning of his relationship with Sylvia had proven this to be a fact.

True Sylvia was a schemer and Keith had been ripe for the picking. However, he had been at Sylvia's side from the moment he learned she was pregnant and was ever present throughout her pregnancy. He suffered through her crankiness, the false alarms, and the sleepless nights. Now the reward was near. This soundless mysterious person would soon materialize and the realness of it all was suddenly hitting him.

The receptionist dialed a number and announced that the father had arrived. She listened for the instructions then, hung up the phone and told him to go to room 4 and scrub up and grab a gown. Keith hurried off to prepare himself. When he had finished dressing, he was ushered into the birthing room. Sylvia was on the birthing table barking and screaming obscenities. However, when she saw him enter the room, he could see in her eyes that she was happy to see him. She reached out her hand toward him, and he rushed to her side and kissed her on the forehead.

"What took you so long?" she complained.

"Traffic," he explained.

"Oh, oh, oh," Sylvia began to cry out in pain.

Keith whispered instructions in her ear on how to breathe. She began to breathe as she had been told to in the birthing class. She was sweating profusely and suffering through a great deal of pain. Every so often she would squeeze his hand so hard it cut off the circulation. Keith never felt more helpless or useless than he did at those moments. He kept coaching her to breathe and Sylvia, who was beside herself, was trying. Tears were flowing out of the corners of her eyes, and from time to time, she would scream out with a furry of one who was undergoing torture. During each of these sessions she would begin to breathe the way she had previously been taught. This went on for what seemed like an eternity. And then Keith heard the doctor say to the nurses, "She's crowning." The doctor looked up at Sylvia and instructed her to hold it, and not to bear down until he told her. Sylvia shook her head to acknowledge that she understood.

Then moments later she said, "I can't hold it."

But the doctor said, "Yes you can, concentrate."

"Ooh", she said, managing tremendous self control.

Then the doctor said, "Push."

And Sylvia began to push.

"Keep pushing, keep pushing."

And then as if on cue, a baby girl made her way into the world. The cord was cut and the nurse carried the baby over to a table where they proceeded to clean her off. The doctor firmly pressed on Sylvia's stomach to assist her in releasing the after birth when Sylvia cried out again.

"I feel another one coming out," she said.

The doctor looked and started to say it was the after birth when he stopped in mid-sentence and cried out, "Oh no, I see another head crowning."

Again the doctor instructed Sylvia to exercise control and to resist the urge to push.

"I can't, I can't," she cried.

"OK," the doctor said. "You can push now."

Sylvia pushed and gave birth to the second baby. This time it was a boy. Afterward, she laid her head on the pillow and the nurse put the little girl in her arms and the other nurse headed over to the table to clean up the boy.

An absolute birthing surprise and without a doubt, the happiest moment in Keith's life. Tears clouded his eyes as he kissed Sylvia on her forehead. Then he leaned over and kissed the baby. The nurse approached him and put the tiny little boy in his arms for a second. Sylvia who was exhausted had drifted off to sleep with their daughter yet in her arms. The second baby came as a complete surprise to everyone. Sylvia had refused to have a sonogram because she feared it would harm her baby. No one could convince her otherwise. The boy was a great deal smaller than the girl, which might have been the reason they did not detect a second heartbeat. At any event, here he was. He would have to be treated as a premature baby, because he wasn't five pounds. He was exactly four pounds six ounces. Keith handed him back to the nurse and they took him away.

Keith looked over at Sylvia who was resting after the ordeal and an overwhelming feeling of love enveloped him. She had delivered not one, but two babies. He was happy that he stood by her throughout the pregnancy. Every minute of her unreasonable behavior, and every hour of sleepless nights he had endured, had been more than worth it. Keith was thinking of taking some time off from work because he knew that Sylvia was going to need some help. The time off would allow him to bond with his new family and give them time to find a proper nanny to assist Sylvia with the twins. Meanwhile he had to see someone in the hospital about changing the last name of his children from Cartier to Huston.

When Keith finally left the hospital the storm was in full rage and the snow was sticking. He went down to the garage, retrieved his car, and headed for Sylvia's apartment in Queens. This had been a busy morning and all he could think about was getting a good night sleep.

HOPE FOR THE FUTURE

I t was late July in New York and the air was heavy with moister. The smoldering heat that mingled with the smog was next to unbearable. Justine moved about slowly, finding it hard to breathe, feeling as though she could cut through the thick hot air with a knife. Marcelo was still in the shower and Justine was checking her list to make sure that she packed everything they would need for the trip.

Things were moving super fast and Justine was having second thoughts because of the reactions she was receiving from Viola and her children. Her daughter Prudence was very upset by her seemingly sudden plan to marry Marcelo. Prudence felt that she should prolong her engagement to Marcelo and get to know him better before rushing off to Africa into marriage. Justine thought this was nonsense because she had been engaged to the man for over a year now and she had known him for more than two years prior. However her daughter felt that Marcelo was a stranger and that, other than what he had told Justine, she really knew nothing about him.

Her daughter, Jackie, had even stopped speaking to her. She just hung up the phone on her one evening without saying goodbye when Justine told her that she was going to take a leave of absence in order to spend a few months in Africa with Marcelo's family. Her daughter Jackie believed that Justine was behaving irrationally, running off to a strange country with a man she barely knew.

"These people have different customs from us," she argued. However, the more Jackie debated the issue, the more determined Justine's resolve was to proceed with her plans. Jackie was so frustrated with Justine she didn't know how to conduct herself. Jackie knew that hanging up the phone on her mother was not the proper behavior to display, especially since her mother was leaving the country. Nevertheless, she just didn't know what else to do to demonstrate her disapproval.

Justine felt that both her daughters' motives were selfish. Jackie wanted her to visit her in California but this trip to Africa would prohibit that. Prudence just wouldn't like anyone who wasn't her father. Their suspicions about Marcelo's intentions were founded on nothing more than outright prejudges. What hurt most was that they cared so little about her feelings. Not one of them had a legitimate reason why she shouldn't marry Marcelo. If any of them could have pointed out a real reason why she should not marry him she might have listened to what they were saying. It was all so ludicrous and she might add pretentious. If they were genuinely concerned about her they would have insisted on accompanying her, if for no other reason than to protect her and be representatives of their side of the family. Viola traveled the world whenever she felt the need. How dare she use her shops in New York as an excuse not to attend the wedding? This really hurt, because Justine knew it was an excuse and was not going to allow any of them to sway her with their unfounded prejudges and or jealousies. This was the first time in her life that she was following her heart. She would not allow fear to play any part in the journey she was embarking. She would think of it as an exciting new adventure.

Besides, she felt that she knew Marcelo well enough. She had observed Marcelo and she knew he could be moody at times. She also noted how he behaved when he was angry. However most of the times he was very thoughtful, he listened to her when she spoke and responded to her needs in kind, he was funny and smart and very ambitious. No side of his personality gave her any cause for real concern. She believed that he genuinely loved her and she loved him.

She had been in love with her first husband, but she was very young when she married the first time and she didn't know what to look for in a man which she felt was the reason the marriage didn't last. What she was feeling for Marcelo was very different. Of course there was passion, but it was more than that, Marcelo was her soul mate. He had traveled from another part of the world bypassing thousands of women to meet and complete her.

That April when she had first laid eyes on Marcelo after he consumed her every thought, she never dreamed that it would have come to all of this. Before Marcelo came into her life, Viola, Jackie, and Prudence were living their lives and doing what they thought best for themselves and they certainly weren't checking in with her for approval. In fact, when she had offered her advice, the girls too often rejected it. As for Viola, she never ran her plans by anyone for approval before she acted on them. She pretty much did as she pleased and maybe, if you were lucky, she would tell you about what she had done after the fact. The last serious conversation she had with her daughter Jackie, before this business with Marcelo, ended with Jackie telling her that she should attend to her own life and to stop worrying about everyone else's. As fate would have it, she was doing just that.

After Marcelo presented her with an engagement ring,

which she accepted, her life had changed. Justine had been afraid of change in the past. However, now she was actually excited to find out what life had in store for her. Although she must admit that with all of this unrest around her getting married, it sometimes caused her to doubt herself. What kept her on track these days was Marcelo's enthusiasm. He actually beamed with joy and they would sometimes stay up until sunrise just talking about their plans for the future. Justine believed in Marcelo, she believed in their union, and she was determined to do whatever it took to secure their happiness together. It's not that she didn't value the opinions of her friends and family, it was just that she felt they were over reacting and that they were completely non supportive of her.

The person that surprised her most was Viola. Viola was present the night Marcelo proposed. She participated in their celebration toasting their future and now she refused to support her decision to follow Marcelo to Africa to meet his family. Viola actually told her that she was surprised that she accepted Marcelo's proposal. "You've always been a rational person, the voice of reason," she had said. When Justine asked her what she meant by that; she retracted the statement and said that she was no one to judge anyone else's life. What did all of this mean?

When Justine recalled the whole episode of her engagement party, she remembered that Viola didn't behave as though she was happy for her. As a matter of fact, now that she thought about it, Viola had very little to say that night. Which in and of itself, was very strange for Viola. This was not the kind of reaction she expected from her best friend, and especially not from a person like Viola. Viola was a free spirit. She believed in living one's life to the fullest and not worrying about what other people thought. She always said that in the end everyone paid the price for their failures and reaped the benefits of their success. So where was all this new found caution coming from? Did Viola know something about Marcelo that she wasn't telling her? No, she dismissed that thought. There would be no reason why Viola would keep important information from her. She wouldn't, it was all mere nonsense. Viola has traveled all over the world and dealt with men and women from many different cultures. So what was so different now? Viola owned her own businesses and could certainly take off time to be her maid of honor if she so desired, so what was the problem? Here she was on her way to Africa to meet Marcelo's people, where there would be a ceremony in the village, and there would be no one to represent her from the States.

If Salina hadn't offered to accompany her, she would have no one there to represent her. One would expect their children and best friend to be happy for them and to support them in this life changing ceremony.

Instead her daughter, Jackie, broke down and cried acclaiming that she was suffering from mid-life crisis. "You don't really know this man, Mom. Does he have a spell on you or something? Please don't go to his country to get married, at least wait until Anthony gets back from Germany," she had begged. Anthony was Justine's youngest child. He was in the Marines and had traveled most of the world. He spoke seven languages and was fluent in French which was the language spoken in the Ivory Coast where Justine was going. Justine would have been only too happy to wait for Anthony to come if he were coming to support her. However, the girls had managed to turn him against the idea of the marriage as well, so what was the point in waiting?

Oddly enough, the only one who seemed to be happy for her was Salina. She had offered to fill in as her maid of honor if Justine would have her. Of course she would have her; she was very grateful for her support. However, Salina's decision to support her had driven a wedge between Salina and Viola. Viola began to behave strangely toward Salina as a result of her accompanying Justine to Africa. The whole thing was bazaar. Salina was clearly Viola's friend. Justine would not have known her if it not for Viola. Yet, Salina took a stand alongside Justine and completely supported her.

Justine remembered that Salina had been somewhat of a project for Viola at first. Salina bore her fair share of troubles and Viola was like a big sister to her. Viola helped her out of a difficult situation after which Salina totally looked up to her. Viola was flattered by the young woman's admiration of her and they became really good friends. Salina had grown up in foster homes and had no real family to speak of.

Salina had encountered some very awful experiences coming up that way. She had been raped in several of the homes and most of the people who took her in were doing it for the money. One of the homes where Salina stayed, the father figure was heavily into computers, and he taught her how to use the computer when he wasn't otherwise abusing her. Upon Salina's seventeenth birthday she ran away from that home, but she ended up with another abusive individual that was worse than the one she had fled. She met Viola through a mutual acquaintance.

When Justine first met Salina she merely tolerated her presence in their lives, because Viola was so fond of her and seemed to have a need to drag Salina along everywhere that they went. So it was really surprising to Justine when Salina took offense at the way Viola was behaving toward her marriage to Marcelo. It wasn't that she and

Salina didn't get along. They did. Justine had actually grown quite fond of her. It was just that Salina had always been so devoted to Viola she wouldn't have thought that Salina would ever oppose anything Viola did.

Salina was convinced that Viola was only jealous and being completely selfish and insensitive to Justine's feelings. She had even said, "It is not the job of a friend to approve of every aspect of your life, but rather to be supportive whenever needed, even when they weren't in total agreement. It was one thing to disagree but to be non supportive, well, that was something else altogether. She told Justine that she couldn't understand why everyone was giving her so much opposition. If this was something that was making her happy, then she, Salina, would do her part as a friend to make it a joyful reality and whatever came of it good or bad, she would be by her side every step of the way." Those were the words that Justine felt should have come from Viola's mouth. However, it seemed as though the people who were closest to her were determined to find ways to destroy any ounce of happiness she might derive in marrying Marcelo. Not to mention how unwelcome it had made Marcelo feel.

Marcelo was building a house on a piece of land that he had purchased in Ghana. He was excited about marrying her and starting up his own business. They decided that they would get married in Africa and then return to the states and get married by the Justice of the Peace as well. Afterward Marcelo would start to build his import and export business. When the house in Africa was completed they would have somewhere to live when they returned to Africa. Justine's daughters were totally against that idea. What were they all afraid of? She couldn't for the life of her understand where all the concern was coming from.

Jackie didn't know any more about Greg when she married him and she moved all the way to California where his family resided. She never gave a care that she was leaving Justine alone in New York, and Prudence lived in Washington! Anthony was in the service. What exactly did they all want from her? It really got on her nerves how Jackie and Prudence kept calling Marcelo a stranger. Everyone is a stranger until you get to know them. It was hypocrisy. The only reason she could think of for their negativity was that Marcelo was not an American. They wouldn't come out and say it, because they knew that that would get her started. Everyone knew her views on that subject. Justine felt that American Blacks should be more tolerant of their brothers and sisters from other countries due to the unfair prejudice that had been doled out on them as African Americans. Justine felt that as African Americans they should have empathy for their foreign brothers and sisters. She felt that Blacks, no matter where they were from, had suffered some type of discrimination or social injustice therefore they should all be one nation at heart. At the very least, they certainly should not take part in prejudges against one another. They got enough of that from everyone else.

Justine planned to keep her apartment in New York no matter where she and Marcelo decided to live. Marcelo had said that once he got his business on the way that they would spend part of the time in Africa and part of their time in the States. The reason for this was that Marcelo had learned his lesson with his first wife and he didn't intend to repeat the same mistake. When his business demanded that he stay in Africa for a prolonged period of time, he wanted his wife to be with him. However they did have one small issue, Marcelo wanted her to leave her job and work with him in his business. When

Justine explained this to Prudence she practically lost her mind. The conversation got so heated that Prudence pulled Jackie's trick and hung up the phone without saying goodbye. Justine was no fool. She understood the point her daughters were trying to make concerning her job, and she was in no hurry to give it up. However, Justine thought that Prudence was over reacting and her actions were totally uncalled for. She was getting a little tired of the girls disrespecting her in that manner. It had been three days now since the incident and neither of them had picked up the phone to call the other. And her best friend, Viola, one of the most opinionated people that she knew, had completely shut down. When she told Viola of the incidence with the girls hanging up the phone on her, she neither offered support or criticism. She simply shrugged her shoulders and shook her head. It was as if Viola silently disapproved of her marrying Marcelo, but just wasn't voicing her opinion. Justine felt completely abandoned by her friend and family. What did they expect her to do? Marcelo wasn't going anywhere and would soon be her husband. He was an African. Did they think that he would never revisit his country? Did they think that she would never go to see her in-laws? She couldn't believe how ignorant they all were behaving. Even in her stance concerning the matter, all of the fuss was giving her cause to doubt herself. Was it she who was being unrea-sonable? she wondered. She had to snap out of this mood, she couldn't allow them to steel her thunder. If Prudence and Jackie wanted to end on this note, so be it. She, Justine, would be following her fiancé to Africa. She would finally be doing what everyone, including Viola, had been advising her to do for years, she had gotten a life! And, by God, she was going to live it.

Marcelo came out of the bathroom with a towel

wrapped around him and water trickling from his head.

"A penny for your thoughts," he said as he leaned in and kissed her on the lips.

"As usual," she said, "I was thinking of you." Then she gave him several pecks on his lips in return.

"Oh no," he said. "I'm not buying that one. When you're thinking about me you always look happy, as well you should. You were thinking about your family and Viola weren't you?"

She looked up at him and shook her head admitting that he was right.

"Look honey," he said. "We can postpone this trip until you get your family on board. Getting married is a very important day in your life. I want you to be happy. We are not just marring each other; we have an extended family to consider. Our families are going to play a very important part in our marriage and we have to at least try to get everyone on board with this."

"Don't you think I've tried?" she said, fighting back the urge to cry.

Just then the phone rang and she walked across the floor and picked up the headset and said, "Hello."

"Hello, Mom," Anthony said.

"Anthony," exclaimed Justine. "How are you?"

"I'm fine Mom. But I'm guessing that you could be better?"

"Why are you saying that?"

Justine braced herself for yet another attack against her marriage to Marcelo.

"Well, we haven't been giving you an easy time of it and I just got to thinking that we were all being inconsiderate of your feelings."

Justine was completely taken aback by his words and was momentarily unable to reply. He sensed that she was at a loss for words and chuckled then continued, "That's why I have decided to accompany you to Africa and give you away. I know the culture and it says a lot when the men in the woman's family show support and approve of the marriage. I'll bring a case of brandy and some cigars." He laughed and said, "Mom, I love you and for better or worse, I'm going to stand beside you on this. I tried to convince my sisters of the importance of all of us being there. But they seemed to be set in their stance. There is nothing I can do about them, but I can do something about me. So when are we leaving for Africa?"

"Oh gosh," Justine said, and the expression on her face spoke volumes to the fact that she was receiving over-whelmingly good news.

"What?" Marcelo said, anxious to know what was being said.

Justine put up one finger to motion him to wait.

Anthony not hearing a response to his question said, "Mom, Mom, are you there?"

Justine regained her composure and said, "Yes, oh yes I'm here. Darling I'm so happy that I couldn't quite believe my ears. You have made your mother very, very happy," she said. Her eyes began to fill up with tears.

"How long will it take you to get here?"

"I can be there by tomorrow night. My flight is sched-uled to land in New York at 9:30 p.m."

"Oh my goodness, I can't wait to see you, baby you have really uplifted my spirits."

"I'm glad, Mom. I'll see you tomorrow then."

Marcelo was beside himself having been held in sus-pense,

"What is happening, Justine, tell me?"

Justine turned toward him and said joyfully, "Anthony is coming to the wedding!"

"God bless you," Marcelo yelled out loud in order for Anthony to hear.

Anthony heard and said to his mother, "He sounds like one happy camper, Mom I can't wait to meet him. See you both tomorrow."

"See you tomorrow and I love you."

"I love you too, Mom," and then he hung up.

Marcelo picked her up and swirled her around.

"You see darling," he said happily. "God is smiling on our union. They will all come around, you'll see. We were meant to be together."

Justine began to feel better about everything. She clung to his neck and kissed the side of his cheek repeatedly as tears of joy streamed down her face.

THE TRIP TO AFRICA

J ustine, Marcelo, and Anthony were leaving with their luggage in hand just as Keith and Sylvia were approaching his apartment with their new babies.

"Oh my," Justine said, looking back and forth between Keith and Sylvia, surprised. "Sylvia you had two babies?" She was surprised to see that they were carrying two babies.

"Congratulations!"

They both smiled proudly, and Sylvia replied, "I had twins," Keith was holding the boy.

"Do you mind?" asked Justine as she approached Sylvia to get a closer look at the girl? Sylvia proudly lifted the blanket from over the baby's head so that Justine could get a look at her.

"Oh she is beautiful," exclaimed Justine.

Keith approached lifting the cover off the boys head so that Justine could get a look at him as well.

"They are beautiful," Justine said, smiling.

Keith said hello to Marcelo and Anthony and motioned in the direction of their luggages and asked, "Leaving town?"

Marcelo smiled and said, "Yes we are going to Africa where the lovely Justine will become my wife."

Keith was momentarily taken aback by the news, but quickly recovered with a timely response. "Hey, man, congratulation," he said as he grabbed Marcelo's hand to shake it. "Thank you, thank you," Marcelo responded and said, "I'm a lucky man."

"Yes you are," Keith said, nodding his head in agreement as he eyed Justine.

"And so are you," Marcelo said, motioning toward Sylvia and the babies.

"Yes, I know," Keith said, looking over at his new family and beaming. Sylvia asked Justine if she could see her engagement ring and Justine thrust her hand forward proudly displaying her two and a half carat diamond.

"Girl you are so lucky," Sylvia said, looking at the diamond in admiration.

"You don't have to sound so envious," Keith said. "I have one for you as well here in my pocket. I was going to present it to you tonight. But since we have an audience, I might as well ask you here and now." Then turning and placing the baby in Marcelo's arms he knelt on one knee, there in the hall, and produced a little black velvet box from his pocket and opened it revealing a beautiful round four carat solitaire diamond ring. Sylvia was in shock. Her eyes immediately welled up with tears.

"Sylvia, will you do me the honor of being my wife?"

"Oh yes, yes Keith I will," and her hand shook as she held it out for Keith to put the ring on her finger.

"Here, let me take the baby," Justine said as she lifted the infant from Sylvia's arms. Sylvia was outwardly crying as Keith put the ring on her finger, she was overcome with joy. When he stood up, she threw her arms around his neck and held on to him as tight as she could. Her whole body trembled. She truly loved him and all she ever wanted from the moment she laid eyes on him was to be his wife. She knew that she had gone about it the wrong way but given the way that Sylvia's mind operated, she didn't know any other way that she could get Keith to settle down. Both she and Keith were players in their own special way. The only difference was Sylvia played the game to win and not just to score for a moment in time. Sylvia did whatever she had to do even if it entailed manipulation; it was her way of accomplishing the overall big picture. They stood there like that for a moment. Then she kissed him on his lips and whispered in his ear, "Thank you Keith. I love you with all my heart and you have made me the happiest woman in the world. You won't be sorry." Anthony began to clap and Marcelo and Justine stood there smiling holding the babies. Sylvia, who always felt a little threatened by Justine, released her grip on Keith and went over to Justine who was holding the girl, and put out her hand so that Justine could see her ring. Justine was genuinely delighted for Sylvia as she looked at her ring joyfully,

"It's beautiful, I'm so happy for you," she said.

"Thank you Justine, and I'm, I'm sorry for the way that I've acted toward you in the past. I was just…"

"You don't have to say anything, we both have what we want and whatever may or may not have existed between us in the past is over."

Sylvia kissed Justine on the cheek and took the baby from her arms. She turned and looked at Marcelo and said, "Congratulations, I wish both of you all the best."

"Thank you," Marcelo said, and he turned and handed the baby back to Keith. Then Anthony said, "Well I hate to breakup this little love fest, but we have a car downstairs waiting to take us to the airport." They all began to laugh and Marcelo and Keith shook hands again and then Keith shook Anthony's hand and everyone said goodbye.

When they arrived at their gate at the airport, they saw that Salina and Claudio were already there seated by the window drinking coffee. Claudio had called Justine last week and told her that he had decided to accompany her and Marcelo on the trip to Africa in support of their marriage. He did not, however, tell her how he and Viola had quarreled bitterly over his decision. Viola felt Claudio's going to Africa in support of Justine made her look bad. His reply to her at the time was, "Jou look bad whether I go to Africa or not. Justine is supposed to be jour best friend and dere is no reason dat, I can thin of, jou are not going other then jealousy, and frankly, I thin dat is small of jou. I had believed jou were a better person than dat."

With that, Viola went into a rage, "How dare you say that I am jealous, jealousy has nothing to do with it! The reason that I am not going..."she stopped short and said, "Screw you! I don't have to explain myself to you or anybody else. I know why I'm not going and if you accompany Justine and Marcelo on this trip I'll consider it a grave disloyalty to me."

Claudio's reply to that was "I have no intention of being loyal to some sing I don know about. If you don feel dat you owe me an explanation as to why jou don want me to go, den I don feel I owe jou any loyalty concerning de matter." With that, he walked out of the house returning late that night after she had gone to bed. They had not discussed it again until she saw him leaving the house this morning and realized that he was not bluffing. He had packed his suit case while she was at the salon the morning before and placed it in the hall closet.

"So," she said when she saw that he was already packed, "You are really going through with this."

He looked at her adamantly and said, "I told you I was going. Jou can still change jour mind and join me. It would really make Justine happy to have jou there. Even your good friend Salina is going."

Viola completely disregarded what he said about Salina going, she treated it as though she didn't hear it and said, "I really don't know how you think. You stand there telling me what would make Justine happy. Have you ever once thought about what would make me happy? You are supposed to be my man!"

"Jeah, I know," Claudio said. "Somehow you always manage to make everysing about jou," and then he picked up his luggage and headed for the door.

Viola called after him, her voice softening as she said, "You're just going to leave without kissing me?"

"I didn know jou wanted me to kiss jou," he said. He walked back over to her and gave her a quick peck on the lips.

But she grabbed hold of him and kissed him hard and long on the lips and then whispered in his ear "please don't let this cause a wedge between us. I still love you, remember that."

He pulled away from her gently and said, "If dere is a wedge between us, it's not because of de wedding." Then he walked back toward the door, opened it, and stepped out into the hall.

Justine was happy to see him and Salina. She went directly over to where they were seated.

"Hey, American family," she said playfully. They turned toward her and then smilingly they stood up and greeted everyone. Marcelo and Anthony approached them. Justine turned and introduced Anthony to Claudio and asked Anthony if he remembered Salina.

Anthony said, "Do I remember Salina? Of course I remember Salina. I used to have a big crush on her when I was younger."

Salina looked at him devilishly and said, "Used too?" Teasingly she winked at him, and Anthony said,

"Don't tempt me, I'm a man now!" and everyone laughed.

Salina was very pretty. Her eyes were not large, but she had wonderfully long lashes that framed them and they were beautifully shaped. It was like looking into brown crystal. Her skin was a rich dark golden brown which looked as though it had been kissed by the sun. Many of her Latino associates called her India because of her coloring. All at once Claudio was taken by her beauty which he had never really noticed before today. Their eyes met when she turned her head. There was an awkward moment that passed between them. She quickly looked away from him and greeted Marcelo who was coming up on her from the opposite side, grinning proudly as he grew nearer leaning down to give her a kiss.

"Hey there handsome, you look very happy," Salina said.

"I am," Marcelo said. "I think I'm the happiest man on earth." They all began to chat merrily as they waited to board their flight.

They landed safely on the Ivory Coast in the city of Abidjan. Marcelo booked everyone rooms in the Pullman Abidjan hotel where they would spend the night before their long hard drive to the Village in the morning. When they all had finally settled down in there suites for the night, Justine was so excited she found it difficult to fall asleep. Marcelo had to give her a sedative to calm her nerves. She finally settled down around 1:00 a.m. and Marcelo was able to fall asleep as well.

The next day, they arrived in the village where there was a great reception. It seemed that the whole village had turned out in celebration of Marcelo's wedding. Marcelo's father was one of the chiefs a much respected member of the community. He was the second brother to the village's head chief. Justine had never seen anything like it. The ceremony took place in Marcelo's father compound. It was beautiful. There were three houses in the compound. The largest one was where they would take their vows. They were escorted to the smaller building where Justine and her bridesmaid, Salina, would prepare for the ceremony. Marcelo and the men were taken to the main house. After Justine and Salina were ready, two of the women escorted them to the larger house which had central air and high cathedral ceilings. Crystal chandeliers hung from the ceiling in the foyer. They passed by a spiraling staircase as they went straight through to the courtyard in the back. There was a canopy of lilies attached to a round arch which was placed directly over the area where the bride and groom would be seated. Justine was happy that Anthony was here to see how nice everything was. He could let his sisters know she was not marrying a wretch. Not that it would have mattered to her, it was just a plus in her favor. Marcelo greeted her and Salina as they stepped out into the yard. They were dressed in African garb. Justine's and Marcelo's garb had been cut from the same cloth. His family was already seated on one side of the table. Marcelo took Justine and whispered. "You look beautiful." Justine and her party of three were ushered over to the table to be introduced to Marcelo's family. They approached the table where they greeted everyone.

Marcelo's daughter, a small graceful woman whose almond colored skin was smooth as satin, smiled and embraced Justine, "Welcome Momma," she said, and then Marcelo's son Jon, a tall lean and lanky young man approached and greeted her. He had Marcelo's eyes. Afterward they approached the Chief, a short and burly man whose whiskers where mixed with black and grey hairs. His head was completely bald and he greeted her with a kiss on both cheeks. Anthony and the rest of her party trailed behind them shaking everyone's hand. Then Marcelo's father Tutee stood up and Marcelo took Justine's hand and approached his father with hopeful eyes. Tutee was a handsome man and Justine could see where Marcelo got his looks. When they were standing before him, he put his hands on Justine's shoulders and kissed her on each cheek. Then he stepped back in order to get an overall look at her. His eyes scanned over her, thoroughly. Holding her hand he gently turned her around in a circle and then he said something in French and nodded his head in approval and everyone laughed. Laughingly Marcelo leaned in to Justine and said, "He says I done well, you are beautiful and you have nice bottom." Justine blushed and gently elbowed Marcelo and everyone continued laughing. Tutee and his Baba, a gentle little woman with a beautiful smile, greeted Justine's family. Then they were all ushered over to the center of the table to be seated. It was decorated with a fresh flower canapé. Tutee gave Marcelo a nod of approval and embraced him giving the onlookers a show of his blessings. At that moment Justine was so grateful to Anthony, Salina, and Claudio for coming to support her, as they were seated on the other side of the table which was designated for the bride's family. She would have felt so ashamed if she had no one there to represent her. Justine still could not understand how her daughters and her good friend Viola stayed back and allowed her to face this experience alone. She had truly believed that they all would come around at the last moment. But they all insisted on standing their ground, whatever that was. Now that she was here getting ready to take her vows, she knew that she would not feel the same about any of them. What they had done to her was very self serving and had nothing to do with anything, but stubborn ignorance and in Viola's case she feared it might even be envy. Justine was a firm believer in "You reap what you sewed." And she believed in giving as good as she got. If it had been financial reasons that kept them from coming, she would have understood. But to reject her wedding strictly based on their feelings was totally unacceptable. As far as Justine was concerned, at this time, it was unforgivable and she would never excuse it.

After the ceremony, everyone sang a song in French. Then the dancing and drinking began the celebration. Anthony was simply having a ball with the beautiful village girls who were openly flirting with him. He was tall, handsome, and in his prime. He looked like his father, lean and muscular with thick curly hair and fair skin. The ladies regarded him as a very good catch as he was from America and he was wearing his military uniform. Anthony took full advantage of the leverage that it afforded him with the ladies. He danced with three ladies at the same time and held conversation with groups of them. The ladies seemed to have lined up in a matter of speaking and he was savoring every moment of it.

Salina took a flute of champagne from one of the servers who was meandering through the crowd and went around the corner into the garden. She thought the house was beautiful and stately with four white columns. The garden was breathtaking and so peaceful; it was plush with foliage. She walked down the pebbled path, taking care not to lose her balance in the high heels she was wearing. She carefully maneuvered herself over to the stone bench which was stationed by a man-made water fall that cascaded down into the pool. There were two thick palm trees on either side of the bench that formed a canopy like covering as the leaves overlapped in a matrimonial intertwine making them one. Lilies decorated the surface of the pool while a tall maze like hedges encompassed the area closing it off from the rest of the house, forming a room like quality. Salina was wearing a formed fitted African print gown that had a split on one side that stopped mid thigh revealing her well formed legs. The top of the dress was designed to fall off her shoulders emphasizing a majestic v shape that pointed to her cleavage revealing the plump round curvature of her breast. She walked over to the bench and pulled back her long wavy mane and twisted it so that it flowed down over one shoulder onto her lap. Her hair seemed to go on forever. It had grown so long that it was somewhat of a problem. If she were not able to visit Viola's salon every week she would not be able to manage it. It hung well beyond her waist and covered her bottom. She sat there alone somewhat melancholy sipping out of the champagne flute and staring down into the pool. Claudio saw her when she wandered off toward the garden and followed her.

"Hi," he said as he approached and sat down alongside her. "What are jou doing here by jourself?"

"Oh, I don't know," she said, looking up at him sheepishly. "I guess I just needed a moment to reflect," she said, looking away from him and down at her Patent-leather shoes.

"Reflect?" he repeated. "Wha does someone as beautiful as jou are have to be pondering over while everyone else is celebrating?"

"I don't know," she said softly, this time looking directly into his green eyes as she exhaled.

"Sure jou do," he said. "Why don jou share jour thoughts with me?" he said persuasively.

"It's nothing, really. I was just thinking how lucky Justine is to have someone love her as much as Marcelo obviously does."

"Ooh, jour day will come," he said, smiling devilishly.

"I don't think so," she said seriously. "A person like me can never hope for real love to come."

"Now wha would make jou say some sing so ridiculous? Jou're beautiful." Claudio was able to express himself in English now quite eloquently.

"Thanks for saying that," she said, looking directly into his eyes. "But beauty is not everything. I have done so many awful things in my life in order to survive, things that no young girl should ever have had to do, and if you knew, you would look at me differently. Then you would understand why someone like me could never hope to achieve what Justine has accomplished here today." Then she looked away from him back down into the pool. Suddenly he felt an even stronger connection with her. She looked up and saw him intently staring at her.

"Viola must have told you about how…" He put his finger to her lips and shushed her.

"Viola told me nosing and dere is no need for jou to drudge up any unpleasant memories from jour past." He pointed to himself and then pointed his finger toward her and said, "I – feel – jou! I know were jou are coming from, because, not too long ago, I was feeling exactly the same way dat jou are feeling now. I felt dat no one could ever love me if dey knew the tings dat I had done in order to survive. But, looking at jou now, I know dat I was wrong and dat it is not true." "How do you know?" she said, looking at him quizzically.

His smile was sincere when he leaned in toward her and stroked her hair as he kissed her tenderly on the lips and Salina felt as though she was floating. His kiss was so soft and so sweet. He pulled away from her looking directly into her eyes and said, "I know dis because jou are quite lovable despite anysing jou may have done in jour past. Jou and I are not so different. Wha jou did jou did because jou were in a survival mode. Some sing the privileged know nosing about, because survival is primal. Dey have never had to go dere."

Salina stared deep into the green pools of his eyes and she knew. She felt as if she knew all the awful secrets that he held within his soul and she said, "I know." She then returned his gesture and said," and I- know -you, and I know that what you have said here tonight is true, because I think that you are quite lovable as well. My god, what am I saying? You're Viola's man!"

"Jou didn say anysing wrong; anyway I don feel the same about Viola anymore. She disappointed me."

"Yeah, right," Salina said. "I mean the way she's treating Justine is despicable."

"Jeah, dat too, but I was not referring to dat. Jou don know all about me and Viola. Jou only know what she tells jou and knowing Viola it couldn't be much. I've done a lot of awful tings in my past, tings I've never told Viola. So jou don know all dere is to know about me. One day, I will tell jou."

"Why don't you tell me now? I promise you I won't be shocked, and I'd be the last to judge you," she said, looking at him knowingly.

"How can jou say that?"

"I can say it because you and I are cut from the same cloth. We have lived similar lives." This time she leaned into him and pressed her lips on his and he parted them with his tongue and they kissed long and tenderly. Salina swooned as she allowed herself to feel emotions that she had withheld all of her life. She knew that what she was doing was taboo and it would undoubtedly bring her friendship with Viola to an end but she couldn't resist. Maybe it was the wedding? Maybe it was seeing the love between Marcelo's parents and the festiveness of the hour, the atmosphere in the garden, or the champagne. Whatever it was, she simply was unable to stop what she was feeling for Claudio. She didn't even want to try. Claudio didn't consciously desire to hurt Viola. But he knew that if he continued, to venture in the direction that his heart was leading him, he was definitely going to hurt her. While yet in the process of thinking these thoughts, part of his mind was pondering what it would be like to be inside Salina. He wanted to take her right then and there in the garden, on the bench under the canopy if she would let him, but he would not try. He wanted their first time to be special. Someone could walk in on them and spoil it, thus concluding in his mind that there would definitely be another time. He could not and would not deny himself what he was feeling for this woman. Not even for Viola.

"Let us join de others," he said. "Sounds like dey're having a good time. Do jou want to dance?"

"Dance," laughed Salina, "in these heels?"

Claudio looked at her six inch platform stilettos and said, "Well anyone who could manage to maneuver their way out trough a pebbled walk-way could find dancing to be a breeze."

"Yeah, well I'll try, but you better not let me fall," she said, laughing as he led her out of the garden.

"Ooh, there you are," Justine exclaimed as Claudio and Salina entered the courtyard hand in hand.

"We were looking for you two earlier. Where were you?" asked Justine.

"We were out back in the garden. Oh, Justine you should see it, it's beautiful," Salina said.

"Really?" Justine said, turning to take Marcelo's hand, who was inches behind her. She looked at Marcelo playfully and said, "Come darling I would love to see the garden."

Marcelo then led Justine out onto the garden path, but was momentarily distracted as he looked back at Claudio and Salina. He leaned toward Justine and said, "Wonder what's going on between those two? They certainly look awfully chummy," he said, still gazing in their direction. Justine pulled him further into the privacy of the garden's green wall foliage and said, "Oh it's probably nothing. They're just having fun." Marcelo quickly lost interest as Justine rubbed her bottom up against his private parts; he pulled her in closer to him as he landed a barrage of kisses onto her neck. She broke free of his grip and ran playfully into the garden. He chased after her joyfully, both of them relishing in their new found happiness.

Viola moped about her condo apartment Sunday morning wondering what she had done. I really made a big mistake not going to Justine's wedding in Africa, she thought. I've been so busy licking my own wounds that I haven't properly thought this whole thing through. Why have I been so nonchalant concerning the wedding plans of my lifelong friend? Not attending that wedding is surely going to put a wedge in our friendship. Could Claudio have been right? Could all of my actions have been born out of jealousy? Now that everything was quiet, with Claudio out of the house, she had all of this time to think, and it was the only thing that made any sense. She knew that Justine's children were totally against the marriage, because they thought that Marcelo was only interested in their mother to get his papers. However, she, Viola knew Marcelo. She had been around them often enough to know that that was not the case. She knew that he genuinely loved Justine and she could have cleared that up with Justine's children and they all could have attended that wedding. Am I that petty, she thought, that I couldn't afford my best friend her happiness simply because my own life is so miserable? Was what Justine had with Marcelo so much like what I so desperately wanted with Claudio,

that I couldn't bear to watch Justine enjoy what I myself could not obtain? Is this whom I have become? Claudio had given her the chance to save face and show up alongside him and she stubbornly stayed her course. And, for what, what had she gained? Did Claudio stay at home and become more loving? She wished that she could pack her bags and go to Africa now. She knew that it was after the fact and felt she would not be well received. It would probably look as though she was running after Claudio. And maybe there would be some truth in it. Be that as it may, Viola was wrong. Had she gone to Africa, Justine would have received her and she would have redeemed herself. Her going to Africa would have said something to the girls as well. But Viola wasn't thinking clearly these days and it was going to cost her. Another thing she hadn't thought about in all the turmoil of her emotions was that Claudio would actually be in Africa for a whole month. A lot could happen in a month! What must Justine think of her? Justine had always been there for her when she needed her and how had she repaid her? Viola believed that there was really nothing she could do to make it up to Justine. I really messed up, she thought. The only thing that she could do at this point would be to ask Justine to forgive her.

WALL OF DECEPTION

Three months had gone by since they all returned from Africa. It was early November and the weather was very mild for that time of the year. Salina's present situation made her feel as though she was between a rock and a hard place. She was none too eager to reveal the knowledge of her and Claudio's affair, and didn't know how long she would be able to maintain this wall of deception.

As torn as she seemed to be, she didn't feel that she was altogether at fault considering the way Claudio and Viola had met. However she really did like Viola and she knew that there would be no salvaging their friendship once Viola found out. As it stood now, she could no longer enjoy what she had with Viola, even though Viola was clueless as to what was going on. Salina did everything in her power to avoid Viola and it seemed that these days Viola was more needy than usual, constantly insisting that they meet for lunch. If it wasn't so sad, it would be laughable. Salina could barely get through their telephone conversations much less break bread with her. Viola would always manage to mention how miserable Claudio was treating her or how he hadn't touched her since his return from Africa, and that only added to her guilt.

Viola noticed the difference in her attitude as well and had asked her if she was cross with her because she did not attend Justine's wedding. It was obvious that Justine's attitude had changed toward Viola as a result of her absence so Viola naturally thought that Salina shared in Justine's feelings. Of course Salina assured her that it was not the case. At those times Salina would think to herself, No, I'm just sleeping with your man, other than that everything's fine. Salina dreaded the day that Viola found out. She thought about breaking it off with Claudio, but she felt so alive when she was with him. She just couldn't bring herself to end it. She just didn't know how much longer she could keep up this wall of deception.

Salina became friends with Viola many years ago, through an acquaintance who worked in one of Viola's salons. Salina was eighteen years old and was living with a forty-five year old man who was physically and mentally abusing her. He would sell her to his friends. He would just wake her up from her sleep in the middle of the night to sleep with one of them and would beat her if she dared to protest. Salina's life, at that time, was a living hell. She confided in a friend and that friend discussed her predicament with Viola and introduced the two of them. After meeting Salina, Viola was moved to help her to get out of that situation. Viola provided her with a place to stay and means of support. They became really good friends as a result. Viola and Justine both had been nothing but good to Salina.

Given everything that Viola had done for her, she knew that Viola would see this as outright betrayal. There was no way that Salina could dress it up to be anything other than what it was. Salina never imagined herself being on the wrong side of Vie. She knew that she owed her a lot and so in this respect, she did feel badly about what had taken place between herself and Claudio, but, not bad enough to step out of the picture.

She kept telling herself that Viola didn't really love Claudio in order to justify her relationship with him. She remembered how Viola had openly boasted that the only reason she brought Claudio to the United States was to serve as her boy toy. Salina always had mixed feelings about that even though she would laugh about it with Viola. One side of her felt it wasn't wrong and the other side was repelled by the thought of one human being using another for sex. Claudio had been living with Viola a whole year before she had actually introduced him to her friends. They had all even joked about that too, but it really wasn't funny. She knew that now. Viola felt entitled, because of everything she had done for him. But, Salina reasoned that the relationship was fated for doom from the very beginning. Viola had even admitted it herself how she knew it wasn't going to last. So if it hadn't been her, Salina, then it would inevitably have been someone else. Salina felt, Claudio had a right to his own dreams and desires even if those dreams and desires did not include Viola.

Claudio had confided in Salina how Viola had accused him of bringing women to her house while she was away in Brazil and that they had a really bad quarrel, which changed the way he felt about her. Claudio felt he was just being used, the same way he had been used all of his life. The only difference was that it was subtle and of course an upgrade in his lifestyle. He felt his life was not really his own. It was as though, in some ways, Viola owned him.

Salina reasoned that Claudio was fifteen years Viola's junior. She believed that Viola was doing to Claudio what had been done to her. Oh, maybe she didn't abuse him physically and sell him to her friends, nevertheless it was still a subtle form of abuse. Salina told herself that Claudio's and Viola's relationship wasn't real and that Viola was in denial. Salina reasoned that it was not her fault that she and Claudio had fallen in love. It had to have been fate. What else could it be if not fate? It certainly could never have taken place had Viola been along on that trip. Everything that happened between Salina and Claudio took place after they went on that trip to Africa. Therefore, it was fated.

Claudio said that he would break the news to Vie, when they got back to the States. However it was proving to be a whole lot harder then he initially anticipated. Viola knew that things had gotten worse between them, but she refused to give him an easy out. Claudio was extremely unhappy and moody. He felt that he could no longer pretend to have feelings where they no longer existed. Especially, now that he had taken up with Salina. He hated leaving her to go home to Viola who would always try to engage him in sex.

In the early stages of his affair with Salina, he would give in to Viola's advances, but he gradually began to feel that it was a betrayal of his love for Salina. Now he no longer wanted to be with Viola in that way. He became verbally abusive in his treatment of her. He didn't want to behave this way toward Viola, because he didn't hate her. He realized that she hadn't made him what he was. After all, in the beginning, it was he who had approached her. She only did what came natural. He understood all of this intellectually, nevertheless he was still trapped and he wanted out and didn't know how to go about it.

It would have been much easier for him to break it off if he had not been involved with one of Viola's friends. However, he rationalized, had he not been involved with Salina, there is no telling how long he would have been willing to go on living in limbo with Viola. Ultimately, it would have come to an end. He believed this, and so it eased his guilt. Viola noted a big difference in Claudio since his return from Africa. The sex, when she could get him to perform, was definitely not the same. He was distant and flew off the handle with the slightest provocation. He stayed out a lot. Sometimes all night and when questioned about his whereabouts he would say something mean like, we are not married, or you don't own me. Even though Viola was miserable, she was not about to end it. She felt that she had invested too much in him to just walk away and she wasn't thinking of financial investment, she was emotionally vested. She was desperately trying to fix things. Viola refused to believe the relationship was over.

SECRET PACT

I t was late November and there was a chill in the air that Saturday morning. There was a storm brewing in the Atlantic and it was predicted that it would hit New York City late that afternoon. The temperature was in the low thirties and the meteorologist predicted snow. That morning, Claudio was working in Viola's Manhattan Salon and had just finished cutting a client's hair when he received a call from Salina.

"Hi, honey, how are you?"

"I'm good," Claudio said, surprised that she had called him while he was at the shop. They had both agreed that it was best that she not call him at work or at home, but rather to just wait until he contacted her. Something had come up and Salina needed to see him right away. Claudio took off his duster and told Viola's manager that he was leaving the salon and would probably not be returning. This caused a bit of a ruckus because they had a lot of people scheduled for haircuts and they only had one other stylist who cut hair in the shop that day.

"I'm not taking this Shit from you," Jose said angrily. "I'm going to speak to Viola about this."

"Jou do wha jou have to do," Claudio said flatly.

From the sound of Salina's voice Claudio knew that something was wrong. With bad weather threatening, Claudio predicted that they would suffer a fair share of no shows. He knew that there would be flack about his leaving, but he just didn't care. He would handle it should it become an issue. He didn't like the sound of Salina's voice and he wanted to find out what was wrong. Jose continued to rant, but Claudio proceeded to ready himself for departure and without engaging Jose he simply left the shop.

He reached Salina's apartment in Brooklyn around twelve o'clock that afternoon. She had given him keys so he just let himself in. She had a large two bedroom walk up in a three story brownstone in Flatbush. Her apartment was on the second floor. He entered the apartment into a small foyer. A small mahogany magazine table graced its entrance where Salina rested her keys, in a crystal bowl resting on top of it, whenever she entered. An oval shaped mirror was positioned directly above the table so that one would be able to glance at one's reflection before leaving the house. As he entered the hallway, he passed a small galley kitchen on his right. The living room was a little further down the hall on the left.

Salina was in the bedroom at the far end of the hall. She could be seen from where he stood in the hall, because the door was open. She was sitting on the end of the bed looking out of the window at the grey skies. Snow had already begun to fall. When he walked into the room she turned and looked up at him and smiled wanly. "What's the matter?" he said, realizing that he was about to hear something unpleasant by the look on her face.

"I don't know how to tell you this," she said sadly. Lightning flashed and the light in the ceiling flickered and thunder rumbled in the far distance.

"Just say it dat's why I'm here. I could tell dat some sing was wrong from the tone of jour voice over ze phone. So let me have it."

She looked away from him back out the window as

fine hale began to form and hit up against it. Then she turned and looked up at him and said sheepishly, "I'm, I'm pregnant," her eyes searched his face for a reaction.

Claudio was stunned. He had thought that she was going to tell him that somehow Viola had found out about their relationship, and he had braced himself for that. He exhaled and shook his head as though to clear it.

As the full understanding of her words began to register in his mind, all he could manage to say was, "Jou' re kidding me."

"I'm not," she said sadly. "What are we going to do?" She asked.

"Jou are going to have our baby," he said flatly.

"But what about Vie?" she said nervously.

"Wha about Vie,?" he stated adamantly. "Listen Salina, we are just going to have to own up to ze fact dat we are a couple. We are going to have to face Viola and deal with ze outcome. We both knew dat des was going to happen and dat drama was going to follow. Viola is in denial about our relationship. We both know dat she is not just going to bow out gracefully."

"I know… I just keep on hoping that she'll break it off with you so we wouldn't have to tell her. I know it's going to be messy when she finds out." Salina said, looking miserable. "She is going to feel betrayed. I don't know how to face her. Claudio we have broken an unwritten rule. You and I should never have happened this way. Viola has done so much for both of us. Claudio, she actually saved my life," Salina said, fretfully as she sat there wringing her hands. "If it wasn't for her, I don't know where I'd be today."

Claudio crossed the room and sat down on the bed beside her and said, "Jeah, I know." She rested her head on his shoulder and he put his arm around her, and said,

"Dere is no telling wha she may do. Whaever it is, we are going to have to face it."

He stood up abruptly and walked over to the window and stood there looking out at the building across the street. The window was cloudy with sleet. He turned and looked at Salina and said, "I'm going to tell her tonight. We have to decide. Eider we're going to be a couple or we are not! We can't keep on hiding from Viola, it's crazy. Even if we were willing to do so, the life growing inside jou dictates dat we face ze music."

Salina rose and walked over to where he was standing. The storm was in full force as hale rained down from the heavens. She put her arms around his waist and rested her head on his lower chest and he embraced her, kissing the top of her head. Suddenly as though struck by lightning, Salina looked up at him in a panic. "No," she said. "You can't just go home and tell her like that. We have to plan this. I mean no matter what we do she's not going to take this kindly."

"I know dat," he said. "But, we can't just keep putting it off, Salina."

"I know that, Claudio, but we can at least be smart about it. You have a lot of things in that house. You've worked hard to get where you are now. Remember what happened the last time you tried to leave? We don't want to sink our own ship. After you tell her, there's going to be hell to pay. Viola is not just going to take this laying down. You need to start looking for work elsewhere. It is not likely that she will continue to let you work at the salon once she finds out about us. I think you should keep quiet for now and start to remove your things from the house a little at a time. You can bring them here. Claudio, both our lifestyles are going to change. I only hope that Justine doesn't fire me."

"I don thin dat Justine will fire jou. She's not exactly one of Viola's fans at ze moment. But, jou're right about everysing else. I need to remove my thins from the house and look for another job. How far along is jour pregnancy?"

"Just about six weeks," she said.

"OK," he said, "than we still have a litt'l time before jou start to show. I'll do like jou said."

And thus they sealed their secret pact. Claudio stepped away from Salina and began to pace back and forth and then he turned and looked at her and said, "I have some money saved so we will be alright for a while."

"So have I," Salina said.

"If nothing else, thanks to Viola I can get a job as a barber. As I said before I have a feeling dat Justine is going to remain neutral. Maybe she would have fired jou on de spot in de past, however, thins are not the same between her and Viola since de wedding and remember jou stood in as her maid of honor!"

"I know," Salina said, "but they still speak."

"I know dey still speak, but Justine is a little chilly, if jou know wha I mean." Salina nodded her head because she had also noted the difference in the way Justine acted toward Viola. She exhaled and asked him if he were hungry and he said that he was. So she scurried down the hall toward the kitchen to make him something to eat. Claudio not wanting to face Viola's wrath about him leaving the shop, and with the storm in full force, decided not to go home that night. He turned off his phone so that he wouldn't have to speak to Viola. He knew she would be calling relentlessly.

CHRISTMAS CHEERS

The holiday spirit permeated throughout the Okonedo household. Christmas music played "Deck the Halls," and Justine and Marcelo were busily decorating their Christmas tree. They had invited Justine's family and their friends over for Christmas Eve. At the office, Justine had even instructed Salina to call Viola and invite her and Claudio at Marcelo's request.

Viola and Justine were still somewhat estranged as was Justine and her daughters. Justine was always polite whenever any of them called. But, she had been guarded and somewhat reserved. Justine decided that she would put her differences aside for the Christmas holidays to please her husband, besides she really missed her daughters and Viola too for that matter. She was happy that her daughters were coming and would be meeting Marcelo for the first time. Anthony, however, was in Germany and would not be able to make it for the holiday festivities. Although things would never really be the same between Justine and Viola, Justine didn't want to keep holding a grudge just because Viola had been too selfish to wish her well in her marriage. That being said, Justine no longer held Viola in as high esteem as she had in the past. Nevertheless, she decided to give no more of her time and energy to past anger and hurt.

Marcelo was happier than he had been in years. Marriage to Justine proved to be good for him. The two of them had fussed over the Christmas tree as much as they could and had finally agreed that the masterpiece was finished, so they stood back to admire it. "Ah," Marcelo said, "this is the best tree I have ever seen."

"You know, I believe you are right," Justine said, rubbing her nose on his. "Who's coming tonight?" he asked.

"Well you know my girls are coming, however, Jackie's girls are staying home with their father, but all our friends are coming. I even invited Keith and Sylvia, next door."

"Really?" he asked in surprise.

Justine laughed, "I know, you're thinking that I've said some not so kind things about Sylvia in the past, but her family is in St Louis and they can't get away for any extended time due to Keith's job and I thought that I'd show some Christmas spirit and put all things negative behind me."

"Well," Marcelo said, "I'm very proud of you. Did you invite Mr. Fox across the hall too?"

"No, I didn't invite Mr. Fox across the hall. I didn't know you wanted me to invite everyone in the building," she said jokingly.

"You know if Salina brings a date, Marcelo injected, there will be fourteen people here? That's a lot of people."

"Yes," Justine said, "but there is plenty of food and I'm sure everyone will be comfortable."

Justine wanted the setting to be very informal. She had the buffet table in the dining area decorated with garland and holly and it was set up with silver trays and warmers to keep the food hot. She went into the kitchen to make sure that everything was ready to carry into the dining area. When suddenly the door bell rang,

"Marcelo, will you get that for me honey?" she said happily. Marcelo gleefully responded rushing to get the door.

He swung open the door and there stood Salina. She was alone and it seemed to him that she had put on a few pounds. She was wearing an Ann Klein princess cut coat with a classic black velvet collar and cuffed sleeves and black pumps, which were surprisingly low for Salina. Her hair was swiped up in a French twist and she was wearing diamond stud earrings. She actually looked quite elegant standing in the door holding a box which was beautifully wrapped in Christmas paper. "Hello," exclaimed Marcelo, "come in welcome, welcome."

"Here, this is for the both of you," she said as she extended the present to him and stepped in through the door.

"Thank you," he said, collecting the package and resting it on the table in the foyer. "Here, let me take your coat."

"Thanks Marcelo, where is Justine?"

"Oh, she's in the kitchen. Go on in," he said as he proceeded to hang up her coat.

Salina looked really sweet, as opposed to her usual sexy attire. Her dress was A-lined with an empire waist and she looked, Marcelo thought, akin to women in his culture who were no longer available or happily married. Maybe, he thought, she has a boyfriend. But then where is he?

"Hey, Justine," Salina said smiling. "Thanks for inviting me. Can I help you with anything?"

"Girl I am glad to see you. Everything is done, but I can really use some help setting the food on the buffet table."

"Sure and we should turn on some music too."

"Oh, you're right the CD is finished Marcelo," Justine shouted. "We need some more music."

"OK," he exclaimed and slipped in a CD and "Luther

Van dross" filled the airwaves with "A Very Special Christmas."

The door bell rang again, and while Salina and Justine carried food into the dining room, Marcelo got the door. This time it was Grace, Majeed, Keith, and Sylvia. "Welcome, welcome," Marcelo chanted as they passed through the threshold. "Merry Christmas," they all said in unison as one couple handed him a bottle of wine and the other a cake. Marcelo placed all gifts on the table in the foyer.

Grace and her husband were dressed in African garb and Grace spotted Justine and said, "Hello beautiful lady, I brought you a really nice treat, and I hope you like cake because I made it."

"Oh, Grace you shouldn't have. That was really very nice of you."

"Hello Justine," Sylvia said in her high squeaky voice as she wiggled into the room. She was wearing a gold sparkled dressed that hugged every curve on her body. On her feet she wore black and gold stiletto hills. Justine shot a look at Marcelo who was checking the very sexy Sylvia out from behind. Caught in the act he grinned showing all his teeth and began to laugh. Justine plucked him on his arm as he cowered away from her playfully. Keith, who had also busted Marcelo admiring Sylvia's wares, chuckled as he complimented Justine, very respectfully, on her attire. She was wearing a colorful sarong with a jewel clasp which was especially designed to be tied to one side. Her top was a white off the shoulder peasant blouse. Her hair fell down around her shoulder, as she had allowed it to grow, as requested by her husband. She looked very pretty. "Thank you Keith, how nice of you to notice," she said, smiling and cut her eye at Marcelo playfully. Then the bell rang again and it was Jackie and Prudence. Justine opened the door. "Oooh," Justine said as she hugged each girl,

"I'm so happy to see you." She turned swiftly and called, "Marcelo, Marcelo," and Marcelo rushed over to the door immediately putting his arm around Justine's shoulders smiling at the two young women.

"These are my daughters Jackie and Prudence. Girls this is my husband Marcelo." Marcelo took each of their hands and kissed them.

"I'm so pleased to meet you," he said.

"Oh Mom," Prudence said, "he's a heart throb."

"Yeees" Jackie said, "I see why you were so taken."

Justine blushed and said, "You two should know me better than that. It takes more than looks to win my heart. This man is a jewel. Come on in and take off your coats, most everyone is here."

Jackie couldn't get over how good her mother looked.

"You look more like our sister than our mother, Mom. Have you been working out with a trainer or something?" asked Prudence.

"No" Justine said, "but I have been going to the gym with Marcelo."

Jackie bore a strong resemblance to Justine and she was beginning to get a patch of white hair on one side of her hair just like her mother. Prudence more resembled her father. She was tall, slender, and light skinned, and had short curly hair. Justine's former husband was a very fair skinned African American. He was tall and very muscular. He was the kind of person who could eat a horse and not gain a pound. Prudence was wearing a little black dress and grey red bottom shoes. Jackie had on black pants and a red blouse that exposed one shoulder, while the other side covered the other shoulder, the sleeve went down to the wrist and on it she wore a thick gold bracelet. The girls handed their mother their coats and entered into the living room.

They spotted Salina and went over to greet her. "Hey Salina," Prudence said, "I almost didn't recognize you. You look so cute. How are you?"

"Oh, I'm fine, thank you," Salina said, hoping that no one would notice her tiny baby bump. "I haven't seen you too in a long time. How are you both?"

"Actually, we're pretty good considering everything that has happened," Jackie said.

"Oh," Salina said, "has something happened?"

"Don't be coy, Salina," Jackie said smiling. "You know quite well that we have been in the dog house for a while with Mom. I'm glad that she decided to cut us some slack and invite us to her Christmas party. For a while I thought that we had lost our Mom due to our stupidity."

"Oh that," Salina said halfway under her breath.

Then someone made a request that they play the CD, "Blame it on the Alcohol," by Usher and Marcelo went to put in the CD. Keith and Sylvia started dancing then the doorbell rang again. Justine opened the door and Viola and Claudio stood in the doorway with a case of Dom Perignon. Claudio had argued with Viola that a case was a bit much, but Viola insisted that they bring it.

Justine gasped at the sight of the case and said, "Oh my Viola, you shouldn't have."

"I told her that it was too much," exclaimed Claudio.

Viola waved him off and said, "Someone had to provide the Christmas cheer and there can never be too much champagne." Then she looked directly at Justine and said, "How are you? You look beautiful. It's been too long," as she performed her ritual kiss to the air.

"Welcome, come in," Justine said, gesturing them through the threshold. "Sit that case down on that counter in the kitchen," Justine ordered Claudio. Viola handed her full length Versace mink.

"Ooh," Justine gasped. "This is beautiful! I'll hang this in my bed room."

"Don't bother yourself. Just throw it across the bed. It's no big deal."

Justine shook her head in disbelief as she headed toward the bedroom with the plush fur. Viola's Vera Wang dress was charcoal grey and the shine made it look like liquid metal. It had a plunging neckline that went well past the cleavage line revealing the sides of her well shaped breast. The dress was about four inches above the knees showing off her long shapely legs which were adorned with silver tone stockings that glittered and shimmered as though they had been sprinkled with stardust. Her boots which only came up to her ankles were charcoal Chanel platform heels and the top hugged tightly around her ankles. Her ears were adorned by diamond chandelier earrings and her platinum hair was fashioned into a ponytail. She looked stunning and every head turned when she entered the room. She walked straight over to Salina and blew kisses to the air then she leaned back to get a look at what she was wearing.

"Well, darling," she said, "don't we look…quaint. This certainly is a new look for you!" Viola said facetiously.

"Well, you know, a girl has to change it up sometimes," Salina said, and she flashed a nervous look at Claudio who was standing behind Viola, then quickly focused her gaze back to Viola.

"Hi Salina," Claudio said, and Salina gave him a quick nod and a hello which was so inaudible that it was swallowed up by the music playing in the room.

"Well," Viola went on, "would you care to tell me why I see so little of you lately?"

"Ooh Viola, it's nothing. You know how it is."

"No, I don't," said, Viola seriously. "I don't know how

it is…I know there have been times when we haven't seen each other for a month or so, but that was because one of us was out of town. We both have been here in New York and it has been four months since you've returned from Africa and you haven't even had an hour to spare?"

"I'm sorry, Viola, really…

"Aunt Viola," Jackie interrupted and embraced Viola from behind before she could produce one of her air kisses…"At the same time Justine made an announcement for everyone to help themselves to the food.

Salina was so thankful for the distractions, because she was beginning to feel really uncomfortable. Viola was really getting ready to zero in on her. For a moment Salina had a feeling that Viola knew about her and Claudio, because it was clear that Viola was annoyed with Salina. Salina also thought that Claudio was really acting strange and that he seemed to be overly occupied with Viola. He hadn't even given her a second glance since their initial greeting. If this was an act he was really good.

As if on cue, Claudio led Viola over to the buffet table; she leaned into him and gave him a peck on the cheek. They had made love just before they left the house and Viola was still basking in the afterglow of it. It was different this time. He was passionate and caring and she felt a glimmer of hope for them. All night long she fluttered around him touching his ear, holding onto his arm, sitting on his lap while Salina felt Viola was marking her. Only Viola was completely unaware that Salina had betrayed her. Viola was just feeling good about Claudio. And the way Claudio gazed upon Viola made Salina feel sick. She had witnessed just

about as much of it as she could stomach before begging everyone's pardon and taking her leave. When Salina was making her rounds to say goodnight, Claudio knew instantly that the whole situation had gotten to her. He wanted to go after her, but to do that would certainly be announcing to Viola, this is the woman that I have been leaving you alone nights for! Viola was no fool. She was already convinced that he was cheating. But, in order to keep the peace she had not pressed him on the matter. He had to admit this was not the Viola he knew in the past. He had never seen her operate this way. He was convinced now that Viola truly did love him.

His change in attitude had begun earlier in the evening when he came out of the shower and told Viola that he was in no mood to go to Justine's party, therefore he wouldn't be accompanying her. Viola approached him from behind and planted a soft and tender kiss on his shoulder. He started to pull away, but instead, he turned around to look her in the eyes. It was then that he saw that there was an expression there that he had never seen before.

"Look," she said in a soft voice. "I'm no fool. I know that you have somebody else. In a way, I guess I deserved that."

He made an attempt at denying it, but she shushed him and said, "Listen," before he could speak she placed a finger over his lips, "I have said I'm sorry in every way that I know how. I love you Claudio, that's why I haven't thrown up my hands. I'm willing to do anything to save this relationship. I love you so much! I know that sorry doesn't erase the things I've said to you. But that's all I have. I really am sorry. Claudio I am so in love with you that it hurts. I lie beside you at night and cry aching for your arms to hold me the way you used to. Believe me when I tell you that I have never in all my life felt this way about anyone! If I could go back in time and undo all the hurt that I caused both of us by my words, I would do it without hesitation. You are the only family I have." When she said this her voice cracked and her eyes welled up with tears. Her voice elevated when she said, "I have no one if I don't have you." Then she lowered her voice to continue. "I know that I'm older than you and that you are probably thinking about leaving me. Claudio, I'm begging you not to do that. Give me a chance, babe. Give us a chance and I promise you, you won't be sorry...I love you so much. How many ways can I show you? Tell me what I have to do! I miss you. If you don't want to go to the Christmas party I won't push it, but I'd like us to go."

Claudio stood there really listening to her, this time, and his heart went out to her. She wasn't the mean bitch he was trying to make her out to be, he thought. Viola paused searching his eyes to see if she was getting through and then she went on to say.

"I'm losing Justine as well Claudio. I love her too and I don't know why I acted like such an asshole about her wedding. I want to go to her party and try to mend fences with her. I don't want to lose her friendship because of some stupid phase I was going through."

This was a perfect time for Claudio to break it off with her, but listening to her words, really hearing the urgency of her delivery, he couldn't bring himself to do it. She had touched him and when he looked in her eyes he realized that what he had been doing, all this time, was holding on to his hurt feelings, his anger with himself and projecting them on to her. Why was he holding her to such high standards? She was human, just like he was. She had made a mistake and he could see that she was sorry.

She put her arms around his waist and pressed her lips ever so gently against his moistened shoulder and kissed him tenderly. A feeling of warmth enveloped him. He was filled with emotion and he turned and wrapped his arms around her and her lips found his. He was overcome with passion. Hungrily he kissed her and lifted her off the floor and carried her to the bed. Their lips touched and their tongues were furiously probing, interlocking in a furious fit of passion. Oh how he had missed her. He hadn't realized how much until she kissed him. It was that kiss, and the expression on her face when she did it, in combination with all that she had said that brought all the emotions he was feeling to a head. He couldn't think of anything except to be inside her. For the first time, since he came back from Africa, Claudio was intoxicated with passion for Viola. He fumbled to remove her bra. She hastened to free herself of all her clothes. Feverishly she loosened the towel that was wrapped around his waist. He heard Viola calling his name telling him how much she loved him over and over. He kissed away the tears that were in her eyes then he heard himself saying

" I love you, I do," and her body trembled beneath him as he entered her with an urgency and all his senses were heightened so that he pre-ejaculated. Viola was so overtaken with joy to see that she could get him that excited she bombarded him with kisses. Afterwards they lay together talking; Viola asked him if he had forgiven her. He said that he had, and then he kissed her and began groping her breast as he drew the nipple into his mouth. Aroused again he lifted her to him and entered her and made love to her in a way he had never done before. They avouched the love they felt for each other. It was so intense until Claudio cried out upon climax. Tears were in his eyes as he burrowed his face into her neck. They had to break away from each other after their third round. They realized that they would never get to Justine's Christmas party if they continued in like fashion. Viola for one would have loved nothing better than to stay home with

Claudio that night, but she didn't want to miss this event. She knew she was in the dog house with Justine and wanted to redeem herself.

Salina knew from the moment she laid eyes on Claudio and Viola that night, something was amiss. The vibe between them was super strong. Viola was simply glowing and Claudio's hands kept rubbing her shoulders or finding their way to her bottom. It was as if he couldn't help himself. He couldn't seem to keep them off of her. Everything they did, the way they looked at each other, told Salina that they had been intimate.

She felt small and insignificant; her stomach felt tight. A feeling of immense anxiety washed over her and if she did not leave when she did, she would have burst into tears. Claudio could see the hurt in Salina's eyes when she said good night and in that single instant she allowed her eyes to rest upon his, he knew that she knew about him and Viola. He felt badly and lowered his head so that she couldn't make further eye contact with him.

He wanted to go after her but he dare not take the risk. He had made a mess of things. He knew now for sure that he was still in love with Viola. But what baffled him was the realization that he also loved Salina, however in a different way. He hadn't consciously used Salina. He just was unaware, at that time, how complicated his feeling were for Viola. He had been angry with Viola for a lot of reasons. And there they were, himself and Salina, alone in Africa. And now, Salina was carrying his child and he knew that he would not be able to abandon her. But how was he going to work this out? He was in a fix and just didn't know what he was going to do.

That night Viola and the girls cornered Justine in the kitchen and begged her forgiveness. The girls confessed to their mother about all their fears concerning Marcelo and admitted that it was all based on ignorance. Viola admitted that she was having so much trouble with Claudio that the last thing that she wanted to do was attend a wedding. Viola admitted that it was mean and selfish of her to have treated someone that she loved so dearly in that manner and she promised never to let Justine down again. They all told Justine that they were ashamed of the way they had acted and would always regret not having taken a part in her wedding ceremony. They wanted to know if she and Marcelo were planning on having another ceremony here in the States. Justine told them that they were saving their money now and had already gotten married in the States by the Justice of the Peace a week after they returned from Africa. Disappointed they all kissed Justine, and the girls promised they would be more supportive in the future.

Justine seemingly accepted all their apologies. However, even though they had made up and Justine pardoned them, Justine had changed. Of course Viola would always be her friend and she would always love her daughters. But the friendship between Justine and Viola had officially changed and she would always be somewhat guarded even with her daughters. She had been burned once by these ladies whom she loved so dearly and she wasn't about to leave herself vulnerable to any of them again.

She knew that there would be challenges in her marriage, but she hoped with the help of God she would have the strength to weather any storms that would come their way. Marcelo was her family now. Justine was happy that they were all able to have closure and the rest of the night was festive. Everyone was in high spirits. Sylvia, Keith, Chide and Patience, who all had arrived late, happily danced all night. Majeed couldn't stop telling jokes and Grace and the girls couldn't stop laughing. Viola and Claudio behaved like young lovers. Marcelo and Justine happily entertained the lot and all and all everyone was spreading Christmas cheer. All except for Salina, that is. Her pillow was wet from tears which spilled until the dawn of Christmas.

SECRET BURDEN

It was the middle of April and the winter months were long behind. The weather had been exceptionally warm so Salina had to shed her winter garments which cloaked the presence of her baby bump revealing to the world what she had been concealing all winter. She had become the buzz of the office as she moped about carrying the fruit of her untold secret. Naturally everyone wanted to know who the father was. She had guarded her secret so jealously, that even her closest friends Viola and Justine were mystified as to with whom Salina had laid. Salina dared tell no one. That would mean exposing Claudio which would without a doubt turn him against her. They would all look down upon her and Claudio would be given a pass. Sure they would be mad at him at first.

But Viola would forgive him anything. She was obsessed with him and had no intension of letting him go. She, Salina, would lose everything. Viola's forgiving heart would not extend to her, not when it concerned her precious Claudio. Better to bare the anguish of being his dirty little secret, than to be banished by them all. Ironically, these people, Viola, Justine and Claudio were all she had in this world. She had no family or friends she could turn to. She felt she had no other choice then to remain silent. The secret burden was hers to bear.

Viola Banks was in good spirits this Saturday afternoon. In fact she was a much happier lady these days. Claudio was being very attentive and loving, though Viola still suspected that he had not stop seeing his secret lover. He was still moody at times and he stayed out late at least twice a week. Sometimes he would come home when the sun was rising. Viola felt this was indicative of a person who had taken a lover. The night that they reconciled, he never admitted to having another woman. She hadn't given him the opportunity to confess, and when questioned about it later he became hostile and distant. Because things were much better between them now, Viola didn't press him. She could see he had no intention of revealing his lover to her. Maybe he felt that he was in so deep and didn't know how to get out of it. So Viola chose to leave well enough alone for now. After all she didn't know for sure that he was having an affair. It was only a strong suspicion. And even if he were, she felt it would eventually fizzle out. She believed that if she harped on it, it would only push him away from her. And anyway, aside from the occasional nights of him coming home late, things were great between them. They attended functions together, he was sweet and funny around the house and the sex, the sex was simply fantastic. She didn't like the thought of him loving someone else, however, she wasn't about to take the risk of coming out the looser this time. If pushed into a corner he might grudgingly choose the other woman. She decided to wait it out. If in fact he was truly having an affair, and she wasn't absolutely certain that he was, he would eventually lose interest and no one would be hurt or, more to the point, she wouldn't be hurt.

Viola hurried about putting on her make-up as she had a lunch date with Justine at Giovanni's an Italian restaurant in Manhattan. She wanted to talk to Justine about Salina because she couldn't for the life of her understand why Salina was concealing the identity of her baby's father from her closest friends. She grabbed her black leather Coach hand-bag and scurried to the door taking one last look at her reflection in the mirror as she fluffed her hair and went out of the door.

Viola arrived at the restaurant before Justine so after she was seated she ordered a drink. When she was well started on, yet, her second drink Justine rushed up to where she was seated and pulled out a chair and sat down.

"Sorry I'm late," she said, breathlessly blowing a kiss at Viola threw the air as was their custom.

"Yeah, well what kept you?" Viola said, mildly affected by the alcohol.

Justine looked at her devilishly, smiled and said, "It's Saturday darling and Marcelo took off work so don't ask any questions."

The two ladies looked at each other knowingly and began to laugh. The waiter approached and Justine ordered a glass of white wine and asked to look at the menu. After a few minutes the waiter returned with the wine and they ordered their food.

When the waiter walked away to put in their order, Viola looked up at Justine and said, "So what do you think about this business with Salina?"

Justine shook her head and said, "I don't know what to make of it. It is quite the mystery. The only reason I can think of for her being so secretive is that the man is probably married."

"OK, so he's married. "Why would she feel the need to hide that from me," Viola said, obviously annoyed?

"Justine I'm her best friend and I have never judged her. Hell I don't judge anyone. If she couldn't tell anyone else in the world, she certainly could tell me!" Viola said incredulously.

"Well, maybe she doesn't want me to know. Maybe she's afraid that if she confides in you that you might let it slip when talking to me."

"No offense, Justine, but if Salina told me something like that in confidence, I wouldn't tell you."

When she said that Justine didn't even flinched she just shrugged her shoulders and went on to say calmly.

"Maybe not, but you might tell Claudio. You know, pillow talk, and then Claudio might mention it to Marcelo, and Marcelo might mention it to me, you know pillow talk," she said, smiling humorously.

Viola laughed and said, "Justine you know you can be a bitch sometimes."

Justine smiled saying in a sing song voice.

"Well you know the saying. It takes one to know one. Anyway, the best way to keep a secret is to tell no one. The untold secret is a secret indeed!"

Viola rolled her eyes and leaned back in her seat. The waiter arrived with their orders. After he sat their food down and walked away Viola leaned forward and said.

"What if I hired a private eye? You know a dick."

"What?" Justine said, astonished! "Girl, if you ever did that to me…That's totally inexcusable. I can think of nothing more despicable."

"Oh come on Justine, you make it sound like I'm a monster."

"Well what you speak of is monstrous," Justine said indignantly!

"Well it's not as though I mean her any harm. How else can I help her if I don't know who he is? I mean Salina is like a little sister to me. I can't just let some creep take advantage of her.

"Viola, Salina is a grown woman and she is not your

little sister. It's none of your business. If she doesn't want us to know who the baby's father is, we just have to respect it."

Viola pushed her plate away and sat back and folded her arms. After about a minute of silence between them she signaled for the waiter to come. When he came over she said.

"Can you bring me another screwdriver and tell them to put in a double shot of Vodka." Justine ordered another glass of wine. They remained silent until the waiter returned with their drinks and then they just changed the subject and started talking about Marcelo and Claudio as they dined.

It was eight p.m. that same day and Marcelo sat at the bar turning his drink around in his hand. He was not much of a drinker and had been nursing his drink for half an hour. Claudio was working on his third drink wondering what he was going to do tonight concerning his women. Marcelo knew that Claudio had another woman aside from Viola he just didn't know who it was. Claudio didn't want to risk telling him that for fear that Marcelo might let it slip to Justine. Claudio told Marcelo about the other woman only because he had needed someone to talk to and he trusted Marcelo fairly well. He needn't have worried though, because Marcelo never discussed the affairs of his friends with Justine. He didn't want her getting any undo notions about him. "So how long do you think you will be able to keep this up? You know how women are. They love to cut in on another woman's territory and are willing to be second for a while, but then ultimately, they almost always want to be number one. This kind of thing is wrong you know," Marcelo said.

"Tell me about it," Claudio said. She wans me to come over tonight and dat's going to be hard, because Viola wans to go out."

"Man, I'm glad I'm not in your shoes. I mean it's easy when you only love one of them, but when you love them both!" He shook his head.

"I know," Claudio said, "and I do love them both. Viola has been so good to me, Marcelo...But the other one is pregnant for me and I don like leaving her alone so much. I wan to go dere tonight and be with her. But, if I do dat I'm going to have to fight with Viola. It's crazy, I don wan to fight with Viola, I just wan to make her happy, jou know?"

Marcelo looked at him quizzically and said, "Man, why don't you just tell Viola about the other one and leave it up to her?"

"Wha do jou mean?"

"Well, you said that Viola suspects you have a lover right?"

"Jeah, but I still don understand wha jou mean?"

"Tell her you have someone else! You know how Viola is. Who knows she might accept it and you won't have to run around beating your head up against the wall."

"Man, are jou serious?" Claudio said, looking at Marcelo disbelievingly.

"Of course I'm serious. You're driving yourself crazy. Men do it all the time in my country. Viola is not your wife!" Marcelo said, shrugging his shoulders looking at Claudio matter-of- factually.

"Jou don't like Viola very much do jou?" Claudio asked Marcelo defensively.

"I have nothing against her," Marcelo said. "She is Justine's friend. I'm just saying she's not your wife so why put yourself through this. Just tell her! What can she do divorce you?"

"The times for having two wives are over," Claudio

said. "Maybe that's why God put a stop to it."

"You mean in this country," Marcelo said. "But I agree anything more than one wife is a headache." Claudio said nothing he just laughed.

Then Marcelo added, "The other one is pregnant right? You should marry her. Make her your wife. See Viola on the side. Where I'm from there would be no question. The one who is bringing forth the fruit is the one you marry. If you stay with Viola you will never have children. The other one might throw away your kid, you said so yourself." Claudio laughed until tears came out of his eyes.

"Wha does children have to do with it African Man? I don see Justine having jour children," Claudio said pointedly."

Marcelo laughed and said, "Claudio, we are not talking about me. I have children. I don't need children from Justine. We are happy the way we are. The way I see it now, Justine is the only woman I'll ever need for the rest of my life. That's why I married her. You don't feel that way about Viola or we wouldn't be having this conversation."

Claudio laughed and said, "Man jou are crazy. I see right now dat jou are trying to get me killed. All this time I tought jou were my frien.

Marcelo laughed in turn and said. "I am your friend you are making too much of this my friend. They are only women. What can they do to you?"

Claudio looked at Marcelo unbelievingly and said, "Man I guess jou don really know Viola. She is no ordinary woman. She eats men like me and jou for dinner and despite wha you may thin, I do love her."

Marcelo laughed, "Sure you love her. Everything you do proves your love. You can speak for yourself concerning Viola. If she were my woman I would handle her. Its' plane to see, she will never leave you."

"Jeah," Claudio said, "maybe jou can handle Justine, but jou have never had a woman like Viola. I'm telling jou. This woman can make or break Jou. I'm not trying to cross her in dat way."

"You don't act like a man who is afraid of being broken. If that were the case you wouldn't be cheating on her. From what I can see you've already crossed her." Marcelo said laughingly. "Let's just forget I said anysing," Claudio said, annoyed. "If I listened to jou, I'd end up getting myself killed." He motioned for the bartender to bring him another drink and pointed at Marcelo and said, "Give him another one too. Dis man has a lot of jokes."

Salina picked up her cell phone and dialed Claudio. She was fed up with this game he was playing. I'm having his baby dam-it, she thought. Why must I endure all this stress about, Viola? How could he do this to me? Had I known that he was still in love with Viola I would never have allowed this pregnancy to go this far. What am I supposed to do once the baby is born? hide it? The phone rang three times and Claudio answered annoyed,

"Hey, I tought we agreed dat I would contact jou."

"Oh really" Salina said, perturbed and just how do we manage to get you to call me when I'm having contractions?"

"Are jou having contractions?"

"Y e a h, that's why I'm calling!"

"How far apart are they?" Claudio asked nervously.

"They are five minutes apart, Claudio. I need you to come over right away. I don't care what you have to tell Viola, you can't just leave me here alone," then she started to cry.

"Don't cry, babe, don't cry. I'm coming. I'm on my way right now, OK? I love you." and then he hung up the phone. He turned to Marcelo and said.

"Look man, I've got to go."

"Is everything alright," asked Marcelo?

Claudio looked at him worriedly and said, "I thin the baby might be coming tonight."

"You see what I mean," Marcelo said. "If Viola knew, you wouldn't have a problem."

Claudio shook his head and said, "Man, jou don know de half of it," meaning that Marcelo didn't know the baby's mother was Salina. He shook Marcelo's hand, clapped him on the back and headed for the door.

Claudio reached Salina's house an hour later. It was Saturday and he didn't have the car and all the trains were running local because they were fixing the express tracks. He climbed the stairs two at a time and reached the apartment and let himself in. He could see Salina from down the hall. She was lying in a fetal position on the bed and she didn't look good. He ran down the hall and came around the bedside and asked.

"Are jou alright, Baby?" Salina had broke-out into a sweat she felt warm to the touch and seemed to be in a lot of pain. She was moaning softly on her side. "How many minutes apart are the contractions now?"

"I don't know I stopped counting."

"Well the last time jou counted how many minutes?"

"I think they were two minutes apart."

"Oh shit," he said, "why didn't you call me sooner, honey?"

"I did call you sooner. I didn't think it would take you this long....Ooh, ooh."

"Are you alright?"

"Call a cab, Babe you've got to get me to the hospital."

Claudio pulled his cell phone from his pocket and dialed a cab. Forty-five minutes later Claudio was carrying Salina into the emergency room. He carried her up to the window and told the clerk "She's in labor." The clerk ran inside and came out with an orderly and they put Salina in a wheel chair and hurriedly pushed her in to one of the rooms to be examined. Shortly after the exam they rushed her off to delivery, she was fully dilated the baby was coming tonight.

At twelve thirty-five p.m. little Aden Rivera was born into the world. Claudio had called Viola around nine p.m. to tell her he would not be able to accompany her to a party. Of course, they quarreled about it and Viola ended up telling him not to bother to come home at all tonight to just stay with his bitch if that's who he preferred to be with. Then, she slammed the phone down into its' holder. Claudio pondered over it for a while and thought to himself maybe Marcelo is right. Maybe it would just be better to tell her. But then he thought better of it. If she found out about Salina, it would be all out war. No, whatever he did, he could never tell Viola about his affair with Salina. It was just too explosive a thing to do. Although a secret burden such as this, was almost doomed to be discovered. It was just a matter of time.

Viola had not seen or heard from Claudio for three days. She was blowing up his cell phone. However, Claudio just let it go to voice mail. She called Justine. But Justine had changed since that whole wedding thing. She listened to her over the phone, but she wouldn't come over. She had cried so much until her whole face was swollen. She tried to get in touched with Salina. Justine said that Salina had called in sick, but for some reason she was not able to reach her either. Now I know what it feels like to need a friend and the friend not be there for you, she thought. All of my troubles seem to have intensified after refusing to go to Justine's wedding. Maybe it was karma.

"Why did I tell him not to come home?" Viola said out loud. It was just a stupid party is, all. I could have let him have his night out on the town without making a big issue of it, she thought. Then again he doesn't have to be this mean. Oh God I hope I haven't lost him, she thought. Then she picked up the cell and dialed his number again. Viola had not gone to the shop in three days. She just couldn't face the world not knowing what was happening between her and Claudio.

At around ten a.m. Wednesday morning she heard Claudio's key turn the lock. She held her breath as she heard his footsteps coming toward the bedroom. Please, please don't let him be coming to say he's leaving, she thought. He walked to the bedroom and stood in the doorway and said, "I'm sorry. I guess you want me to leave." Viola jumped up and ran to him and threw her arms around his neck and began to cry. He folded his arms around her and kissed her hair. He was perplexed. He didn't want to cause her this kind of pain. He just didn't know what to do. He really was in love with two women, and one of them had just delivered him a son. He loved Vie and wanted to be with her. But he wanted to be with Salina and his son as well. He had a hard time tearing himself away from his little family in Brooklyn today. He was totally in love with his son. The only reason he came home is because he knew that Viola was probably beside herself with worry. If Viola had asked him to leave, he would have gone back to Brooklyn and hoped that after a time she would take him back as Marcelo suggested she might. It was not as if it wouldn't have hurt him to leave her. The truth is he didn't know how he would feel if she'd told him she was through and really meant it. He was really banking on what Marcelo had said to him. He was hoping that she would accept him even if she knew there was somebody else even if she found out it was Salina. Deep down inside he felt this was a possibility.

Viola was a hard woman to figure. He knew for certain that she loved him and that she would tolerate a lot. But how much, that he did not know? He really wished polygamy was legal in this country. He would marry Viola and take Salina as his second wife. Yes, he would marry them both. They should have a law like that in every country, he thought wistfully. Two wives might be a headache, but it would solve his present dilemma.

LIFE'S LITTLE REWARDS

It was mid May and Arlene Shapiro was fluttering about her house in the Hampton's instructing the cook as to where she wanted the caterers to set-up. She and Samuel owned an English Tooter styled home with five bedrooms, three master suits, and five bathrooms. The living room was massive and it could hold up to a hundred people easily. This was Marcelo's last week with them and they were throwing a party in his honor. They were very fond of Marcelo and thought of him like family. In all the time that they had known Marcelo, he had never asked them for anything. Instead he was grateful to them for giving him the opportunity to exercise what he had learned in school. He was a hard worker and true to his word. He had proven himself dependable. The Shapiro's owned two other businesses in mid town which they were better able to manage since Marcelo had taken over the store in Brooklyn. He had worked for them for three years and had made a lot of improvements. He was so dedicated many people in the neighborhood thought that he owned the store. The Shapiro's were getting on in years and decided that when Marcelo left that they would sell the stores and move to Florida.

The Brooklyn store was actually worth much more now that Marcelo had brought it up to the 21st century with his marketing skills. Arleen's feeling's was bitter sweet, on the one hand this was a joyous time for all, but on the other hand she felt that they probably would never see Marcelo again. They had invited some of their close friends. They encouraged Marcelo to invite his friends as well. Many of the store owners in the downtown area of Brooklyn, where their store was located, were expected to attend as well.

Arlene, a tall woman with a mountainous flock of unruly curly salt and pepper hair, talked with many of her friends about the young African who had saved her husband's life. Of course she greatly exaggerated, because Marcelo had actually arrived on the scene well after the assault had taken place. However, in Arlene's version, it all happened quite differently. Marcelo arrived in all his glory and scared the burglars off. Arlene was a colorful woman and felt the need to embellish on facts and since it seemed to make her happy, Samuel and Marcelo indulged her.

Justine was at Viola's salon getting her hair done. Viola and Claudio were going to be picking her and Marcelo up from the house. Marcelo invited her African friends, Grace and Majeed. They had a car and were more than happy to give Chide and Patience a ride out to the Hampton's. After Justine's little Christmas party last year, she and Sylvia had become quite chummy. She had even watched the twins for Sylvia on several occasions. So Justine invited, as she liked to put it, the Parkers to the party. She started calling them that after she and Marcelo accompanied Sylvia and Keith to the Justice of the Peace and witnessed their marriage. This party was really a big deal to Marcelo, because the Shapiro's wanted him to meet some of their friends who were interested in investing in his business.

Justine had tried to invite Salina, but Salina was being very stand-offish these days. She took a leave of absence after the baby was born and never returned to work. Justine still couldn't, for the life of her, figure out what was wrong with Salina. All she knew for sure was that Salina was hiding something and she had changed.

Salina's love for Viola had metamorphosed into extreme jealousy and hatred. It was ironic because initially it was she who was hesitant to tell Viola about their affair. Now she was very resentful of the fact that Claudio could not bring himself to leave Viola thus causing her to remain in the background, and live in Viola's shadow as the dirty little secret. She couldn't believe how Viola was allowing Claudio to get away with what he was doing either. He slept over at her house at least two nights a week. Viola had to know that Claudio had another woman. Claudio agreed that she probably knew and had just accepted it. So did this mean that because the grand Viola had accepted the fact that he had someone on the side that she should accept being on the sidelines indefinitely?

Salina had put up with it for two years and her patience was beginning to wear thin. If Claudio did not make up his mind by the end of the month who he wanted to be with, Salina was going to pull out of the relationship and count her losses. She just couldn't go on allowing herself to be treated in this manner. In the beginning she had been so in love with Claudio she was willing to take any part of him that she could get. Now, the joy she felt in being with him had turned to agony. She was not happy.

She had given up too much for him. Yet he got to keep everything. He had two families. He was able to attend all of their friend's parties with Viola on his arm. And even if Salina elected to accept the invitations she received from their friends, she would have to appear alone, because he couldn't bear to see her with another man. It wasn't fair. She wanted a man she could call her own. Maybe it was she who had been in denial and not Viola. Maybe Claudio never had any intentions of giving her up. Viola was in the blood that flowed through his veins. Taking him away from Vie was far from easy. She had greatly underestimated Viola's hold on Claudio. How could she ever have thought that someone like her could take anything away from someone like Viola? Viola was the type who cared little for what was going on behind the scenes. She was an upfront person. As long as she could keep up appearances, she was willing to share a few crumbs with some little beggar. She as much as said so one day when Salina inadvertently took her call, it was eerie, Viola was talking to her about the other woman. It was the most uncomfortable of feelings. All the while she was talking, Salina wondered does she know it's me? Is she sending me a message? She openly voiced her suspicions about Claudio having another woman. She said that she didn't like the idea of someone else being in the picture. But, if the little beggar was that desperate for her crumbs then she would tolerate it for now so long as it didn't interfere with their social life. But even worse than that, Claudio enjoyed the life style he shared with Viola. It was one of life's little rewards which came along with being with Viola. Why should he settle for the dull life style of a peasant when he could live the life to the fullest with Vie? Because of the nature of Viola's business and her enormous success, Viola knew many celebrities. She was always being invited to different events. There was always something going on in her world. It was actually one of the things she, Salina, had enjoyed about being a friend of Viola's. All the lavish dinner parties she attended with the beautiful people and the elegant surroundings and plush, plush living. Viola got to rub elbows with people of power and means. She was forever jet setting around to different countries. And now that she had the salon in Brazil, she was expanding her horizons. Vacationing in the most luxurious spots and just enjoying the best of everything. Salina just couldn't compare with the glamour which surrounded Viola. Salina had now come to despise her and all she stood for.

It was nine o'clock and Arlene was at the top of the stairs when the guests began to pile in. She resembled Barbra Streisand. Her nose a fairly dominate feature on her face. She wore a pastel blue silk Ann Klein evening gown that had a chocked lace collar. Her hair was swept up in a cluster on top of her head. She was wearing pearl earrings which matched the string of pearl beads that draped down around her neck to her waist. The maid ushered her guests into the grand living room as she gracefully descended the stairs.

By eleven o'clock the party was in full force and everyone that was coming had arrived. Samuel was a rather small man with smooth olive skin and, except for a few white hairs growing around the corners of his temple and lower part of his head, was fairly bald. His eyebrows were thick and bushy and completely white and he also had a rather thick mustache. He stood in the doorway and clanged a spoon against his glass to get everyone's attention. "Everyone listen I have an announcement to make," he said proudly. A hush came over the crowd and every eye was on Samuel.

"I would like everyone to accompany me to the garden."

"What's going on?" different ones began to whisper.

"Come on, come on," encouraged Arlene. "You'll see when we get there." When everyone had managed to make it out back through the threshold, one by one they were struck with awe. There in the middle of the yard rapped in a humongous red bow was a 2013 Lexus S.U.V. "Aaaah," everyone said in unison.

Samuel gestured toward Marcelo and said, "Marcelo, you have been none-other than a blessing to me and my wife from the very first time that we laid eyes on you. I for one, and I know that I speak for my wife as well, will miss you immensely. What I wish for you and your lovely wife is success in your business and most of all I wish you a binding love as the love shared by myself and Arlene." Arlene blushed and looked around the room at everyone bashfully. "This," and he pointed toward the Lexus, "is a small token of our appreciation of you. May you live a long time and be prosperous." The room was completely silent. Everyone was in shock. Marcelo stood motionless in the middle of the yard speechless.

And then someone in the crowd broke the silence and said, "Hear, hear" and everyone clapped and cheered. Caterers weaved throughout the crowd with flutes of champagne on their trays while Marcelo embraced Samuel. Later he made his way over to his new car and Justine joined him.

Later on that evening Samuel privately presented Marcelo with a sizable check. It was an investment to jump start his new business. He also put him in touch with another interested investor. Marcelo was taken aback by all the Shapiro's were doing in his behalf. He was determined to succeed and do them proud. He knew that they believed that he would disappear from their lives, but that was far from the truth. He intended to keep in touch the same way he did with his family in Africa.

CLAUDIO'S CHOICE

I t was late September and the leaves were beginning to fall off the trees and carpet the ground with their array of colors. Children had returned to school flooding the trains and buses with their loud and noisy chatter. Aden had turned two and was starting pre-school. Salina had just offered Claudio an ultimatum, either he told Viola about the two of them and leave or he could pack the things he had in her house and go back to Viola completely. He could do whichever was most comfortable for him, she didn't care which. She had technically already lost all of her friends and she was through with hiding in the shadows. One way or another, this train had pulled into the station and she was getting off. She needed to get on with her life now. As it stood now, he had reduced his overnight stays to when Viola was out of town. Other than that it was a stolen day here and there. This wasn't even fair to baby Aden. It was actually worse than when they had first started seeing each other. At least then he would spend an occasional night causing Viola a little grief. If he couldn't bring himself to leave Viola, then as far as she was concerned it was over, she would get rid of this second child that yet grew within her womb. Claudio could tell that Salina meant to make good on her threat to abort his child. There was a resolve in her eyes and if she had not been the mother of his children, he would be OK with letting her go. She had become a bit of a nag and not much fun to be around anymore. Besides, she knew when they first started out that he was Viola's man and yet she proceeded with the affair. Now, after they had finally figured out a way to co-exist with Viola, she wanted to throw a monkey wrench into the plan. Ironically, the only place where he found real peace and happiness was with Viola. She seldom questioned him about where he was when he was away from her and she always welcomed him home whenever he returned. As a result, he didn't spend too much time away from home because it was so pleasant there and she had a kick ass body to sit back and admire.

On the other hand, he adored his son and didn't want Salina to get rid of his unborn child, because he liked the idea of having children. And when Salina wasn't getting on his last nerve, she wasn't so bad. But, the truth of the matter was he preferred Viola.

He walked down the street with his shoulders slumped forward, his brow line wrinkled with dread. Each moment grew closer to the insidious deed he was about to do to Viola. He knew he would break her heart and he hated himself for creating this problem.

The truth was his heart would be breaking as well; it wasn't as if he blamed Salina for her position. It was just an awful situation and it never should have happened. He had no one to blame except himself. He reached the building where he and Viola resided and stood outside making idle conversation with the doorman prolonging the awful task that lie ahead of him.

Claudio had to face the fact that he was a coward. He was now able to tell Viola that he was having an affair. But, he couldn't bare the look in her eyes if she knew with whom. That part he would withhold from her. It was because of his cowardice, he had to rip both their hearts out. It was a losing situation as far as he was concerned. Claudio's choice was proving to be a painful one. He could not believe how low he had sunk.

Claudio entered the apartment and walked through the living room into the bedroom. He walked toward the mantle. His footsteps cushioned by the plush carpeting on the floor. Viola heard him come in and came out of the kitchen into the bedroom to greet him. "Hi honey," she said as she approached him and gave him a peck on the lips. She was wearing very shear linen Pajamas with the top being slightly tapered at the waist showing off her curves. The see through linen fabric created a silhouette revealing her rounded breast, strong firm bum, and shapely legs.

He looked down at her lovingly, his eyes were sad though, "Sit down Viola," he said, "we have to talk."

She could tell by the expression on his face that it was serious. "What's the matter?" she asked concerned.

"Just take a seat," he said, gesturing toward her off white Victorian chaise lounge by the window.

But she wouldn't comply, "Claudio, I don't want to sit down. Just tell me what's going on."

"I'm leaving," he said abruptly, and then walked over to the window and began fidgeting with the trim around the edge of the pale gold brocade drapes.

Viola stood motionlessly in the middle of the room. There was a lump forming at the back of her throat as she processed what he had just said. "What are you saying Claudio?" she said. Her heart began to thump rapidly.

"Look Vie, I know dat jou know I've been seeing another woman. We have never discussed it but..."

"What are you telling me? Are you saying that you don't love me anymore?"

"No, no, dat's not wha I'm saying. Vie, please I din

mean for it…"

"What did you mean, Claudio? Did you think I was going to like getting dumped? I mean I knew it," she said. "What man stays out all night as frequently as you did? I knew you had someone, but I thought that you had stopped and came to your senses. I don't understand, I mean the way you treat me… I thought you loved me. I knew you were younger but I thought you were just sewing wild oats." Viola legs refused to hold her and she shakily walked over to the chaise and sunk down. Tears formed in her eyes and she could not contain herself any longer; she allowed them to pour. Her body trembled and Claudio could feel her pain as she cried out in anguish. Aaaaaaaaaaah! He wished that he could retract what he had just said. He knew how much he loved her now. He even knew that if he retracted what he had said that she would have forgiven him. But, he could not retract it. Salina already mothered his son and now she was expecting another. He could not ask her to keep baring his children under these circumstances. It was the only right thing to do for the sake of his children.

"Vie," he went on to say, "We have a child together and now she is pregnant with another. It is not dat I don't love jou, I do. It just I wan to be with my children. I have a family," he said pleadingly.

"Is that it?" she asked, tears streaming down her face. Is it because I can't give you children?" Viola had just turned fifty that week and threw a big party celebrating the event. She had even invited Salina who again rejected her invitation. She just couldn't figure Salina out these days. She must really be having an affair with a married man and just relinquished her life to it, she thought. Viola had dental surgery three months before her party. She looked beautiful, but she knew that she couldn't compete with a woman who was breeding. She hadn't taken into consideration that Claudio might want children, because she had never had a desire for them herself. Besides his family in Brazil was quite an expense for him. She had never imagined that he would want children of his own. She would have taken some fertility drugs years ago and tried to conceive if she knew it meant that much to him. If only he had expressed a desire to have children before it had become too late for her.

"Who is she?" she asked.

"It's not important who she is we…"

"What do you mean it's not important who she is?" Viola shouted. "It's fucking important to me! You and she are tearing my whole world apart!" And then suddenly, as though she were suffering from a mental disorder, she rose from the chaise. She clasped her hands together franticly as though in prayer, and tried to reason with Claudio.

"Look Claudio, I can talk to her. I can give her money. We can take care of the children. Claudio I'll help you to raise them. You and I…"

"Vie," he said, walking over to her and gently taking her in his arms.

"She, she can't be bought off with money. She loves our son. She's not going to hand him over to jou for a price."

Still crying Viola looked up at him and said, "The child is a boy? You have a son?"

"Jes, he's two."

"What's his name?" she asked.

"Viola, why are jou asking…?"

"Why am I asking questions? Do you hear yourself? I mean Claudio, don't you think you owe me something?"

"Of course I owe jou everysing. I just don see how it

makes thins any better for jou to have names."

"I want to know! I want to know their names, I want to know everything. I want to know how it started, when it started and how it got to this. Oh Claudio, I'm no fool. I knew things were a little shaky between us after we had that fight three years ago when I brought you back from the airport, but to think that you hated me and harbored this much resentment and animosity toward me...Claudio if you wanted to hurt me, if you wanted to get me back, you have succeeded."

She was frantic; her whole body was shaking. "I will never recover from this. You have killed me." She pushed away from him and sank back onto the chaise again and began to cry hysterically.

"I don hate jou, Vie," he said, helplessly realizing that his friend Marcelo was right. He should have told her before. She would have accepted it and this all wouldn't be such a shock. He could have spent more time with Salina and the baby and maybe Salina wouldn't have resorted to the threat of aborting their child. He just stood there watching her not knowing what to do. She was in anguish and he wanted to comfort her. He sat down beside her and took her into his arms again and she surrendered laying her head in his chest and gave way to her sorrow showering him with her tears. He rocked her back and forth as he kissed the top of her head. They stayed like this for a long time until her tears subsided and she was able to ask him.

"When are you leaving?"

"I'll stay de night if jou wan me to," he said.

"I want you to," she said, looking up at him helplessly. He kissed her softly on the mouth and tears flowed from her eyes and he kissed the tears and picked her up from the sofa and took her into the bedroom.

Morning brought with it a gloomy haze of dread. Viola woke and looked at Claudio lying beside her asleep and peered outside the window at the grey sky. She knew that she should hate him, but she could not. Her love was of the purest form where it concerned Claudio. She loved him unconditionally. Ironically there was nothing Claudio could do to change that. He could honestly have told her who the mother was and she would have been angry, but after she had time to process it all, she would have come to terms with it. So long as it meant that she wouldn't lose him. She loved everything about him, his smile, his eyes, his body, the sound of his voice, his scent. Claudio had a profound effect on Viola. Since meeting him, she had changed in many ways. She knew that her money had limitations and that there were certain things that she just couldn't control. She had almost lost him once before and she would do anything to keep him now. She would have been happy to go on the way they were if that was what he wanted. This other woman had placed some demands on him. She had gained leverage because of the children and forced him into leaving her. If only she knew who she was. If only she could come to some terms with her. She got up and went into the kitchen and put on a pot of coffee. It was Saturday and the maid was off for the weekend.

She was standing at the counter scrambling eggs when Claudio came up behind her and put his arms around her waist and kissed her on the back of the neck. She moaned and sighed. To think that after today, he would be gone and she would no longer feel his arms around her.

"The maid is off this weekend," she said, "stay with me. I don't want to be alone just yet. I can't bear losing you today. I need to get my head wrapped around this whole thing." Without hesitation, Claudio said, "OK, Vie,

I can do dat. I hope jou know I still love you. It's..."

"Shush, I don't want to talk about this right now. If you are not going to tell me who this person is, then all I want to do is be with you. Let us say goodbye in a quiet way and I'll let you go on Monday without a fuss. Just give me this little cut of time. That's all I ask," Viola's mind was racing. She needed time to figure something out. He kissed her neck and she closed her eyes and inhaled his scent. Her heart was heavy with despair, but she would not allow herself to think of her plight just yet. She would love him and figure out what to do on Monday. This weekend he would belong to her and her alone. She didn't know how she would ever be able to let him go. There had to be a way she could keep him.

Claudio left early Monday morning while Viola was yet asleep. He loved her more now than he had before. He only wished that he had come to this realization before he involved himself with Salina. His feelings for Salina were complicated. He loved her also, but in a different way. They had a special connection because of their past and she was the mother of his children. Having noted that, he also resented her. She was, after all, supposed to be Viola's friend. She hadn't been angry with Viola at the time they had begun their affair, he was. He behaved like a prick coming onto her in Africa, but if she was Viola's true friend, she would have turned him down. She would still be in their circle and all would be right with the world. He knew on an intellectual level that he was just trying to justify his own guilt in the matter. Looking at Viola lying there asleep he realized that he could have had everything with her. It was she who had saved his life and had given him so much. If he had asked her for a child she would have done it without hesitation or died trying. When he had turned thirty-five this year she had gifted him a 2013

Porsche. But it wasn't just the material things. He really loved being around her. She was exciting and funny and she was giving in every way a person could possibly think of, especially the way she so freely gave him her love. He had heard other men complain about how their wives weren't giving them enough sex to justify why they had taken a mistress. He could not complain about that with Viola. Even when they quarreled she never used an argument to withhold sex from him. Her age was just a number. She was young, vivacious, funny, and electrifying. He had really messed up; she was one of a kind. However they had started out, Viola had changed along the way and she really loved him. If he knew nothing else he knew that.

HOUND DOG

The weather was fairly nice for an early morning in September. The wind was whipping and twirling the leaves about on the ground. Viola looked out of her window and released the pulls on each side of the drapes so that they would block out the light of the sun. Claudio had been gone for hours now. She walked back over to her bed and picked up the phone and sped-dialed a number. "Hello, Viola's beauty Haven," a voice sounded into her receiver.

"Hello Kathy, this is Viola, look, I'm not feeling well so I will not be down to the shop today."

"Oh, sorry to hear it, do you have a cold?"

"No, but I probably will not be in at all this week. Cancel any appointments I may have and reschedule them with Sonia."

"Oh, OK. Is everything al....?"

"Thank you Kathy," she said as she hung up the phone. She sat on the edge of the bed in her darkened room and sighed. Then she picked up the phone and called Justine. Justine was bustling about the house getting ready to go to work when the phone rang. "Now who can that be?" she said, looking at the caller I.D. "Viola," she said out loud. "Now what does she want this early in the morning?" She hesitated a moment trying to decide whether to answer it or let it go to voicemail. Then she picked it up and said, "Hello."

"Hello, Justine I need to talk to you."

"Is anything wrong, because I'm on my way to work?"

"Yes, something is very wrong. My whole world has just caved in."

"What are you talking about Viola?"

"He has finally left me, Justine. I'm finished."

"Stop talking like that Viola, you're not finished. Look, I can't get away right now, but I promise to come over right after work, OK?"

"OK, I'll see you later," Viola said, and she placed the phone back in its cradle.

Viola crossed the room and sat down at her desk and turned on the computer. She knew Justine would frown on what she was about to do, but she had to know who it was that had taken from her the only man she had ever loved. She googled the word "detective agency" and "Hound Dog" detective agency popped up with a host of others. "Hum," she said as she picked up the phone and dialed the number.

Claudio did not go in to work either that morning. He climbed the steps to Salina's apartment and put his key in the lock. Salina met him as he entered the hall. She had been calling his phone all weekend. He had turned it off so all of her calls went to voicemail.

Salina was angry and she lashed out at Claudio as soon as he got through the door.

"Couldn't you tear yourself away from that old bitch long enough to answer my calls?" she yelled. He walked past her toward the bedroom where Aden was fast asleep in his crib. Salina followed close behind him ranting.

"You just can't get enough of that old cobweb pussy," she shouted tears gathering in her eyes.

Claudio turned around slowly and shook his finger at her. There was a look in his eyes that Salina had never seen there before. His voice was low but threatening as he said, "Stop, jou just stop. I left her, OK! She doesn't know dat it's jou, but she knows I have a family and dat it's over between us."

"How did the bitch take it?" Salina said harshly and uncaring.

Claudio approached her slowly and positioned her up against the wall, he held her there firmly. He bent over and looked directly into her eyes, he hissed at her, "Jou will not refer to her dat way. I won allow it." He looked at her and said quizzically, "Wha is wrong with jou Salina? Viola has been nothing but kind to jou. WE, JOU AND I, HAVE WRONGED HER!" he shouted. incredulously. Then his voice lowered and he was almost inaudible when he spoke, "I was her man. Jou were supposed to be her friend. We are at fault. Viola has done notsing wrong. Jou have no real reason to resent her and I won let jou disrespect her." He continued to speak in a whisper "We hurt her, Salina. I've never seen her like dat before. Dere is no fight left in her." Then he released her and walked over to the window, he turned around and looked at Salina. There were tears in his eyes when he said, "I left her because of my responsibility to jou and our children. I love jou, but make no mistake, I love Viola and I always will. All I ask is after all dat we have done to her is dat jou respect her. Jou don't have to worry. I will marry jou and I will honor our marriage because jou will be my wife. But don jou ever say anysing derogatory about Viola to me." If jou do dat, jou will push me away."

Salina knew by the look in his eyes that he was a man in pain and she thought better about crossing him. "I'm going to put on a pot of coffee. Do you want something to eat," she asked. "Jeah, I can use a cup of coffee," he said as he pulled his shirt off and lay down on the bed. He was so exhausted, he had not slept well the night before. He stayed up most of the night holding Viola in his arms. Now when he laid his head upon the pillow the cloak of sleep enveloped him within seconds of closing his eyes. Salina returned with the coffee in time for the symphony of snores. She sat on the end of the bed and sipped on it worriedly as she pondered over her present situation.

THE RECKONING

Justine had come to the end of a long hard day at the office and was regretting her promise to go by Viola's house after work. She decided to call before venturing all the way to up town Manhattan to Viola's apartment. Maybe she and Claudio had made up. She really wasn't in the mood for another of Viola and Claudio's sagas. She picked up the phone and dialed the number.

Viola picked up, "Hello," her voice sounded calm.

"Hi there," Justine said cheerfully. "You're sounding much better. Can I go home? Is everything alright with you now?"

Viola didn't answer right away. She was taken aback by Justine's attitude. She realized she had not only lost Claudio, but she had lost Justine as well. This was not the caring friend she once knew. Well, she thought to herself, I guess I deserve it. Besides, Justine has her own life. "Yes, I'm fine. You can go home."

"Are you sure? Justine questioned.

"Yes, I'm sure," Viola replied. "You can go home to your husband."

"Well, OK," Justine said, "I'll call you tomorrow."

"Yeah, sure," Viola said, "call me tomorrow."

Two weeks had passed since Viola and Claudio's break-up. Claudio had called her a few times to see how she was doing. Finally she asked him not to call her unless it was to say he was coming home. Viola received a report from the detective agency she hired. She was sitting in her office at the beauty salon when she opened up the file. After reading the contents she sat back in her chair letting the paper fall on the floor. She sat gazing out the window, not really seeing anything for a long time. She picked up the phone and called her lawyer. After talking for awhile she picked the report up off the floor then put it back into the folder and grabbed her coat and headed for the door. The receptionist called after her as she was leaving, but Viola heard nothing but the thoughts racing through her head. Later that morning Viola called her receptionist and told her she wasn't coming back to the salon. Then she went into the bathroom and took a long hot shower. She stepped out of the shower onto the mat and grabbed a towel and wrapped it around her. She sat at her dressing table and rubbed lotion onto her body. Looking into the mirror she saw a stranger staring back at her. "Why?" she asked. Tears welled up in her eyes and she wiped them away. Patting her face gently with a cotton pad she began to apply her makeup. During the process she would break out crying and would have to begin the process anew. When she was finally finished she went to the closet and took out a plain white pant suit and got dressed.

Carmen had made some tea. When Viola came into the kitchen Carmen greeted her. "Miss Viola," she said smiling. "Do jou wan some sing to eat?"

"No Carmen, I'll just take some of that tea."

"Is some sing wrong? Why jou come back des morning?"

"No, nothing is wrong Carmen, I'm taking the rest of the day off. I thought I'd go shopping. Bloomingdale's is having a sale." Viola picked up the tea cup revealing her freshly manicured fingernails. They were painted fire truck red. She took a couple of sips of the tea, then she walked down the hall and took her jacket out of the closet and walked out the door.

After browsing around in Bloomingdale's for an hour, Viola finally made a purchase and asked the sales person if she could cut the tags as she wished to change there. The sales girl cut the tag and Viola changed, leaving her former clothing on the bench.

"What should I do with your clothes?" asked the sales girl.

"Oh just throw them in the trash."

"But there is nothing wrong with them," she answered puzzled.

Viola had no more words for her and left the store without so much as looking back.

Viola pulled up in front of the brownstone around one o'clock in the afternoon. She had purchased the brownstone way back in 1989 for the small sum of one dollar. The government was giving them away to anyone who would commit to restoring them. She initially purchased it to rent it out. It was sort of an investment. But when she had met Salina she really felt for her. They became very close and, after a time, Viola thought of her like a sister. She kind off adopted Salina. She became like family. Viola actually gave the Latin beauty the property. Viola felt that Salina had such a raw deal in life and Viola wanted to make it all right and give her a sense of power where she would never have to be put in a compromising position again. When Viola renovated the building and installed some modern appliances, she rented one of the apartments to Salina. They steadily became closer and then one year Viola just gave the brownstone to Salina. Viola figured that Salina could live in one apartment and the other two would provide her with additional income. When she drew up the papers it stated that Salina would have to give Viola 30% of the prophets earned from the two rentals. Salina was floored by the gesture.

Viola sat outside in her brand new 2013 Mercedes Benz working up the courage to go inside and confront Salina. Her heart was heavy and she couldn't believe that Salina could do such a thing to her. However, it all was making sense now. She knew that the report was true. There was no question in her mind. After Claudio and Salina had returned from Justine's wedding in Africa they both had behaved differently. This explained Claudio's moodiness and his lack of intimacy. Salina's pregnancy, all the secrecy concerning the baby's father, Salina's sudden withdrawal from all her friends, everything was making sense now.

Viola never connected the dots, because never in a million years would she expect something like this from Salina.

Viola approached Salina's apartment and rang the door bell. She knew that Salina was inside because she could hear the television and Salina interacting with the baby. She rang the door bell again. After a few minutes everything became silent and she heard nothing. She waited outside the door for about a minute more. Then she went into her handbag and pulled out a set of keys. She hoped that Salina hadn't changed the lock. Viola had these keys for years. She had made three sets of keys and gave two of them to Salina when she put the deed to the property in her hands. Viola inserted her key into the lock and turned the tumbler and the door opened. She walked into the foyer and headed down the hall. Salina came out of the kitchen and halted her, she was wearing her hair short these days as it had become too much to manage with the baby since she no longer visited Viola's salon.

"How dare you," shouted Salina.

"You dare me?" Viola questioned. "I can't believe your gall. On my way over I told myself that you avoided me out of shame. But it's not shame at all is it? It's just plain insolence. You don't even have the decency to be sorry."

Just then the little boy came out of the bedroom and said, "Mommy," and Salina ordered him to go back into the bedroom. He looked up at Viola and she knew at once that this was Claudio's son. He had Salina's coloring, but everything else was Claudio, even down to the green eyes.

"Claudio's son," "Viola heard herself saying. Her eyes gorged with tears. She blinked and they trickled down her cheeks. Salina noticed that there was something very odd about Viola's appearance and then it struck her. Viola was wearing a red dress. Viola never wore that much color. In all the years that she had known Vie all she had ever wore was white, beige or taupe, maybe an occasional muted gold, or the palest of blues, but never a red dress. Why Viola thought she was living on the edge if she wore a black dress and red shoes. Salina had never seen her wear loud colors. Nevertheless here she stood in Salina's hallway dressed in crimson red. Everything was red right on down to the stiletto heels she was wearing. Even her red toenails peeked out of the opening of her open-toed shoes. Salina picked up her son who would not obey her and carried him to the bedroom, shoved him inside, and closed the door behind him. Immediately he began to whale. Salina felt uneasy about the whole situation of Viola all dressed up in red, coming there to her house, letting herself in with a key Salina didn't even know she had.

"What do you want Viola?" she asked.

"What do I want? What do I want? I want my fucking man back," Viola shouted! Then she lowered her voice and hissed. "And an apology couldn't hurt." She then began to laugh hysterically as tears filled her eyes. It was as if she had gone mad. Aden began to beat his little hands upon the door as he continued to cry.

"Mommy, mommy!"

"Look, Viola you're scaring me," Salina said, shaken as she looked back toward the door hoping that Aden wouldn't be able to open it and come out.

"Ooh I'm sorry. I wouldn't want to scare you! After all you only managed to finish me. I'm done, Salina! Claudio was the one thing in this world that made me want to get up in the mornings. Did you know that? Do you know how much I love him? Hum? Do you know that I love him more than life itself?"

Aden continued to cry. It was like a gnawing growl that played on in the background and wouldn't stop.

"What am I supposed to do now that you have presented him with the one thing I can never give him? HUH? Tell me, what would you do if you were me?" She glanced toward the door where Aden was whaling away and then cut her eyes back toward Salina. "Tell me Salina?" she shouted! "What would you do if someone who you considered to be your best friend, your sister just ripped your fucking heart out? What would you do?"

"Look, Vie," Salina said nervously, "y-you should j-just leave this isn't…" She stopped short when she saw Viola pull the gun out of her purse. "Oh God," she said.

"No Salina, God had nothing to do with this! I loved you Salina," Viola said. "Hell, I loved both of you. If he couldn't control himself couldn't you have thought of me? How, tell me how, could you do this to me? How, Salina? I just want to know!" Tears were streaming down Viola's face.

"Viola please," Salina, wined "I'm sorry, o-OK?"

"You're sorry? Sorry?" She began laughing again as

tears poured from her eyes. Salina was afraid. She dare not make any sudden moves because Viola was pointing the gun straight at her.

"Mommmy, mommy, ahhhhhhhhhh!"

"Look Vie, I didn't think you were really in love with him. I thought he was just a fling for you. You said so yourself that you weren't tripping and you knew it wouldn't last," Salina said, glancing over at the door where Aden continued to render his gnawing symphony.

"Really, So I shouldn't trip huh? I don't think that this was your call to make, Salina. How dare you judge me and help yourself to my man. You didn't even ask me how I felt. You just figured I didn't deserve him. Hum, is that it?

You are young and beautiful. You could have had any man you wanted.

Why would you even think to lay with my man? You were supposed to be my friend, I trusted you. All this time I've been worried about you and you've been laughing at me. I feel like such a fool." She was breathing heavily and the hand that was holding the gun began to shake. Tears were streaming down her cheeks and Aden's relentless whaling continued in the background. Salina knew that she had to be careful; she didn't want to say the wrong thing.

"Well, no Viola, I wasn't laughing at you. I didn't plan for this to happen. I didn't go after him."

"Oh so you think it would make me feel better knowing he went after you?"

Not knowing what else to do Salina blurted out, "Why can't you just let it be? You're rich, you have everything."

Viola was astonished by her reply, "You really don't understand, do you?" Viola said, shaking violently. "Everything is nothing without Claudio. Can't you see that? I have nothing that means anything if I don't have him."

Salina was really scared now. Viola looked insane. Her eyes were glaring, her face wet with tears and snot. Salina could see that she had lost it; she snapped. This was not going to end well. Viola was actually moaning. Her words were incoherent and no longer made sense.

"Though you ... you don't even...I hate ... Whhhhhhhhhhy?"

Salina whom she had loved, had committed the ultimate betrayal. Justine no longer loved her either. Why had Claudio, whom she loved with every part of her being, left her for Salina. How could he do this? In her mind these people were her family, and now she felt it was over. Viola could actually feel herself drowning in a sea of hopelessness and despair. She, unlike Justine, had never learned the art of prayer. She didn't know how. She didn't believe in it. The walls seemed to be closing in on her. She let out a scream of pure anguish.

She looked at Salina and shouted, "This is the reckoning,"

She fired a shot at Salina and then turned the revolver around and, with both hands on the gun, placed it in her mouth. Salina, whom she had grazed in the shoulder, fell to the floor. She was stunned, but had recovered from her stupor in time to shout, "No Viola, please."

Viola's eyes were shut and a deep moan escaped her throat before she pulled the trigger.

THE FUNERAL

I t was early October and the wind was whipping about creating a miniature whirlpool of the fallen leaves. Angry clouds hovered low in the sky swollen with moisture that would soon become a torrential outpour. Wednesday morning's gloomy sky matched Justine's mood as she glanced out of the bedroom window. With a heavy heart she packed the last of their bags. She and Marcelo would be journeying to Africa by the end of the week and she wanted to make sure they had everything that they needed.

She had been crying for days now. She was riddled with guilt, because Viola had reached out to her in her final days and she didn't go to her. The truth of the matter was Justine had been harboring some resentment left over from what she had believed to be Viola's betrayal. It all seemed so petty now, as she looked back on it. Viola was desperately in need of her forgiveness and she had allowed false pride to stand in the way of giving it. She had pretended to forgive, but true forgiveness offers total pardoned and Justine knew that she had not given Viola that. Viola was never completely resolved of, what in Justine's mind was, an act of selfishness and uncaring. She felt she had not taken Viola back into her bosom as in the Bible story of the prodigal son.

In that story his father forgave him after he demanded his inheritance, then willfully squandered it abroad, and returned home an impoverished failure. Justine had actually taught that story in Sunday school. In the story this father had forgiven his son, received him with open arms, and even threw him a party upon his return. Viola had humbled herself and apologized and Justine didn't forgive her. Justine's heart was drowning in a sea of sorrow and regret. She would give anything for a do over if it were possible.

She would have gladly gone to Viola's house that evening had she known how desperate Viola had become. She must have been beside herself with anguish and blinded by emotion, which Justine believed, could have been defused if Viola had someone with whom she could have confided in, someone who would have helped her put things into perspective. She had probably been riding an emotional roller coaster with Claudio for years. No wonder she didn't want to attend a wedding. She must have been in a great deal of pain which she managed to hide from everyone. Claudio must have meant the world to her and she must have felt that she couldn't face life without him.

How could Salina have allowed this to happen after everything Viola had done for her. And Claudio, what was he thinking? He must have known how desperately Viola needed him. Poor Viola, Justine thought, feeling so alone in her final hours. Justine knew that she had not made herself available to Viola.

Justine burst into tears yet again when she thought about how Viola planned her death right down to her attire. It was so creepy and oh so sad. What was she trying to say by dressing up in red? Did the red represent blood or a broken heart? Or was she saying that she had the power of life and death? Why did she have to shoot herself in the head? What did it all mean? Justine just didn't know what to figure; she knew Viola had no family to speak of. Her parents were long dead and she had no siblings. Justine, Claudio, and Salina had been her family and they all had let her down.

Yet despite their treatment of her she left all of her businesses to Justine. All accept the one in Brazil. That she left to Claudio. She also left a nice little nest egg for her maid Carmen. Viola had called her lawyers before she did her gruesome deed and brought her estate up to date. Salina was due to inherit half of what Justine had received, but she changed that before she ended it all leaving everything to Justine. She left a note on the passenger seat in her Mercedes which read:

Dear Justine,

If you are reading this letter then that means that I am dead. You are probably calling me a coward and you would be right. Everyone thought me to be the strong, cold, hard business woman, but I'm really not as strong as you all believed me to be. I guess that was why I always guarded my feelings. I always knew that if I let down my guard that I would fall hard. I'm sorry that I was unable to bare this burden that life has dealt me. I just couldn't do it. I'm 50 years old, I'll never recover from this loss. I can't even envision life without Claudio. I'm so angry with him. Yet I love him with all my heart. I tried to pray Justine. I wish that I knew your God. Whenever I tried, I just felt like I was talking to myself. I'm really sorry I couldn't have been a better friend to you. I really still love you, you know. I left most everything I have to you darling. I know money can't make up for the way I acted, but I hope that it brings you more happiness than it did me and that you can find it in your heart to finally forgive me.

I know you are probably mad with Claudio. But he is a good man. He wasn't mean to me in the end. I will take the memory of our last night with me. Salina got what was coming to her, she never loved me, Justine. All the time I thought she was my friend and she took my man. I don't forgive her.

Forgive me, Justine.

Viola Banks

Love Viola Banks

That was all. What she said about Salina made no sense to Justine. What Salina had done was low down as far as Justine was concerned. What Justine did not know was Viola had fully intended to kill Salina, but when Viola saw Claudio's son, she made a switch in plans. She could not bring herself to injure Claudio's child by killing his mother. So she shot Salina so that she would carry a scar to remember what she had done to her, but she didn't kill her. Viola took a fatal journey to the edge of love and could go no further.

Justine picked up a picture that was taken years ago of herself, Viola, and Salina. She touched Viola's face, then held it to her chest. They were so happy and they were all so close. Justine loved Viola and it was evident that Viola had loved her and desperately needed her friendship that day when she called. What hurt even more was that now she and Marcelo would never want for anything financially, because of Viola's death. Justine would give it all up if she could just go back in time. Tears streamed down her face as she put the picture in the suitcase that she was taking to Africa. Justine had always turned to God when things seemed unbearable. And now she has learned what that lesson meant she taught so often in Sunday school. However, she couldn't offer that to Salina and Claudio right now. But she did know God and she knew prayer changed things. And she was praying. Justine pondered in her mind. If Viola had prayed, who knows maybe Claudio would have come back to her? She had tried to impart this belief to her friend Viola. But, Viola's view of God was sketchy at best. Justine overcome with grief began to cry. Her whole body shuck with anguish as she lowered herself to the floor. Marcelo walked into the bedroom and rushed over to her and lifted her from the floor and cradled her in his arms. "Shush," he whispered over and over as he kissed her hair, because her face was buried in his chest.

Viola knew a lot of people. The rain had finally started to fall and a small crowd of people were gathered outside the funeral home holding up their umbrellas. Viola was christened as a Catholic, but she could not be buried in the church due to the circumstances surrounding her death. The funeral was held at Holland's Funeral home in Harlem. There were so many people that they were not able to house them all.

A video screen and speaker system was set up outside in the lobby of the funeral home so that the people who were unable to enter the chapel, where the funeral was being held could see and hear the service. Claudio, who had not fully moved out of the apartment he shared with Viola, was seated on the front row. Justine and Marcelo were to be seated there as well. Salina was sitting beside Claudio. Little Aden was sitting in Claudio's lap. When Justine and Marcelo were ushered to the front to be seated, Justine never looked their way. Justine sat at the opposite end of the same pew. Marcelo, however, did stop and kneeled beside Claudio, who was slumped forward in his chair, holding onto his son, openly crying. Little Aden, not knowing what was happening clung onto his father trying to console him as he too was crying and totally confused.

Marcelo put his hand on Claudio's shoulder and whispered in his ear; "don't mind Justine. She will come around eventually. I can imagine how badly you are hurting, man. If you need anything, someone to talk to, you know my number." Trembling Claudio reached out to Marcelo and wept on his shoulder. Afterward Marcelo walked over to where Justine was seated and sat beside her. She was weeping and he attempted to console her. He placed his arms around her and she wept openly and unrestrained.

When the funeral was over Salina tried to approach Justine, but Justine put up her hand, stopping her in her tracks. "You got what you wanted," she said coldly. "Just stay away from me. I can't trust myself around you right now." Salina, whose arm was in a sling, stepped back away from Justine and hurriedly walked back over to Claudio. What must I have been thinking? she thought to herself. What could I possibly say to Justine? I betrayed someone who had literally saved me and I destroyed her. I owe Viola my life, and who would know that better than Justine? Never in her wildest dreams could Salina have forecasted this outcome. She had no idea how much Viola needed Claudio. She would never forget the way Viola looked, or the words she said, before she took her life. "You have killed me!" Salina would take those words with her to her grave.

Bringing little Aden with them to the funeral seemed to add coal to the fire that had ignited in Justine. She felt it was egregious and insensitive of the couple. But as awful as it seemed to her, there was no disrespect intended by Claudio or Salina. They didn't have anyone to watch Aden and Salina wanted to come to give Viola her last respects.

However, her gesture was looked upon with distain by those who knew the story. As far as Justine was concerned, it would have been far better if Claudio and Salina both had just stayed away. In any case, it simply wasn't an option for Claudio, because Viola had given Justine and Claudio burial rights over her body. So they had to collaborate in order to make the funeral arrangements. However, Justine could have no more to do with him once Viola was buried.

Justine's friends had all turned out and Anthony, Prudence, and Jackie were also there to pay their last respects. They all went back to Justine's and Marcelo's apartment after the burial. Marcelo had tried to talk Justine into allowing Claudio and Salina to come, but Justine would hear none of that. Every time she would allow herself to even look in their direction she would grimace. So Claudio and Salina went their own way after the burial service was over.

Justine, who would always have feelings of regret whenever she thought of Viola, went back to the house and served as a perfect hostess to those who gathered there to mourn Viola's passing. Though everyone told her to relax and allow them to serve her, Justine could not be still. She had to be doing something in order to keep her mind busy, otherwise she would end up in tears.

Sylvia elected to help her out in the kitchen. When they reached the kitchen Sylvia turned and said, "I'm so sorry, Justine." She placed her hand over Justine's.

Justine smiled wanly and said, "Thanks, Sylvia."

"Look I didn't know Viola well, I only saw her a couple of times at your Christmas party, and the Shapiro's but you could clearly see that she and Claudio were very much in love."

"Yes, it was certainly obvious they were in love," Justine said, "that's why this whole thing is so shocking to me."

"It is shocking," Sylvia agreed. "Viola didn't strike me as a person who would kill herself."

"She didn't," Justine agreed, "I had no idea she was that vulnerable."

Sylvia walked over to the table where the food was and began scooping up potato salad from the large container seated on the counter and placed it in a serving bowl. She turned and looked over at Justine and whispered, "She should not have killed herself. She should have went over to Salina's house and beat that ass!"

Justine laughed for the first time since Viola's death and looked over at Sylvia and said, "Yeah, I know that's what you would have done."

Remembering how Justine had witnessed the fight between her and Chichi, Sylvia threw her head back and laughed. "You know that's right," she proclaimed. "Viola should have called me up. I would have set her straight." Sylvia's last statement threw Justine back into a funk and she burst into tears. "Oh baby," Sylvia said, totally confused, "what did I say?" as she put the large spoon down on the counter and approached Justine to comfort her.

"It's just that she did call me and I should have been available to her. What you said was right, Sylvia she just needed someone to set her straight. If she had someone to talk to she would probably be alive today and that someone should have been me. I couldn't forgive her for not attending my wedding in Africa so I didn't go to her when she called me! How stupid was that?"

"Oh, now honey," Sylvia said as she embraced Justine, "there is no way you could have known her state of mind. You can't take this on yourself, nobody can. In the end it was Viola's choice. Clearly she was in a bad place and needed professional help. You couldn't have known that. And you did forgive her, honey. You were still angry, grant it, but you did forgive her. You invited her to your party and you were talking to her again. I don't care what anyone says. It takes time to fully get over some things. You forgave her Justine, do you hear me? You did forgive her. That's why you are here today." Justine stopped crying and was truly comforted by Sylvia's words, because she felt that if she would have known Viola's state of mind, she would have gone to her straight away. They embraced and Sylvia kissed Justine on the cheek and went back to preparing the food.

Claudio now understood why so long ago Viola had attacked him so viciously with her words. Viola was not the tough hard woman she portrayed herself to be. She was very vulnerable. She had lost her mother and father in a car accident when she was sixteen. She had no brother or sister, not even an Aunt or Uncle. At least he had his family in Brazil, he thought. Viola was literally all alone in the world. She wanted to love and be loved, but she had shielded herself against it for so long because she was not able to go through the pain of losing another loved one. Somehow she had unwittingly fallen in love with Claudio. All she ever wanted was his love, and forgiveness. Claudio didn't know how fragile she was, or he would have never left her. He had only been thinking about himself and what he wanted. He didn't blame Justine for her distain of him. Viola had been good to him and to his family and he paid her back with disloyalty. He should have stayed with Viola. He knew that now. He could have still been a father to Aden and if Salina aborted the baby then that would have been on her. He deeply regretted his decision to leave Viola. Salina was stronger and would have been able to handle a breakup much better than Viola. In fact it was she who had given him the ultimatum. He and Salina were cut from the same mold. They had undergone life's worst and never once gave suicide a second thought. They were survivors who scraped and clawed at life. They hung on to it for all it is worth. Be it good or be it bad, they handled whatever life threw at them. If he had a do over, things would be different. His heart ached for her. He thought he was doing the right thing by choosing Salina for his son's sake. He was so overridden with guilt that he could not allow himself to be close to Salina. He knew that Salina must be going through her own bit of hell, but he was unable to comfort her. What they had done to Viola was much worse than anything she had done to them. He had chosen to deal with someone with whom Viola dearly loved and that person was happy to join him in this betrayal. They drove Viola to the edge where she felt she had no other recourse.

After the funeral they drove back to Salina's Brooklyn brownstone in total silence. Claudio would leave Salina and the baby there and return to the condo he had once shared with Viola. There were still a lot of things he needed to do there. Since Viola had left the apartment to him, he would have to sell it. Knowing how she felt about her place, there was no way he would bring another woman to live with him there. He needed that time to be alone there. Every moment of every second that he was able to be there, though it was painful, it helped him to come to terms with the whole awful turn of events.

Here he could relive the wonderful moments they shared and the memory of their last night together. Claudio knew in his heart that it would be a long time before his life would have any semblance of normalcy. Viola had actually left him a lot of money. The will was updated the very day she took her life. If there ever was a doubt about her love, it was erased. Knowing that he had betrayed her, she still gave him the one thing he wouldn't give her when she needed it, forgiveness. She made sure that he would never want for anything even though he had broken her heart in the cruelest of ways. Viola visited him in his dreams every night that he stayed at the condo. Each night he cried until sleep stole in and carried him away to a place where he could be with her where she waited for him in the land of dreams. In one of the dreams he decided to stay with Viola and they were both happy and then he woke up. Some of these dreams were strangely real, that when he awakened later to find it all a dream, the pain of his loss would fill his heart with despair all over again.

EPILOGUE

After Viola's death, Justine and Marcelo went to West Africa to start Marcelo's business. The couple would return to the States from time to time with Marcelo's children. After a time, Marcelo's children were able to get visas to attend school in the United States.

Sylvia and Keith eventually moved to California with the twins so that Keith could be near his sister Joyce.

Claudio and Salina got married and moved to Brazil where Claudio would take care of Viola's business and Salina gave birth to a baby girl.

Justine and Sylvia kept in touch by phone and actually became very good friends. They even traveled back and forth on holidays to celebrate and met each other's extended families.

Claudio was never really ever the same after Viola's passing. He and Marcelo however, did keep in touch and they would meet up from time to time. They had formed a very close bond. Marcelo knew that in those last days that Claudio was conflicted, and that he was very remorseful for having gotten himself into that situation, and he felt for him.

Marcelo was the only one that Claudio could talk to about the subject. Justine never could quite understand Marcelo's interpretation of Claudio's dilemma, though she eventually came around as Marcelo said she would, and managed to be civil toward Claudio and Salina. They even spent the Easter holidays together one year. She gave both Claudio and Salina the forgiveness they needed from her. She reasoned that Viola was gone, and there was nothing any of them could do about that. Justine had learned a hard lesson and that was nothing good ever came from holding grudges. She embraced the two in a way that she had not done for Viola and hoped that God would have mercy on Viola's tortured soul.

Claudio turned out to be a good father to the children and tried to be the best husband he could be, under the circumstances, to Salina. He did love her, but Salina was never able to fully capture his whole heart. Viola owned a piece of him even in death. Salina would sometimes observe him looking off into space and she knew that in those moments his thoughts were with Viola. Salina was sorry she had allowed herself to become involved with Claudio, because stolen love was never certain and kept you just on the edge of love.

ACKNOWLEDGEMENTS

To Jack Lesko, John A. Pease, Deloris Chapman, Nina Yip Pease, Rhonda Morris, Faye Waiters, and Yvonne Graham, thank you all for your help, your time and tireless support. I appreciate everything each and every one of you contributed to the success of this book. Thank you from the bottom of my heart. May God richly bless all of you.

ABOUT THE AUTHOR

JOY ROBERTS-PIERRE was born and raised in New York City. She attended Bronx Community College and graduated with honors with a degree in Liberal Arts. She currently resides in Society Hill, South Carolina. She has always loved art and as a child she enjoyed creating comic strip stories for her classmates.

She was one of the lead singers in the radio choir at the Greater Refuge Temple church in Harlem. She now sings with the worship team at Union Baptist Church where her husband is the pastor.

She dabbles in all forms of the arts such as sculpting, painting, drawing, and doll art.

As a doll artist, Joy noticed that there were not a lot of Black dolls featured in any of the doll shows she attended. So she co-produced the first Black doll show in New York City in 1995 and continued her shows up until 2010. Her shows featured many Black doll artists largely from the Eastern United States.

Her doll art has been displayed in galleries such as the Black Doll theatre, in Harlem, the Interchurch Gallery, in Manhattan, the Hub-Robenson Gallery, at Penn State University, the Riverview Park Tower Art Show, in Harlem and many of the shows she herself produced in the Bronx, Manhattan, and Brooklyn. Her dolls have been featured in magazines and books such as *Soft Dolls & Animals*, *Doll World*, *Dolls*, *Contemporary Doll Collectors* and the book *Black Dolls Proud, Bold & Beautiful*.

Joy is now extending her love for art in the form of writing. *Journey to the Edge of Love* is her first book and she artfully uses language to create a picture in your mind's eye.

www.ingramcontent.com/pod-product-compliance
Lightning Source LLC
Chambersburg PA
CBHW050016180626
46810CB00002B/449